My Darling Elia

My Darling Elia

Eugenie Melnyk

 St. Martin's Press ✿ New York

THOMAS DUNNE BOOKS.
An imprint of St. Martin's Press.

MY DARLING ELIA. Copyright © 1999 by Eugenie Melnyk. All rights
reserved. Printed in the United States of America. No part of this
book may be used or reproduced in any manner whatsoever without written permission except in the case of brief quotations
embodied in critical articles or reviews. For information, address
St. Martin's Press, 175 Fifth Avenue, New York, N.Y. 10010.

Design by Nancy Resnick

Library of Congress Cataloging-in-Publication Data

Melnyk, Eugenie.
    My darling Elia / Eugenie Melnyk. — 1st ed.
        p.   cm.
    ISBN 0-312-20565-1
    1. Treblinka (Concentration camp) Fiction.   2. Babi Yar
Massacre, Ukraine, 1941 Fiction.   3. Jews—Canada Fiction.
4. Warsaw (Poland)—History—Warsaw Ghetto Uprising,
1943 Fiction.   I. Title.
PR9199.3.M4278M9   1999
813'.54—dc21   99-13110
                                                            CIP

First Edition: June 1999

10 9 8 7 6 5 4 3 2 1

For my daughter, Jenny Shepherd

Descriptions of the events at Babi Yar, in the Warsaw ghetto, and at Treblinka are all based on the true stories of very real people who endured and survived to testify.

My Darling Elia

Chapter 1

The flea market vendors all knew him by sight, though not by name. He was one of the dozen or so regulars who came to the market week after week and drifted from table to table, buying nothing, spending only their lonely Sunday hours. Unlike the others, who snatched at any opportunity to engage the vendors in conversation, he spoke to no one.

He appeared, usually, between ten and eleven each Sunday morning, and if he happened to catch our eye, mine or Cia's, his head dipped in a formal nod, then he retreated into a slow and methodical inspection of the merchandise we had for sale.

As we had with all the regulars, Cia and I had given him a name. Between ourselves, we called him "*Stahray*," the Ukrainian word for old man.

Although neither of us is really fluent in the language, we are both of Ukrainian extraction and have retained enough of a vocabulary to make private comments on the looks and habits of people passing our tables. We fill in the gaps with French or English and, since our facility in all three languages is equal, we understand one another perfectly.

The name suited him.

He was aged in a way that had nothing to do with his years. We guessed him to be in his late sixties or early seventies which, at forty-eight and well on the way there myself, I don't consider all that old. But there was a fast fragility in his thin, stooped frame and in the careful way he walked, leaning on a knobby cane, that made him seem aged.

He was gray, all gray.

Gray tweed overcoat. Gray fur wedge hat. When the weather turned warm, gray trousers and gray cardigan. Gray hair receding from a high forehead, skin dusted with the film of poor health. Thick gray eyebrows thatched over pale eyes. A high-bridged nose thinning to transparent nostrils.

Two harsh grooves bracketed a pale mouth and a white scar curved from the corner of his lower lip to the deep cleft in his chin. They were the only memorable features of an unremarkable face.

Looking back, I realize he was the only regular none of us knew anything about. And to tell the truth, we had no real reason to care. If he had failed to appear, weeks could have passed before we'd have been aware of his absence.

And yet, before the summer ended, there wasn't a vendor or a regular in that particular flea market and in the city's flea market circuit whose imagination wasn't captured by him.

His search for Anna became an obsession with Cia and with me. And he had a profound effect on my daughter, Jenny.

Chapter 2

Indoor flea markets are quiet during the summer months. Vendors and flea market buffs are inclined to go to the outdoor markets, particularly on a beautiful Sunday morning in June.

Had it been autumn, when the mall aisles are crowded and noisy, I doubt I'd have heard the old man's choking gasp.

He was balanced precariously on his cane, trembling visibly. His right arm was braced against the easel on which we had hung our junk jewelry, and his clenched fist was white against the black velvet. Two bright spots of color burned under his tightly closed eyes.

"Are you all right?" I touched his arm hesitantly. "Are you all right?"

His eyes flew open and they were a blazing blue, not gray at all. He nodded shakily.

"Yes. Thank you. I am fine. Please. Just give me a moment."

"Here." I gestured to the folding chair on which I had been sitting. "Sit down. You look a little wonky."

"Thank you." He took two unsteady steps, dropped into the chair, and peered up at me from under the shaggy brows. "Wonky? I don't know the word. Is there really such a word?"

"It's in the dictionary," I assured him.

Cia, returning from the delicatessen with two mugs of coffee, raised a questioning eyebrow at me as she sidled past.

"Something wrong?" She handed me my coffee, glancing from me to the old man. "Something happen?"

"I don't know." On impulse, I offered my coffee to the old man. "Would you like some?"

He raised his hand in a gesture of refusal, his fist still clenched.

"Thank you, no," he said and unclenched his fingers. "This happened."

Cia's eyes flickered and I knew she had caught the trace of accent I had, the difficulty with the "th" sound that comes out faintly "dh." Most old country Ukrainians have it, no matter how well they learn to speak the English language. Cia claims it's a dead giveaway, that she can spot a hunky by it a mile away.

I grinned at her, knowing the same thought was passing through her mind. How often had we made remarks in Ukrainian about this old man, banking on his inability to understand?

"What is it?" Cia frowned down at the object in his palm. "I mean, I know what it is. What made it a happening?"

It was from our jewelry display, a pendant and chain, the pendant a white metal disk, approximately the size of a twenty-five-cent piece. A yellow bead, embedded in the disk's center, was surrounded by lines of radiation, etched into the metal.

With a little mental effort, one could imagine the bead as a sun, the etched lines as rays. It had an amateurish look, not particularly attractive.

The old man drew a deep breath. He pressed the bead and the disk sprang open. His fingers were trembling as he spread it wide. He glanced down, then turned his head away, his lips pressed in a bitter line.

"It's a locket!" Cia's surprise mirrored my own. "May we see it?"

Wordlessly, the old man handed the locket to her.

The face of a handsome young man looked up at us from the left side of the locket. The photograph had yellowed, but there was no mistaking that high-bridged nose, the cleft chin.

It could only be the old man as a youth.

The photo on the right had been destroyed by moisture. All that remained was a wave of fair hair curling around a small, feminine ear.

"I wanted to see her face just once more." The old man's whisper was hoarse.

Cia looked at me, closed the locket, and placed it gently into his palm.

"Please. Keep it," she said. "It was yours, wasn't it."

For a moment he didn't answer, didn't seem to hear. Then he heaved a ragged sigh.

"I made it for my wife over fifty years ago." There was a sudden flash of pure mischief in his eyes. "In Kiev."

He waited, watching our reaction, his glance dancing from one to the other, thoroughly enjoying our discomfort.

"Uh huh," Cia finally said with resignation. "In Kiev. In the Ukraine."

"In Kiev." The flash was now a full-fledged gleam. "In the Ukraine."

"And you speak Ukrainian. Fluently, of course."

"Of course." He nodded. And then he smiled.

There are people whose faces are transformed when they smile. Who smile with such singular sweetness that your heart can lift right out of your breast if the smile is meant for you. I felt my breath catch in my throat.

"And my name is Elia Strohan. Not Stahray," he added. The smile faded. His fingers closed over the locket.

"Please," he said. "Where did you get this?"

Cia shrugged. Knowing she could only disappoint him, she answered with a trace of impatience in her voice.

"Who knows? We could have bought it at any of a hundred garage sales. Or moving sales. Or church bazaars. Any of the places we buy all this junk." Her arm swept our laden tables. "I can't even remember what we bought last week, much less where we bought it."

The old man flinched at her tone but persisted.

"You can't think where it might have been? Which section of the city? The West Island? East end? Downtown?"

"We never buy downtown. It would have to be somewhere on the West Island."

"Could you possibly remember when? When you bought it?"

Cia looked at me helplessly. "Liz?"

I shook my head. "But it would have to have been within the last three months. We didn't have any jewelry until after Easter. Remember?"

"That's right!" Cia brightened. "The aurora!"

The aurora was a brooch we bought from a divorcée who was selling out and decamping to Florida. I picked it out of a shoe box full of costume jewelry. Not because it was attractive; it was dark and dirty; or because I know anything about jewelry; I don't. But under the tarnish I had spotted the sterling mark.

We paid fifty cents for it, spent two hours cleaning it, and sold it for thirty dollars to Betty, our flea market neighbor.

The heavy backing proved to be vermeil, a gold wash over sterling. The pear-shaped stones, cleaned in an ammonia bath, sparkled purple at the perimeter, through mauve and rose to pale pink at the brooch's heart.

Betty sold it the following week for ninety-five dollars and we've dug through a ton of junk jewelry since.

We've never had another such find and the entire episode has taken on an air of unreality. Every so often we revive it to reassure ourselves it can happen.

The old man listened politely, his thumb caressing the locket. He nodded appreciation of our story.

"So you bought it in the last three months, then." There was a tremor in his voice. He cleared his throat and added, with a sort of helpless doggedness. "But you don't recall where."

On the verge of giving him a sharp reply, Cia suddenly heard the bleakness in his words.

"Is it so important?" she asked quietly.

For a moment I thought the old man wouldn't answer. He gazed past us, unseeing, the locket tightly clenched in his fist. When he spoke, it was in a voice heavy with desolation.

"Wherever it was, wherever you bought this, my Anna must be there." He turned his eyes on Cia, and once more they were a foggy gray. "Yes. It is so important."

"You made the locket for Anna," Cia said softly.

"Yes."

Cia frowned. "You said she must be here. Doesn't she know you're here?"

The old man looked down at the locket in his hand. His head moved in a helpless gesture of negation.

"On September twenty-ninth, nineteen forty-one," he said, his voice thin, "the Nazis shot thirty thousand Jews at Babi Yar, in Kiev. Anna believes I died with them."

As I said, indoor flea markets are slack during the summer months, the hours languid.

Cia wanted to hear all about Anna and so did I. Between us we cajoled and bullied the old man into sharing our lunch and answering our questions.

At first his answers were almost monosyllabic, his voice thready. Then memory took hold and he talked as much to himself as to us.

Chapter 3

*E*lia Strohan was the only child of Itzak Strohan, a fruit vendor at the Bessarabka market in Kiev, and of his wife, Rose Boretz Strohan.

Itzak and Rose had long given up hope of children when, to their astonishment, Rose became pregnant.

The prospect of becoming parents unnerved rather than delighted them. They had been married twenty years and were set in their ways. Itzak's life was centered on his shop and his synagogue, Rose's in her kitchen and women's groups.

When Elia was born, on January 7, Ukrainian Christmas Day, in 1911, Rose was thirty-eight years old, Itzak forty-nine. The fair hair and blue eyes of their newborn son puzzled them until Itzak recalled the half-forgotten family legend of a great-grandmother raped by a blond Cossack giant.

The advent of a child caused no ripple in the Strohan household. Itzak had his world, Rose hers. Elia was expected to find his own and he did. In books.

In primary school his teachers recognized his ear for language and in secondary school he was encouraged to develop the gift. Elia financed his higher education by tutoring the children of a wealthy Armenian family.

When he met Anna Romanovich he was twenty-four

years old, an assistant professor of languages at the University of Kiev. In addition to the Yiddish he spoke at home, he was fluent in Ukrainian, Polish, French, and German. His Armenian was sketchy, his English adequate.

He was tall for a Ukrainian, almost six feet, and handsome in a scholarly way. He was aware of some of his female students found him attractive but their flirtings were lost on him. Like his parents, he lived a circumscribed life. He taught, he studied. His superiors at the university praised him as a dedicated teacher and a properly serious young man.

(The old man wasn't as kind in referring to the young Elia. "I was a pompous, pedantic ass," he described himself.)

Anna was seventeen, a new student in one of his French classes. She was seated in the front row, her chin resting in the palms of her hands, her elbows planted on the desktop, studying him.

When Elia raised his head to begin the class he found himself looking directly into eyes so blue they were almost navy in color. Their gazes locked for a moment. Then she dropped an eyelid in a broad, bawdy wink.

Elia's scalp tingled with shock. His heart gave a great leap and he had a sudden, frantic need for air to breathe. It was a new and completely strange sensation for him. He came to his senses writing on the blackboard, the chalk trembling in his fingers, and did not look in her direction again that day.

He woke next morning in an unfamiliar state of excitement. She was in his first class and he studied her furtively each time she bent over her assignment, looking away quickly when she raised her head.

For the first time in his life he was struck by the ineffable wonder of a woman. The slim ankles, sweetly crossed. The slender hands, rosy tipped. The satin skin, flushed peach on high, lovely cheekbones. Brows like wings, lashes dark and thick. Her hair dark blond, tied back with a ribbon. Upper lip short, lower full. A dimple came and went at the corner of her mouth when she spoke and he was entranced by it.

When the class ended he watched her leave, enchanted by the glossy fall of hair bouncing as she walked.

He checked. She was a music student, a gifted violinist. He learned she was a member of the Kiev Symphony Orchestra and began attending their concerts, picking her out in the violin section, not hearing the music, aware only of her.

She was a laughing girl, outgoing and lively, with a sunny nature that drew others to her. If Elia saw her with a man—a student at the school or a musician at the concert hall—his stomach filled with sour bile he recognized as jealousy. And yet he could think of no way to approach her.

He had visions of rescuing her from the jaws of a mad dog, of saving her from the wheels of a runaway tram. Knowing they were adolescent melodramas, his mood would veer to anger at her and contempt for himself at his inadequacy.

He tried ignoring her, convincing himself it was undignified for a professor to be panting after a silly young girl.

A week before the Christmas break the problem was taken out of his hands.

Leaving class, Anna's ankle twisted. She staggered toward him, her armload of books flying in all directions. A heavy volume struck Elia on the shin. He bent to rub his leg, she bent to pick up a book, and their heads cracked together.

Clutching his forehead, he stepped to his right. She, hand pressed to her head, stepped left. Confused, he retraced his step at the same time she returned to her original position.

Face to face still, they burst into laughter.

Not until after they were married did Anna admit she had planned the entire episode.

"I choreographed it very precisely," she murmured into the curve of his shoulder. "Then I had to wait a whole month to get you into just the right place at just the right time."

"And nearly knocked me out in the process." Elia's arms tightened around her. "Tell me something. Did you know how I felt about you?"

"Of course I knew."

"Oh? You did? How?"

Anna giggled. "Everybody knew."

Elia drew back to see if she was serious. She balanced her chin on his chest, her eyes dancing.

"If you could have seen yourself. You stammered every time you spoke to me."

"I did not."

She tilted her head, grinning. "And your ears turned pink. I loved your pink ears."

"My ears turned pink? You loved me for pink ears?"

She traced the outline of his mouth with a gentle finger, sending shivers through him.

"Listen, husband of mine," she said. "One lovely day I saw you walking after class with the sun in your hair and your nose in a book, so trusting you wouldn't bump into anything or be knocked down by anyone. And I told myself, there is a man who needs someone to take care of him. I told myself, there is the man I will spend the rest of my life with. And then, then, my darling Elia, I told everybody else. Hands off. He's mine."

Chapter 4

It would be incorrect to say that Elia formally courted Anna. They walked together to and from classes. He accompanied her to orchestra practice and concerts. They drank gallons of coffee in student cafés.

In late January, on her eighteenth birthday, Anna invited him to meet her mother, a plump and petulant widow who had difficulty remembering his name. A week later, Elia took Anna to his parents' home. The evening was one of awkward attempts to find some common ground. Elia and Anna left early.

Anna was subdued, and they walked in silence. Finally, she stopped and faced him, forcing him to a standstill.

"They'll never accept me, you know," she said. Her hands were thrust deep in her pockets, her shoulders hunched. To Elia she looked smaller, very young and very vulnerable.

"I don't need their acceptance." It was a simple statement of fact. "Nor do you."

She hunched deeper into her coat. Haloed by her frosty fox hood, her face was pink with cold. She frowned up at him.

"Does it bother you that I'm not a Jew?" she asked, her eyes searching his.

He smiled down at her. "Does it bother you that I am?"

"I asked you first." The words were spoken lightly but her eyes had darkened. She sniffed wetly and dabbed at her nose with a mittened hand. "I really do want to know, Elia."

"Can't we keep walking?" Elia reached for her arm. "We'll freeze just standing here."

"Not until you answer." She evaded his grasp and stamped one foot to the other, her boots squeaking on the hard-packed snow.

"We can walk and talk." Elia circled her shoulders with his arm and drew her to his side.

For a moment she stiffened, resisting, then yielded. Hugging him about the waist, she fell in step. They matched strides, heads lowered against the cutting wind.

Rounding a corner brought them into a street whose buildings offered some degree of protection.

"Well?" Anna demanded, raising her head.

"I'm thinking."

"About what? It's a simple question. Just give me a simple answer."

"But it's not a simple question."

"Elia!" She broke step and would have halted but Elia pulled her along. She hopped to regain stride.

"You're trying to avoid answering," she accused.

"No. I'm not. I'm trying to think how to . . ."

"What's the matter with plain old yes or no? Either you mind or you don't. Is that so complicated?"

Elia glanced down at the stubborn set of her chin.

"I'll try to explain," he said. "I once heard a Ukrainian folk song about a wounded soldier and a flower. Or was it a tree? I've forgotten. Whichever is not important. The soldier and the tree clung to life as long as the sun shone. When the sun set, they died. You know the song?"

Anna nodded. "Yes. But what has . . ."

"Without the sun we would all die. That's the statement the song makes, isn't it?"

"Yes, but I still don't see . . ."

"What it has to do with the question? Let me continue. We are all creatures of the sun. Plants, animals, man, we are all Nature's creatures." He side-glanced. "Do you follow?"

She plodded silently beside him, her head bent. Receiving no response, he resumed.

"Now. Nature's laws are explicit. The sun rises and sets. Seasons change. Every living thing reproduces its own kind. Every living thing must die. Nature sets a pattern and plants and animals abide by the pattern set for their species. Only man does not. The human animal seems unable to accept Nature's simplicity. We invent complex beliefs. We establish arbitrary boundaries. We set up artificial barriers to convince ourselves we are different one from the other. But these differences have no relevance in Nature. The primitive body functions of a Hindu are no different from those, say, of a Jew."

Entering into a new street, they faced a blast of frigid air. Both turned simultaneously and walked backward, clinging together. Elia felt her shiver.

"Look at us." He pressed her closer. "Animals are provided with natural protection from the elements. We are not. A Turk's flesh will freeze as quickly as an Englishman's. The sun will burn a Ukrainian Christian like you as casually as it will a Dutch atheist. Our labels don't protect us. We are simply a species, subject to the laws that govern all species. Birth and death. Male and female. Everything else is irrelevant."

They walked almost half a block before Anna realized nothing more was forthcoming. She halted abruptly.

Elia stumbled, thrown off balance, and she slipped from the circle of his arm. She faced him, hugging herself, shivering and stamping her feet.

"That's all?" Her breath rose in a frosty cloud.

"All?" Elia shook his head, puzzled.

"I asked you a question. I asked if you minded that I am not a Jew."

"And I answered."

"Oh no, Professor Strohan. That wasn't an answer. That was a full-scale lecture. Couldn't you just say it doesn't matter?" Her teeth clicked together involuntarily and she gritted them to stop their chattering. "You've never once said you love me. Is it so d-damn hard to say you l-love me?"

Elia, utterly disoriented, stared down at her flushed face.

He had never expressed words of love, never heard them directed toward himself. His parents, if they loved him, and he knew they did, had been inarticulate and undemonstrative. Until Anna, he had never experienced the tumult of the passions she aroused in him. He knew that a day in which he didn't see her was a lost day but it had never occurred to him to name the thing he felt love.

He pulled her to him and buried his face in the soft fur next to her cheek.

"I thought you knew," he said hoarsely. "My God, Anna, I worship you the way the earth worships the sun."

"S-say it then!" She was stammering with cold. "'I-tell me th-that you love me."

"I love you." Suddenly Elia laughed, a joyous shout of recognition. "I love you, Anna Romanovich. And I will love you till the day I die!"

Chapter 5

They were married in a civil ceremony in April of 1935 and moved into a tiny flat a short distance from the university.

In her estimate of Elia's parents, Anna had been only partially correct. They were not disapproving. They were simply at a loss with a gentile daughter-in-law.

Neither Itzak nor Rose had ever been acquainted with a Christian. No non-Jew had ever crossed the threshold of their home. Anna was a visitor from a world they feared and did not understand. They treated her with the careful courtesy that bridges unalterable differences but precludes intimacy.

In the beginning, at Anna's insistence, she and Elia visited the elderly Strohans once a week, occasionally staying for meals after polite urging from Itzak.

In his parent's home, Elia lapsed into their habit of silence and Anna found herself chattering to fill the empty air, painfully aware of Itzak's faint reproof, of Rose's downcast eyes and sudden bustlings of activity.

After too many such strained visits Anna admitted defeat. All four Strohans were relieved when the weekly ordeal ended.

Anna's mother, more urbane than the Strohans, made a plausible show of welcoming Elia into her family. It was an effort she couldn't quite carry off. Though she prattled her usual small talk at him, her voice was pitched higher than normal and she could never look fully at him.

Shooting furtive glances from china blue eyes, she gave an impression of wariness, as though convinced he was hiding something and if she were to be quick she would see what it was. Probably, Elia thought dryly, the horns and hooked nose of the slavic peasant's concept of a Jew.

She could not bring herself to utter the word "Jew." "Hebrew persuasion" and "Semitic ancestry" were her euphemisms. It amused Elia. It infuriated Anna.

"Elia's a Jew, Mamma," she snapped once. "Semitic ancestry? Arabs are Semites. The Assyrians. The Phoenicians. Babylonians. They were Semites too. Elia is a Jew."

"Of course, dear." Olga Romanovich's plump hand tweaked a ruffle, poked a curl. "I know, dear."

Elia eventually begged off.

"I just make her uncomfortable," he reasoned. "Christmas, Easter, birthdays, all right. Otherwise, why don't you visit your mother alone."

Anna thought a moment, then agreed.

"And on the Jewish holidays, we'll make your parents uncomfortable."

In the first months of their marriage, Elia, who had lived enclosed in the silence of his own body, was bewildered by Anna's quicksilver nature. When she was happy, she sang. Sad, she cried briefly and stormily. Angry, she raged noisily.

He had always weighed every judgment he made. Her decisions were based on instinct and emotion. "Don't confuse me with logic" was her airy defense when he tried to apply reason.

He never moved without careful planning and preparation. She plunged blithely into anything that caught her interest. "C'est la vie," she'd say, and shrug if it didn't work out.

"You don't take anything seriously," he accused.

"Oh, yes I do." She nuzzled him, deliberately provocative. "I take you very seriously."

Slowly he began to understand it was only in contrast with his own dispassionate nature that she appeared frivolous. Beneath the lightheartedness was a brutal honesty she applied to herself and to everyone around her.

When she was home, the air was charged with her vitality. When she was absent, the stillness of the empty rooms echoed in Elia's ears.

The first time the orchestra went on tour and she was gone for the weekend, Elia hammered out the pendant locket from a pewter dish she had brought to the marriage.

She cried over the sun image he had gouged into the soft metal and made a ceremony of hanging the locket around her neck.

"I'll never take it off. Never. When I die I want it buried with me. Don't give it to anyone, not even our grandchildren. Promise me."

"What if I go first?"

"And leave me alone? Don't you dare."

They acquired a small group of friends whose interests paralleled theirs.

Saul Levi, a Gallican cellist, married to a stolid premed student named Marusia. Orest Tokariuk, a humpbacked science instructor, who played the bandura like an angel. Lesia Boyko, a talented artist, whose love for Orest was obvious to everyone but Orest himself.

For five busy, happy years, Elia never started a day without thanking God for Anna.

Chapter 6

On the twenty-second of June, 1941, Hitler's armies invaded Russia. Elia was mobilized into a unit defending Kiev.

On the nineteenth of September, Kiev surrendered.

When the order came to retreat, Elia's unit was stationed on the left bank of the Dnieper. The demoralized army dispersed, the leaderless men wandering into the woods and open fields.

Six hundred thousand were taken prisoner. Others, exchanging their uniforms for rags begged or stolen from peasants, escaped to make their way home.

Elia was one of them. He set out for Kiev, hiding by day, walking by night. He arrived on the night of the twenty-eighth, frantic with fear for Anna.

From miles away, the sky over the city had glowed red. Central Kiev was in flames. For four days, building after building had been blown up by bombs planted by the retreating Russian army. The Kreshchatik, Kiev's main thoroughfare, was a blazing furnace.

Elia circled the cordoned streets and made his way to the flat. He fitted the key into the lock with trembling hands. The moment the door swung open, he knew the rooms were empty.

Propped against a picture of Anna and himself was a letter, dated three days previously. He read:

My Darling Elia,
   Please God you will be reading this. It will mean you are alive and safe.
   I have gone with Mamma to my sister in Lvov. Mamma's flat is gone, fini, kaput. This nest was large enough for us but FAR too small for Mamma and me. Even so, I would not be leaving were it not for the baby.

Baby! Elia's eyes froze on the word. With an effort of will, he continued reading.

I have written to you many times but have had no word from you so I don't even know if you know. We have manufactured a miracle, you and I. Sometime in Spring, the end of March, I believe.
   I'm not sure what conditions are in Lvov, but they can't be worse than here. I'll wait for you in Lvov. Please come soon, my darling, darling Elia.

Always and forever,
Your Anna

Elia sat with the letter in his hand, staring emptily at the eerie glow in the night sky. After a long time, he rose stiffly. Moving like an old man, he fell on the bed without undressing. When he awoke, the windows were still dark. He had slept only a matter of hours.

He stripped off the clothing he had worn for a week and dropped it into the garbage. He bathed and selected a pair of trousers, a wool shirt, and a leather jacket from the closet. He dressed and, while packing a small suitcase with a change of clothing and some toilet articles, he finished the bread from the previous day.

With great care, he cut Anna's face from the photograph and fitted it, together with her letter, into his wallet.

Dawn was a promise in the eastern sky when he reached the flat where his parents had lived all the years of their married life, where he had grown up. He twisted the old-fashioned doorbell, expecting to wait, envisioning his mother rising, donning the heavy wool bathrobe she had worn since he could remember, and shuffling to see what kind of me-shuge came calling before daybreak.

To his surprise, the bell was answered immediately. His father, fully clothed, stood framed in the doorway, wearing an identical expression of astonishment.

"Who is it?" he heard his mother call out from the rear of the flat.

"It's Elia." His father raised his voice without turning his head. "It's our son. It's Elia."

Then, as though he had reminded himself who Elia was, he gestured for Elia to enter.

"Your mother is packing for the trip," he explained.

"Trip?" Elia followed his father down the narrow passageway to the kitchen. To his knowledge, neither Itzak nor Rose had ever traveled farther than the other side of town. "You're going on a trip?"

"We all are. All Jews. You didn't know? The Germans are relocating us."

"Relocating where?"

"Who knows?" His father shrugged. "Who ever tells us? All we know is they are bringing special trains to take us out of the city. We have to be on Melnikov Street, near the cemetery, at eight o'clock this morning. And we must bring everything we will need with us."

His mother looked up from packing a wicker basket with fruit, cheese, bread, and hard-boiled eggs. She tucked a clean towel over the food.

"Are you all right?" Her glance flickered at Elia.

"I'm fine, Mamma."

To Elia, his mother seemed to have aged since last he had seen her. Her face was pale, her eyes blinked distractedly. Her hands moved with a nervous will of their own, picking at the table's wooden surface, bleached white with years of scrubbing.

Her eyes darted to the suitcase he carried.

"You're coming with us?"

"No. I'm on my way to Lvov. Anna is there. I just came to say goodbye." Elia turned to his father. "I'll take you to the train."

His father raised both palms in polite protest.

"It's not necessary," he said. "We're meeting some of the others at the corner."

"Still, you have your things. I can help carry them."

"As you like." His father shrugged but Elia caught the quick relief in the old man's eyes.

"Well, Rose?" Itzak was suddenly brisk. "Are we ready? The others will be there already."

Rose nodded. She picked up the basket and stood absently, her eyes caressing the room she had come to as a bride.

"Come, come." Itzak clapped his hands. "It will all be here when we come back. Come, already."

They emerged into the street, the three of them, Rose carrying the basket of food and her household treasures tied into a pillowcase, Itzak with Elia's lighter bag, and Elia laden with two heavy suitcases bulging with the elder Strohans' belongings.

The others were gathering at the corner, the women huddled like a band of crows in their black shawls, the men arguing and gesticulating, bearded chin wagging. All were old, their children grown and gone on to lives of their own.

There was Solomon Kalish, the butcher, and his wife, Hanka, a couple cast from the same corpulent mold, both of whom Elia remembered with affection, he for his unfailing good humor, she for sweet rolls handed out freely to neighborhood children.

There was Yankel Rosen, the tailor, and his shrewish wife, Rachel, the local gossip, whose long nose, according to her husband, was God's way of warning the world against her.

And Nathan Goretsky, the baker, a thin, dour man who picked unceasingly at his straggly eyebrows, pulling the gray hairs down over his eyes as if to hide the distrust with which he viewed the world. His wife, a hardworking and irrepressibly cheerful woman named Sarah, was pulling a two-wheeled cart packed to overflowing with bedding and boxes and pots and pans.

There was a babble of greeting for Elia and a recounting of offspring, some of whom would join the group along the way. The street was filling with others like themselves and they began to walk, the men determinedly optimistic, the women mistily silent.

"Hey, Nathan," Solomon Kalish boomed. "Did you bring along everything you own? Your old woman will need the strength of an ox to pull that load."

"And who knows if we'll ever come back?" Nathan Goretsky, the baker, snapped. "How do we know where they're sending us? And why?"

"The war. Because of the war. They're moving us for our own protection," Elia's father explained, casting a worried eye on Rose, who plodded mutely beside him.

"So why only Jews?"

"What are you trying to do, you old fool!" Yankel Rosen shouted at him angrily. "Scare the women? Listen, I remember the Germans in the Great War. They treated the Jews decently. They're a decent people, a civilized people. Did you ever hear of a pogrom in Germany? Did you?"

Goretsky shot him a malevolent glance from under his brows.

"We'll see," he muttered darkly. "We'll see."

By now the street was thick with people, a sea of heads all flowing in the same direction. The small group had difficulty staying together and Elia instructed his parents to follow him. He was taller and they could keep his head in view. The others fell into line.

Moving slowly by necessity, Elia had time to look around at the nature of the crowd.

There were howling children and women with babies slung on their hips. There were young girls with anxious eyes and old men and old women, some weeping, some pushing angrily and cursing. There were cripples and invalids being half carried by family members. There were few young men like himself. Those who were fit had been mobilized into the army.

The streets were lined with the curious; gentiles who had come to watch the Jews leave Kiev. Some wept openly. Some laughed and pointed at the heavy-laden old women with strings of onions and garlic slung around their necks like garlands, at religious old men in robes that swept the ground. Some shouted insults.

For the first time, Elia felt a prickle of uneasiness. Where were they being sent? Why only Jews? He pushed the thoughts aside but a tight knot of misgiving was forming in his chest.

On Melnikov Street the crowd faltered to a standstill. There was a barrier ahead. Elia set the heavy suitcase down and seated his mother on one of them.

"Elia! Elia! Elia Strohan!"

Elia turned at the sound of his name and scanned the crowd pressing around him.

Pushing frantically through was Lesia Boyko, her hair disheveled, her eyes wide with panic. She reached his side and clutched his arm, her fingers digging painfully.

"Elia. Listen!" she panted. "There's something wrong! Listen! People are going in but nobody's coming out. Listen!

Orest went through the barrier more than three hours ago. He hasn't come out yet. I've been waiting and waiting. He hasn't come out!"

Gently, Elia disengaged her hands and held them in his own.

"Calm down, Lesia," he said quietly. "Tell me what happened. Calm down. Please."

He felt some of the tension leave her fingers but her eyes remained frightened.

"We were coming to say goodbye to Saul and Marusia, Orest and I. We were to meet but I was late. I guess they decided not to wait for me, I don't know. I saw them go through the barrier and I shouted to them but they didn't hear me."

She stared around, her panic returning.

"My God! All these people! The noise!" Her voice soared in incipient hysteria. Elia tightened his grip on her hands. Her eyes refocused and she sucked in air, her mouth wide.

"Elia," she gasped. "What is happening?"

"Nothing. Nothing is happening," he said soothingly. "It's as you said. There are a lot of people."

She nodded, her eyes fastened on his face.

"Stay here. Wait here," he continued. "I'm taking my parents to the train, then I'm coming back. Anna is in Lvov. I'm going there. I'll find Orest and we'll meet you back here. Wait for us here. All right?"

Her fingers stiffened in his grasp. "I'll come with you."

"No." Elia's sense of foreboding had strengthened. "Wait here. If we get separated, I'll have to search for you as well as Orest. Wait here."

Lesia nodded. "All right. But please don't take too long."

"As quickly as possible," he assured her.

Elia returned to his father's side. He bent his head close to Itzak's ear.

"Papa, I don't like this," he said quietly. "I don't think you should go."

The old man's head turned and Elia saw the fear in his eyes. Before his father could speak, Rachel Rosen, whose ears were as sharp as her nose, began to scream.

"I knew it! I knew it!" She clutched her husband, hysteria mounting in her voice. "I told you! We're going to our deaths! They're sending us to our deaths! This is the end of us!"

The crowd around them stirred like a frightened animal. A woman sobbed convulsively, an old man wailed. Yankel Rosen clapped a hand across his wife's mouth and the strident voice was stilled. She squirmed in his grasp, her eyes dilated with terror.

"Listen to me!" It was Solomon Kalish shouting, his arms held high. "Listen to me, everybody! Stay calm! Look around you. Do you think they can kill all these people? There must be thousands of us. The Germans are not barbarians. Stay calm! Stay calm or we'll start a panic and we will all be killed. By each other!"

His words were effective. The frenzied air slowly subsided into a querulous rumbling of moans and complaints. The crowd was an amorphous mass, surging forward in intermittent waves.

Suddenly, Elia and his group found themselves at the barrier.

Stretched across the street lined with German soldiers and Ukrainian policemen were strands of barbed wire. Antitank obstacles formed a passage through which the throng flowed in a tortuous, disorderly stream.

The noise and confusion were now stupefying. Empty cabs emerged from the passageway, the drivers honking and shouting for clearance, the crowd pushing and screaming abuse. A plane passed low overheard and somewhere the sharp, sporadic fire of a machine gun could be heard.

Elia, now genuinely alarmed, caught his father's arm.

"Papa . . ." he began.

Itzak shook his head.

"We have no choice." His voice was low. His eyes warned Elia, darting sideways at Rose. "Didn't you read the notices? Any Jew remaining in Kiev will be shot. We must go wherever they are sending us."

Rose had walked the entire distance wrapped in silence, her shoulders hunched, her thoughts her own. She lifted her head and her eyes met Itzak's. She turned to Elia and pressed her fist to his chest, the laden pillowcase swinging between them like a pendulum.

"Listen to me, Elia. There's no need for you to come any further with us. Go. Get away from here." Her mouth trembled and she bit her lip, pushing harder at Elia. "We'll be all right. Leave now. Go to Lvov. *Go now.*"

Elia was startled, then shamed at the intensity of his impulse to turn and push back the way they had come. Before he could formulate his thoughts, it was too late. Elia and his group were forced into the passageway by the pressure of people behind.

They emerged near a gateway set into a long brick barrier that Elia recognized as the wall surrounding the Jewish cemetery. He felt his heart lurch with fear. His glance met that of Nathan Goretsky, and the little baker nodded, his eyes bitter, a sour smile on his thin lips. Then he was lost to sight as the tightly packed crowd shifted.

A ragged queue was being formed, those in the rear pushing, the people ahead shouting and complaining. The queue moved and halted, moved and halted, advancing finally into an open area piled high with baggage, boxes, and cases.

German soldiers, shouting to be heard, were ordering the confused crowd to leave their belongings, food packages to the right, all else to the left. Rose's fist tightened on her precious pillowcase. It was torn from her grasp by a soldier and she cried out in dismay when he threw it carelessly onto a pile of boxes.

The soldiers were counting off and sending people ahead, a few at a time. Elia and his group clung together, Solomon

Kalish herding them like a distracted schoolteacher burdened with unruly children.

"We must stay together," he pleaded, pulling Rose to prevent her from retrieving her pillowcase. "Leave it! Leave it! You'll get it back on the train. They'll put it on the train."

"What train?" Goretsky's voice was shrill with rage. "There is no train, you stupid old shit! Can't you hear? They're shooting them! They're not putting them on any train. They're shooting them!"

The intermittent sound of gunfire was louder now but Kalish seemed not to hear.

"Stay together! Stay together!" he screamed. "We must get seats together. Our children will be looking for us. We must stay together!"

They were counted off and sent to join a larger group. Only Yankel was held back. Rachel, her long nose quivering, wailed in despair.

"No! No! My husband, my husband! Let him come! Please! My husband!"

The soldiers, ignoring her anguished cries, pushed her ahead, shouting at her to keep moving.

"I'll wait for you, Yankel!" she shrieked back at the same time her husband called to her to meet him at the train.

She stumbled, blinded with tears, and Elia took her arm. As they marched between rows of German soldiers, the group fell silent. Even Solomon Kalish, his face ashen, was struck dumb. He clung to the arm of his wife, Hanka, who walked in a mindless state of terror, her eyes glazed and unseeing.

Elia, now half supporting Rachel, quickened his step to come abreast of his parents. Itzak and Rose were hand in hand, their eyes cast down, their white faces set and expressionless.

Only Nathan Goretsky, his arm encircling his dazed wife, seemed in possession of his senses. His eyes under the straggling brows were alive, darting from left to right, leaping ahead to where soldiers with dogs on leashes awaited them.

His glance met Elia's and his mouth twisted in a sardonic grin that said "I told you so" as clearly as though he had spoken the words aloud.

They arrived at a corridor formed by the German soldiers and their dogs.

The corridor was narrow, no more than five feet across, and Elia was forced to drop back behind his parents as they entered.

He had only a moment to watch in horror as the soldiers, lined shoulder to shoulder, began beating the old people with clubs. Then he was in the corridor himself, his arm still supporting the wildly sobbing Rachel.

A heavy rubber truncheon descended on his shoulder, numbing his arm, and he felt Rachel slip away from him. He almost pitched over her as a blow from a second soldier split the skin over his eye. Half dazed, half blinded by blood pouring from the wound, he staggered and lost sight of her completely.

There was no way to dodge the blows, no way to go but forward. Pressed by the milling crowd behind him, he stumbled on, his good arm raised to protect his head. Shrieks of pain tore at his ears, blows fell with sickening thuds, the barking of the frantic dogs filled him with sheer animal terror. He saw a man fall and he lurched around him as the crowd trampled the prostrate body.

And then he was through, spewed forth into a small, open field strewed with discarded clothing and crowded with battered people, some naked, some whose clothes were being ripped off by German soldiers and Ukrainian police.

"Strip! Quickly! Take your clothes off! Move!" A young soldier with a sallow, acne-pitted face shouted at Elia, poking him with the butt of his club. "Get moving!"

At that moment, Goretsky emerged from the corridor. His hair was matted with blood, his left arm dangled grotesquely by his side. He was laughing hysterically, a high, harsh sound that scraped at the nerves like a rasp.

The soldier turned on him.

"Shut up!" he screamed. "Shut up and undress! Move!" He swung his club at the useless arm.

Goretsky laughed harder.

The club rose and fell and still Goretsky laughed. He raised his right arm and pointed a long, bony finger at the soldier.

Elia felt the hair on his scalp rise. The baker's eyes, under the wild brows, burned satanically. The savage laughter emanating from Goretsky's broken mouth was chillingly inhuman.

An expression of superstitious fear crossed the soldier's face. He attacked Goretsky in a frenzy, beating the small man to the ground.

The laughter ceased abruptly. Goretsky lay still, his face a bloody pulp, unrecognizable. The soldier swung his boot and kicked the motionless figure. Goretsky's lifeless body flopped like a sawdust doll, then settled facedown into the earth.

Shivering uncontrollably, Elia removed his clothing. Beside him, Hanka Kalish whimpered unceasingly. Her naked husband helped her undress, working with trembling fingers on the laces of her embroidered vest.

Nearby, Sarah Goretsky stood as though turned to stone, her empty eyes fixed on the heap of bloodstained rags that had been her husband.

"Come on! Come on! Don't just stand there." A Ukrainian policeman poked her with his club. "Undress! Move now!"

Sarah seemed not to hear. She made no move and the policeman raised his club.

"No! Please!"

Elia's mother intervened, her arms raised to fend off the blow. She was naked, one eye was swollen shut, and she was bleeding from a deep cut in her chin.

"Please! We will do it. Please." She tore at Sarah's skirt, calling out to Itzak for help.

Between them, Itzak sobbing aloud, Sarah weeping soundlessly, they stripped Sarah, bending her wooden arms to remove her blouse and undervest, scrabbling at boots that seemed glued to her rigid feet. Elia knelt and, with his parents bracing her, removed the boots. For a moment he was unable to rise. He hung on all fours, fighting a wave of nausea.

"Move! Get up! Move!"

A savage kick sent him sprawling. He staggered to his feet and joined the others, averting his eyes from the trembling nakedness of women who had been old when he was a child.

They were herded into a line formed at a gap in the high sand quarry walls.

A young woman with an infant howling in her arms preceeded Elia through the cleft in the sand wall. As they emerged, the distraught mother turned to Elia, pressing her baby against her naked breast. She was blinking so furiously her eyes appeared to be bouncing in her head.

"He's not like this, you know." Her voice was strained, her words tumbled over one another. "He's a very good baby. He hardly ever cries. Unless he's hungry. He must be hungry, don't you think? What time is it? Should I feed him? What do you think?"

Elia gaped at her denial of what was happening around her. Her child would never be hungry again. He would be dead. She would be dead. And soon.

And with that thought, the numbness that had held Elia in a state of near paralysis splintered. He understood. Understood and believed.

They were killing them all and they would kill him too. He would not see Anna in Lvov. He would never see Anna in Lvov. He would never see Anna again.

Elia looked around wildly.

Behind him, his parents led a catatonic Sarah between them, followed by a terrified throng of naked people stumbling through the gap in the sandy walls. There was no turning back. He had no choice but to keep moving along a ledge that grew steadily narrower.

The line halted and Elia pressed against the quarry wall to avoid falling forward. Across the deep ravine, on the other side of the quarry, he saw a soldier pick up a machine gun and start firing. He looked down.

He had only a split second to take in the horror below. The quarry floor was a carnage pit of naked, bloody bodies. He heard the screams. To his left, he saw bodies fall from the ledge.

He jumped.

It was a long drop and Elia fell badly, his leg twisting under him as he struck bottom. He pitched forward, smashing his face on the elbow of a corpse. For a moment his consciousness flickered like a failing lightbulb, then his mouth filled with blood, threatening to choke him. He coughed and spat, then forced himself to lie still.

He became aware of a steady shifting movement under and around him. There was still life in some of the bodies and, as they stirred, they settled one into the other. He was slowly being pressed into the grisly mass.

He had barely formulated the thought of movement when shots rang out above the moaning and sobbing sounds of those not yet dead. Beside him, the body of the young mother twitched, leaped, then lay inert, one arm flung across Elia's chest.

Elia lay rigid. Peripheral vision afforded him a view of the ledge where the soldiers stood, firing pistols at any sign of movement below. He closed his eyes and waited, hardly daring to breathe. The firing ceased. Fearful of moving, terrified of remaining where he was, he waited.

The rattling screech of a machine gun rent the air. The naked body of an old man fell with a sickening thud, one fist thumping the wound on Elia's cheek. Then another body caught him in the back, landing like a sledgehammer blow.

Elia jacknifed involuntarily and the bloodied corpse of a boy no more than eight years of age flopped into the circle of his arms.

Elia screamed aloud. The child's face was set in a rictus of terror. His chest had been torn away by bullets. The splintered ends of white bone protruded through the flesh of his forearm. Shuddering with reaction, his vision bleared with tears, Elia held the frail, warm body close.

Once again, revolver bullets ripped at dying flesh, once more the machine gun rattled and bodies fell. A resolution began to form in Elia's mind, a determination to survive. To survive and see Anna again, to one day hold his living child in his arms.

He matched himself to the methodical pattern set by the Germans, moving during the bursts of machine-gun fire, taking advantage of the rain of bodies to crawl by inches toward the quarry wall. He dragged the dead boy with him, using the small body as a shield between himself and the eyes of the soldiers during the intervals between the machine-gun killings.

He soon lost count of his minuscule advances. Like some obscene nocturnal animal, he slithered over corpses each time the machine gun commenced firing. He was covered in a slime of blood and feces—many of the victims had defecated as they fell. Grimly, he blessed the broken nose dulling his sense of smell. He felt no pain. Only a feverish compulsion to reach the quarry wall.

Dusk was falling when Elia's numbed brain took note of a change in the falling bodies. The new ones were fully clothed.

It puzzled Elia. With night approaching, were the soldiers becoming impatient? Then, as the machine gun chattered above, he knelt on the humpback of Orest Tokariuk. He recoiled in horror.

The clothed bodies were not those of Jews. They were gentiles who had come to see their Jewish friends off on the train and had been caught in the net. The Germans, Elia guessed, intended to leave no live witnesses.

He thought of Lesia Boyko waiting and it seemed a century had passed since he had left her with the assurance he would return with Orest. Lying beside the body of his friend, he knew he would never again hear a bandura played without reliving the anguish of this moment.

He brushed the matted hair from Orest's face and gently closed the wildly staring eyes. When the shooting started, he moved on. He was only yards from the wall when the firing ceased entirely.

He lay still, eyeing the bodies nearest him for clothing. When he felt it was safe, he began the the gruesome task of stripping bloody garments from the corpses—a woolen sweater, a pair of trousers, thick socks from the feet of a chunky woman with dirty ankles.

When darkness fell, black and starless, Elia began climbing the quarry wall, digging footholds, raising himself and digging more. His ascent was slow and tortuous. His injured leg was all but useless, threatening to buckle each time it was necessary to trust his weight to it.

After what seemed an endless time but was, in actuality, less than an hour, his searching hand met empty air and he knew he had reached the top of the quarry wall. With the last strength of his quivering arms, he pulled himself up and over the edge and sprawled forward, his face throbbing agonizingly with each beat of his pounding heart.

He pressed himself into the sandy soil, waiting for his pulse to return to normal, then crawled away from the ravine, not knowing or caring in which direction he was bound, wanting only to get as far from the quarry as possible before daybreak.

He crawled through the night, dragging himself forward

by his elbows. At the first sign of dawn, he crept into the thick growth in a ditch and slept.

He woke, thirsty and shivering with chill. His eyes were puffed shut, sealed by the gummy mucous residue of fever. He picked at the dried pus until he could pry his eyelids open a little. By tilting his head far back, he could peer through narrow slits between his lashes.

The sky was the leaden gray peculiar to both dawn and twilight. For a moment he thought it was morning. As the sky darkened, he realized he had slept throughout the day.

Slowly, cautiously, he raised his head above the level of the weeds. The ditch in which he lay encircled a ploughed field. On the far side of the field was a white farmhouse. Beside the house was a thatch-roofed barn.

Taking a zigzag course, he crossed the field at a snail's pace, following a furrow, heaving his swollen leg over into the next furrow and crawling on.

He blacked out repeatedly. Each time he regained consciousness he pried an eyelid open and sighted on the barn, then blindly crawled a few yards more.

Night had fallen when he reached the barn. By touch, he located a mound of hay. Dimly aware of the sound of barking dogs, he burrowed deep into the hay and lost consciousness once more.

Chapter 7

*T*hat was Babi Yar."

The old man raised his eyes, looked at Cia, then at me.

"One day it was just a ravine on the outskirts of Kiev," he said. "A place where children played. The next day it became the depths of hell. They try to say now that it never happened. But it did. I was there."

Around us, the flea market pace had quickened. It was four-thirty and the other vendors were packing. By five the mall would be empty. Cia and I were late starting.

"Mr. Strohan." I held out my hand. "Give me the locket. I'll check back at some of the places we went. Maybe somebody will recognize it."

The old man rose slowly to his feet. He looked at the pendant, shook his head, and dropped it into my outstretched hand.

"Maybe," he said. "But you must not hope too much." He smiled and corrected himself. "*I* must not hope too much."

"Don't say that," I protested. "We might just get lucky. Come back next week."

The old man nodded. Leaning on his cane, he shuffled to the mall doors. Before leaving, he turned and raised his hand in a gesture of farewell.

"Dopobachynia!" Cia and I both called at the same time.

The old man grinned.

"Dopobachynia," he repeated. His smile took the sting out of his next words. "Your accents are atrocious, you know."

Cia laughed. "We know."

"Be sure to come back next week," I reminded him.

"I will."

He waved and was gone.

Betty, our neighbor, paused in her packing.

"What in hell was all that about?" she demanded. "What was the old guy yakking at you all afternoon about?"

Betty is in her fifties, a big woman we disliked on sight and are now enormously fond of. As my daughter, Jenny, would say, everything hangs out up front with Betty.

She can be crude and she can be very rude, but her rough manner is deceptive. She's a good-natured, generous human being with an extensive knowledge of jewelry and antique silver. Unlike many—or most—vendors she willingly shares what she knows with anyone asking her advice.

"I'll tell you all about it next week." I showed her the pendant. "Does this look familiar to you?"

She peered at the locket and shook her head.

"Nope." Her lips turned down in distaste. "I wouldn't look at a thing like that anyway. It's crap."

She collapsed the legs of her metal folding table, letting it crash to the floor. Every vendor in the mall winced. Breakage is a constant flea market hazard and any smashing sound produces an instant reaction.

Packing with practiced speed, Cia called over to me.

"Liz? Have you any idea what you've let us in for with that locket? Do you how much running around we'll have to do? And do you know what our chances are of tracking it down?"

"I know," I called back sheepishly. "Look, Cia. You don't have to get involved. You didn't make the dumb offer."

Cia flapped her hand at me.

"Yeah, yeah. I know. But if you hadn't, I would have."

Chapter 8

Perhaps, in order for anyone to understand what my impulsive offer entailed, I should describe how flea markets—and flea market vendors—operate.

First, I'll explain how Cia and I became involved in flea marketing. Or rather, slid into it, because that's the way it came about.

My name is Liz Cantrell.

I was born Elisaveta Novasad. Elisaveta became Elizabeth and Elizabeth, inevitably, became Liz. Novasad changed to Cantrell when I married John, an account executive in the advertising agency where I worked as a copywriter.

It wasn't a good marriage.

I imagine, if I hadn't fallen pregnant, as the French-Canadians have it, we'd have gone on with the rather superficial, very expensive way of life provided by two excellent salaries. But I did get pregnant. Jenny was born. And John, increasingly, came home only to change clothes. He died in a drunken auto accident when Jenny was four.

After two or three unhappy experiences with housekeepers, I became a freelance copywriter. Which means I write radio and television commercials, ads, catalogs, industrial films, and so forth. Anything anyone will pay me to write.

It's a living, but it's a feast-or-famine thing. Sometimes a

month, even two, can pass without an assignment. There is
no steady paycheck. I imagine, somewhere back in my subconscious, I was looking for a way to bring in cash on a
regular basis when I met Cia.

Cia was christened Anastasia Kushnir. Thirty or forty
years ago Ukrainian girls named Anastasia were called Ann,
Nancy, or Nelly by their English friends. Not Cia. How Sia
with an "S" became Cia with a "C" I don't know and, until
this moment, it never occurred to me to ask.

Cia married Peter Sutherland. They were divorced, three
years ago, after twenty-five years of marriage and two children—Valerie, who now lives in California, and Barry, an
agriculture student at MacDonald College.

After the divorce, Cia opened a handicrafts shop. Her
choice of location was unfortunate. The venture failed and
she was left with a basement piled high with unsold stock.
Somewhat soured on individual enterprise, she took a job in
a bank. We met at garage sales, to which we were both ad-
dicted, and became friends.

One Sunday we happened on a flea market held in a
shopping mall at Valois, a neighboring suburb. Behind laden
tables were faces we encountered regularly at garage sales.

As we roamed through the mall, the same thought was
taking shape in both our heads, Cia had a mountain of wool
and craft materials. Packed away in my basement was John's
expensive sports equipment and boxes of household articles
left me by my mother.

An elderly couple, selling secondhand books, pointed out
the flea market organizer, a vendor himself. We paid him
twenty dollars advance rent and we were in the flea market
business.

It took eight Sundays to sell off most of what we had.
But by then we had learned from other vendors and were
spending our Saturdays chasing garage sales, rummage sales,
and bazaars, buying anything and everything we thought we
could sell.

Early each Saturday morning we draw a map of all the garage sales advertised in the area we plan to cover. By eight o'clock, we're on our way.

Most sales are scheduled for nine or ten, but we quickly discovered other vendors had arrived before us, so we are always early, often arriving as the garage salers were beginning to set up. I've wondered what those people think of the sudden influx of buyers who dash in early, select quickly, and rush away. Are they aware they've been invaded by flea market vendors?

For a long time after we started, Cia and I referred to the flea market vendors as weird. And it's partially true—by and large they're not your average nine-to-five consumer-type people. They are different, even though I stopped calling them weird after Jenny reminded me I was one of them.

Whatever we make, Cia and I split three ways. One-third to buy more stock, one-third to her, one-third to me. We'll never get rich, but it's all cash and it pays for the groceries.

Driving home that Sunday, Cia laid out the problems involved in my offer to track down the pendant.

"Three months of garage sales, averaging, say, twenty to thirty a week. Do you realize we're talking about close to three hundred? Not to mention church bazaars and rummage sales."

"I know."

"We can forget bazaars and rummage sales," she continued. "There's no way we're going to trace everybody who contributed to them."

"I know."

"Would you stop saying 'I know'? I know you know. So what do we do? I never kept the maps we made. Did you?"

"No. But I saved all the newspapers to roll into logs for the fireplace. We marked the garage sales we were interested in, remember? I'll go through them tomorrow morning."

Chapter 9

I awoke early Monday morning, staggering out of a nightmare in which I had crawled through a sea of corpses, searching for the body of my daughter.

The old man's reporting of the events at Babi Yar had been coolly dispassionate, a detachment acquired, I'm sure, over the span of the five intervening decades.

Maybe that's how evil survives.

Time leaches human outrage out of history, leaving only bare factual bones, and even the most horrifying crime becomes a shadowy episode, distant and unreal.

But to me, Babi Yar had become immediate and monstrous. It had festered in my mind and erupted in my dream. The smell of blood clung to my nostrils. Dying shrieks echoed in my ears.

Remaining in bed was impossible. I got up, made coffee, carried the pot to the basement, and attacked the pile of newspapers, separating the classified sections from the weekend editions of the past three months.

I was restacking the papers when I heard Jenny moving in the kitchen above my head. I called up to her. The door to the basement opened and she came down as far as the landing.

"I thought you'd gone out." She leaned over the railing,

her long hair falling across her bare breasts. "Where's the coffeepot? I can't find it."

"Here." I held up the empty pot. "Make some fresh. I'll have a cup with you. And put on some clothes while you're at it."

"It's too hot to get dressed. Anyway, who's going to see me?" She slouched down the stairs and took the pot from my outstretched hand. "What's with all the newspapers?"

"Go make coffee. I'll come up and tell you all about it. And for heaven's sake, at least put on a pair of panties. You look hairy and lewd and obscene."

She grinned down at me.

"Anybody'd look hairy from down there." The grin broadened. "Hey, can you imagine the view for a midget at a nudist camp? *There's* hairy and obscene."

"Go." I laughed. "Make coffee. I'll be up in a minute."

She left, snickering to herself.

I picked up the garage sale pages. There were forty-three of them, each scrawled with heavy red circles marking the sales we had planned to attend. I carried them upstairs.

Jenny, wearing a bikini bathing suit, set out mugs and poured coffee. Casually defiant, she lit a cigarette. I bit my tongue. The issue of her smoking was a lost war.

I handed her the locket. She opened it and her brows lifted.

"Mm. A hunk. Who is he and where is he?"

"Stop drooling. He's an old man now. That picture was taken long before you were born."

I told her Elia's story.

She listened, but she's of the television generation. Violence has no reality for them. How can it? An actor is brutally murdered in a cops 'n' robbers drama this week and turns up next week as an ambulance driver in a medical series. Brutality is carefully choreographed and death is never final.

"So did he go to Lvov and find Anna?" she asked.

"I don't know. We had to pack up."

"Oh." She yawned and stretched luxuriously. "Man, I sure don't feel like going to work today."

"What time did you get in? I didn't hear you."

As soon as the words were out of my mouth I knew I was making the same old mistake. Her face went blank. Over her eyes, the shutters closed and were firmly locked.

"Late." She butted her cigarette messily in a saucer.

"How late?" I couldn't stop myself.

"Very late," she said flatly and lit a second cigarette.

"Honey, you're not getting enough sleep. You're going to be sick if you keep on the way you are."

I heard what I was saying. I was aware I was going down the wrong road. I knew what her reaction would be. But once you start, it's like riding a roller coaster. You can't get off until you've run the course.

"Jenny," I persisted stupidly, knowing the outcome. "You can't chase around all night, then work an eight-hour day and not pay for it."

She unfolded her long, slim legs and stood up. Hips jutting, arms folded across her chest, she faced me coldly.

"We've been there, done this," she said unpleasantly. "I'm eighteen years old and . . ."

"Seventeen."

"So seventeen. I'll be eighteen in two months." She held up her hand and ticked off her fingers. "I have a job. I have a car. Okay, so I couldn't get a loan without you, but I'm the one who's paying it. I pay room and board. Nobody is going to tell me what I can and can't do. If I want to stay out all night, I will."

"Not as long as you live in this house. Not as long as you're a minor. Not as long as I'm responsible for you."

We were hurtling along all too familiar rails now, but neither of us could stop. It's almost a ritual. It *is* a ritual. I sidetracked.

"Jenny, you know I can't sleep until I know you're safe and sound. I keep waking up, wondering if you're in some car accident somewhere. Maybe you can get along without sleep. I can't."

"It's not my fault you can't sleep. And I don't know what you're so worried about. Nothing's going to happen to me."

"That's what every stiff in the morgue thought."

"I'm a careful driver and you know it. I've never had a speeding ticket. I've never even had a parking ticket."

"It's not your driving I'm worried about. It's Rick's. He drives too fast. And he drinks too much. I don't give a damn what he does when he's alone. But I'll be damned if he's going to endanger the most precious thing I own."

"You don't own me!" she screamed. "*I* own me!"

"You know damn well what I meant!" I screamed back at her.

"You're damn right I do." Jenny's voice was venomous. "All this has nothing to do with sleep. It's Rick. It's always Rick. What have you got against him?"

"What have I got against him? He's a handsome, spoiled nothing. He's lazy. He has no manners. He's a total waste of space. That's what I have against him."

"He speaks well of you too." Jenny sneered with a calculated insolence that was new.

Suddenly I was overwhelmed with a cold rage I had never felt toward her before. I slapped her face, hard.

For a moment we gaped at one another, dumbfounded. I had never in her life struck her, not even when she had misbehaved as a child.

"You hit me!" Jenny gasped, incredulous. Then she howled like a ten-year-old. "*You hit me!*"

"And I'll hit you again if you ever take that tone with me," I gritted to cover my own shock. "You can speak to your friends that way. Not to me. I won't take it from you. Never."

Her eyes filled, her lower lip pouted as it had when she was a baby.

"You hit me," she repeated and burst into tears. Sobbing,

she ran upstairs to her room. I heard the bed jump as she threw herself across it.

Utterly defeated, I poured another mug of coffee and tried to calm myself.

I was angry at having allowed myself to become embroiled in yet another argument. All my resolve to maintain a dignified, adult attitude with Jenny was once more down the drain. I was disgusted at having so thoroughly lost my temper.

And her lusty wailing was beginning to grate on my nerves.

I climbed the stairs, knocked, opened the door to her room.

"Listen, honey . . ."

"Go away!" Her face was buried in her pillow and the words were muffled. "You're a violent, violent person! I hate you!"

"I'm not too wild about you at the moment either, you know."

She raised her head and glared at me.

"Go away. This is my room and I don't want you in it."

Without warning, a bubble of laughter erupted in my gut and I snorted aloud. Moments ago, this snuffling child had been a bikinied young lady, smoking to prove her independence.

"Come on, Jenny. We're being silly. I didn't mean to . . ."

"Go away!" she screamed. "I mean it! I hate you!"

Shaken, I retreated to my own room. I dressed quickly and went downstairs. I prepared Jenny's dinner—today was her three-to-eleven shift—packed it and left the bag on the dishwasher, snatched a sheet of the garage sale ads and fled to my car.

Driving to the first of the addresses, I tried, for the hundredth time, to understand the stranger who had usurped my daughter's body.

From babyhood on, Jenny had been a delight.

As a young teenager, she had spent her summers as a day camp counselor. At fifteen she had transferred her enthusiasm and her energy to work with a senior citizens group. She had been chubby then, with lank hair, adolescent skin, nails bitten to the quick, and braces on her teeth.

And she had been loving, funny, and wildly romantic.

Looking back, it seems to me the good changes took place overnight. She stopped biting her nails, lost forty pounds. The braces were removed. Her seventeenth birthday gift was a fifty-dollar haircut.

The snapshot I took of her that day shows a very pretty, tall, slim girl with honey-colored hair and level blue eyes. She is holding up both hands to display the painted, pointed nails she never thought she'd have. And if it wasn't for the happy grin on her face, the shot could be used by Revlon.

And that's when she met Rick Lawrence, a handsome twenty-year-old brat too insensitive to recognize the vulnerability of the insecure young girl inside the shapely body of the poised young woman she now appears to be.

There are too many Rick Lawrences.

They drop out of school. They drop in and out of jobs. They drive family cars and live free in the homes of their indulgent, indifferent parents. They're aimless, except in their pursuit of pleasure. They're careless with people and possessions. Their response to adults is a thinly veiled insolence. And their morals would make an alley cat blush.

Under Rick's influence, Jenny dropped her plans for college. When I told her she must either continue her schooling or go to work, she found a job as a sales clerk in an airport gift shop and declared her right to henceforth do as she pleased.

The only opinions she seems to value now, the only approval she seems to seek is that of Rick and the vapid clones, male and female, he calls his friends.

I am the enemy. And I don't know how to handle it.

———

I drove to seven garage sale addresses that day. Four in the afternoon, three in the evening with Cia.

The next day, we covered six.

The following day, of the eight we drove to see, three were a waste of gas. No one was home. At the others, the reaction was identical. Suspicion first, then a shake of the head.

"No. Sorry."

Chapter 10

Driving to the flea market Sunday morning, Cia summed up the week's efforts.

"Okay. We showed the locket to twenty-four people. Which is better than I expected, thanks to you. But even at that rate, it could take a minimum of eight weeks to cover all the addresses we have. And that's only if you don't get any freelance jobs over the entire summer."

"Jesus, Cia. Don't say that. You'll hex me."

"Don't be silly. What I'm saying is, do we make a career out of the damn thing? Or do we give the locket back and say, 'Sorry, we tried.' "

"I hate to give up so soon."

"I know. So do I. But how long do you think we should go searching through the great big haystack with our teeny needle?"

"We could hit the right place next week."

Cia snorted. "Yeah. Sure we could."

"Okay," I said. "Why don't we do it this way? As long as I have free time, I'll make the rounds during the day and we'll go together in the evenings. When I don't, we won't. Agreed?"

"Agreed." Cia nodded.

We finished setting up by nine and I went the round of

vendors with the locket. None had seen it before, each wanted to hear the story, and it was close to ten o'clock by the time I returned to our table.

"No luck?" Cia asked.

I shook my head.

"But Ros and Mike Hennessy have a good idea. They do two other flea markets, Lachute and Finnigan's, and if we can give them a picture of the locket, they'll ask around. Did Barry take his Polaroid to Europe with him?"

"No. We'll take a shot tomorrow and give it to them." Cia indicated the mall doors with her thumb. "You missed the Weeper. She just left."

The Weeper is a flea market regular and not to be believed. She is a good-looking woman in her late forties, with large, mournful eyes and carefully coifed auburn hair. She is always tastefully and expensively dressed.

The first time she came to our table, months back, she completely flummoxed Cia and me. She picked up a pretty green glass bowl we had priced at six dollars.

"Is this your best price?" she asked, fixing me with her heavily lashed brown eyes.

"Well, we might come down a bit. Make an offer."

"Fifty cents?"

"Fifty cents!" I was taken aback. "Oh, no. I'm sorry."

I reached to take the bowl from her.

"Please." To my astonishment, two great tears gushed from those tragic eyes and rolled majestically down her cheeks. Her grip on the bowl tightened. She opened her fist and showed me two quarters.

"Please. It's all I have. Please. Take it."

Her eyes were swimming. Tears slid unchecked down her face and fell in drops off her chin onto her tweed suit. I looked helplessly at Cia. She was gaping, open-mouthed, at the woman.

To this day I don't know whether I was hypnotized by her tears or just horribly embarrassed for her. I gave her the bowl for fifty cents and we watched her scuttle through the mall doors.

We looked across at Ros and Mike, wondering if they had witnessed the performance. They had. And they were laughing. She was an old story to them.

"Was she carrying anything?" I asked now.

"A plastic bag. There must be a new vendor this week."

"There is. Up near the deli."

Cia laughed. She nodded toward the doors. "Here comes our old man."

He was carrying a bakery carton tied with white string. He reached our table and handed it to Cia.

"Croissants for your coffee," he said. "Fresh baked and still hot."

"Oh, lovely," Cia crowed. "I'll go get coffee. Why don't you come in and sit down, Mr. Strohan. I won't be a minute."

"Elia." He raised his palm. "Please. Call me Elia."

"Elia it is. I'm Cia. She's Liz."

He nodded. "I know. I remember."

While Cia was gone, I told Elia we had come up empty-handed.

"I'm sorry," I concluded. "But we'll keep trying. Is it all right if we keep the locket awhile longer?"

"Of course." He touched my shoulder gently. "Don't expect too much, Liz. I appreciate what you're doing, but I've learned not to hope too much. You mustn't either."

"I always hope," I said, and smiled at him.

"Yes." He looked at me. "One does. As long as one can."

Cia returned. We took turns serving two or three customers while we ate the croissants and drank the coffee. At the first lull, we sat down.

"Now tell us," I said. "Did you get to Lvov?"

He nodded but didn't reply immediately. He crumpled his Styrofoam cup and tossed it into the paper bag we used for trash.

"Yes," he said finally. "But much later than I expected."

Chapter 11

Buried in his mound of hay, Elia heard the dogs only moments before they were upon him.

Consciousness flickered briefly.

He was dimly aware of a fiery thirst, of pulsating agony behind his eyes that threatened to blow his skull apart. The frantic yelping of the dogs followed him back into blackness.

Several times the darkness swirled to murky clouds of gray, illuminated by flashes of a lurid phosphorescence. He dreamed he was carrying the boy again. Small, dead hands wrapped themselves softly around his wrists. He fought to lay the bloody corpse aside but could not free himself. He dreamed he wakened and opened his eyes, only to find himself looking into the face of the boy. Screaming silently, he slipped away, feeling the child's cold fingers on his burning face, stroking gently.

He came to full consciousness slowly, floating upward on a rivulet of sound that gradually resolved into a soft humming he recognized. It was a Ukrainian folk melody Anna had often sung as she worked at cooking, washing, cleaning the apartment.

A wild streak of hope seared through him. He opened his eyes.

He was lying on a cot in a narrow room.

Sunlight streamed through small casement windows set deep in a whitewashed wall opposite, outlining the figure of a woman bent over a wooden washstand. Her back was to him and she hummed to herself as she wrung a cloth from a steaming basin, her hands pink from the hot water.

From where he lay, he could see only the braided knot of her gray hair. She wore a white blouse, the sleeves rolled above her elbows, and a heavy black cotton skirt. She must have sensed his scrutiny, for she turned quickly, the song dying in her throat.

"Ah!" she cried and bustled across the room, carrying the steaming cloth. "Back in the land of the living!"

Seating herself on a stool, she laid the cloth across his forehead, her eyes intent. She could have been anywhere between forty and sixty years of age. Her skin had the permanently brown look of the outdoor worker. Her plump cheeks were the color of russet apples. Wrinkles radiated from the corners of blue eyes.

Satisfied with her arrangement of the hot cloth, she sat up straight and met his gaze.

"I am Kalyna Zaleschuk," she said. "This is my house." She tapped the cot. "This is my son's bed. The dogs found you."

Elia cleared his rusty throat. "Thank you," he croaked.

"You're one of the Jews they're killing over at Babi Yar." It was not a question. She stated the fact, arms folded across her ample bosom.

Elia was startled. "How did you know?"

She pointed her chin at the area halfway down the cot.

"I brought up four sons," she said. "None of theirs were like that. I've never seen a Jewish one before. Very neat."

Elia could feel his cheeks flushing.

"I didn't mean . . ." he stammered. "I meant, how did you know about Babi Yar?"

Her brows lifted. "How could I not know? How could you shoot people day after day and anybody not know?"

"Day after day." Elia echoed. "How long have I been here?"

"Five days." She held up five fingers. "You've been in that bed for five days."

Elia closed his eyes, shuddering.

"And they've been shooting people?" He choked out the words. "Day after day?"

"Day after day."

He opened his eyes and looked at her, unable to absorb the truth of what she was saying.

"And people know what's happening?"

She nodded. "If I know, then everybody knows. I mind my own business. I'm always the last to know anything."

"And they do nothing?"

"What can they do?" She shrugged. "The Germans will shoot them too."

"They're shooting them anyway," Elia said. "Don't they know it's not only Jews they're killing? They're shooting Ukrainians—gentiles—too."

She nodded vigorously. "I know. I know. And they'll shoot a lot more. Anybody who helps the Jews, anybody who hides a Jew, they'll shoot them all too."

The words sent a chill through Elia. He looked up at her, trying to read behind the bright blue of her eyes. She understood immediately and patted his shoulder.

"Don't worry, don't worry! I wouldn't give those *chorts* the skin off a fart," she reassured him.

Her shoulders lifted and fell.

"I have nothing against Jews," she said. "Some have. Not me. You're no different than me. You want to feed your kids, be a little bit happy. Live. Just like me. Like my cow, out there." She hooked a thumb at the window. "I have to hide her too."

Elia found himself laughing, carefully until he gauged the extent of his tolerance to the pain, then with mirth bordering on hysteria.

Kalyna, startled at first, threw back her head and guffawed. She was missing an eyetooth and the gap gave her a faintly Rabelaisian look. She laughed from the belly, her unfettered breasts jiggling under her loose peasant blouse.

Behind her, the door opened. A young boy peered in, wide-eyed, and joined in the laughter without knowing its cause. He pushed the door and hurried to his mother's side, followed by a girl two or three years his senior.

Kalyna hugged him to her, wiping her brimming eyes on her sleeve.

"This is Bohdan," she said. "This is my baby. The last one. There won't be any more."

"I'm not a baby," the boy protested. "I'm seven. I'm big."

"Of course you're big." She kissed the top of her head. "You are my big baby."

She reached for the girl who stood shyly behind her, eyes fastened on Elia. "And this is Olena, my big girl. She has been taking care of you."

Elia thanked Olena gravely. Over the heads of the children, his eyes sought Kalyna's. Again, without words, she understood. She shook her head.

"They'll say nothing. They keep bigger secrets than you."

Elia learned the first secret from Olena.

Her eldest brother, Taras, had deserted from the army. Ill and wounded, he had crawled home. For two months, hidden and cared for by his family, he had clung to life, then died on the cot where Elia lay.

Had it not been for an accident, he might never have known the second secret.

As his strength returned, Elia became aware of the household routine. Other than when Olena came to see to his needs, the house was empty and silent throughout the entire day.

In the evening, Kalyna came, changed his bandages, fed and bathed him. Her touch was gentle as she probed his swollen leg. She assured him it was not broken. The ligaments were badly torn but they would mend.

His head wound festered and she frowned each time she tended it. His broken nose she could do nothing about except describe the rainbow of colors that went with it.

In the beginning, she would disappear after she had ministered to him. After the first week, she brought her mending in the evening and sat with him, chatting about her own life, questioning his.

She had inherited the farm, married young, and given birth to eight children, three stillborn, before her husband, a man older than she, died.

"No loss." She shrugged and tilted her hand in the classic drinking gesture. "He was a drunk. And a mean one at that. If his liver hadn't killed him, one of my boys would have sooner or later. Maybe even me."

Of her older boys, as far as she knew, only Taras was dead. All three had been inducted into the army.

"Ivan and Dimitri will come home," she repeated. "Maybe soon, maybe when the war is over. Maybe they're prisoners. Maybe they're far away. But they're not dead. I know it,"—she tapped her breast—"here."

By the third week, Elia was making small forays around the room, walking gingerly on the still-weakened leg, and fighting a dizziness that came and went. Kalyna had impressed on him, for the sake of his safety and theirs, that he must not show himself outdoors.

"The dogs will warn us if anyone comes," she explained. "Some of my neighbors, especially those damned Savitskys, would as soon turn you in as look at you."

On the day of the accident, Elia was doing his morning exercise of ten paces forward, ten back, when he heard the dogs.

He hobbled to the window.

Kalyna appeared from behind the barn, running full tilt toward the house. She burst into the room.

"Into bed! Be quick!," she panted. "Germans. A German patrol is coming. Get into bed and look sick. Look very damn sick!"

She slammed the door behind her.

Stretched out on the cot, the covers pulled up to his chin, Elia heard the sound of heavy boots. He let his mouth drop open, narrowed his eyes to slits through which he could see the door.

"What is in here?" a heavy voice demanded in German.

"No! No!" he heard Kalyna cry out. "Please! You mustn't go in there!"

"Open it! Tell her to open it," the German commanded.

The door swung wide. A Ukrainian policeman stepped into the room, followed by a German soldier carrying a rifle. Kalyna remained in the doorway, wringing her hands.

"Who is this?" the soldier barked. "Ask her who it is."

Kalyna needed no translation.

"My nephew," she wailed. "My nephew from Poltava. He's very sick. He's dying." She turned large eyes on the Ukrainian policeman. "It's the fever. Typhus. He's dying."

Blanching, crossing himself, the policeman dived for the doorway, shouting *"Typhus"* at the soldier. Kalyna leaped nimbly aside as both men bolted. She threw Elia a broad wink and closed the door behind her.

Five minutes later, she was back. She dropped onto the stool and heaved a deep sigh.

"They're gone, thank the Lord."

"What are they looking for?"

"Jews. Livestock." She shrugged. "Anything they can steal. Except they call it requisitioning."

"They're hunting Jews?"

She nodded.

"Thank you, Kalyna," Elia said softly.

Kalyna waved a self-deprecating hand.

"You, I wasn't worried about. You, I had it all figured

out. But how do you tell a cow to lie down and play dead?"

They laughed together, then Kalyna crossed herself solemnly and left him. It wasn't until the door closed behind her that Elia realized how different she looked.

She was normally as tidy as a cat, her blouse always white and spotless, her skin shining, her hair clean and neatly plaited. He had never seen her as she had appeared a moment ago, dressed in filthy trousers, soiled shirt. There had been dirt in her hair, on her face and hands, grime under her fingernails.

Harvesting? Too late in the season. He began to wonder what she and the children did, absent from the house all day.

In the early afternoon, the dogs barked again.

Once again, Kalyna ran from behind the barn. She slowed to a walk and Elia knew there was no immediate danger. Nevertheless, he stretched out on the cot and pulled the quilt up to his chin.

Minutes later, the door opened.

Through slitted lids, Elia saw Kalyna in the doorway. With her was an old woman, head wrapped in a flowered, fringed shawl. Beside her stood a pale, gaunt priest with nervous eyes.

"As I said, Pani Zaleschuk—" The old crone's voice was a thin whine. "I didn't know you had a nephew in Poltava."

"As I said, Pani Savitsky," Kalyna replied tartly, "Where is it written that you have to know everything there is to know?"

"The Germans said he was dying of the fever."

"They came to your house, too, did they?"

The old woman nodded. Her face collapsed in a toothless grin. "They're hunting Yids, you know, my dear Pani Zaleschuk."

"They're scouting provisions, my dear Pani Savitsky. They'll be back for those prize pigs of yours."

The old woman's head reared. "What? My pigs? Oh, no,

Pani Zaleschuk. They were very polite and respectful to me."

"They'll be even more polite when they come for your pigs."

The old woman darted a spiteful glance at Kalyna and changed the subject.

"So your poor nephew is dying, is he, Pani Zaleschuk? The fever, you say?"

"Be my guest, Pani Savitsky." Kalyna gestured broadly. "Go burn your hand on his forehead."

Drawing back hastily, the old woman placed the priest in the doorway. The priest cleared his throat apprehensively. He raised two fingers in Elia's direction.

"Bless you, my son," he intoned.

He plucked at the old woman's sleeve and the two hurried away. Kalyna, grinning broadly, followed.

Elia heard a door slam, then Kalyna was back.

"They're gone." She blew a noisy, crepitating sound with her tongue. "Nosy old sow."

"The priest?"

"Her son. A real snot nose. But your troubles are over." Kalyna's voice was dry. "You've been blessed by a Savitsky."

She raised two fingers in mocking benediction and left. The house returned to its normal afternoon stillness.

Elia was hovering between sleep and wakefulness when the door crashed open. Young Bohdan flew across the room. He jerked frantically at Elia's arm.

"Cousin Elia! Cousin Elia!" he screamed. "My mother! My mother! Hurry! My mother!"

Elia scrambled from the cot. Limping, hopping, loping, he followed the hysterical boy through the house, out and across the yard. They circled the barn, the boy dashing forward and back, screaming with impatience.

Behind the barn was a scrub-covered hillock, almost as high as the barn. Bohdan raced to a tangle of brush and yanked it aside, revealing an opening that led to a tunnel no more than three feet in height.

He dropped to his knees, shouting at Elia to follow.

Elia followed, gritting his teeth at the stab of pain in his leg. He emerged in a low, domed room carved out under the hill. At the far end, Olena was sobbing and scrabbling with her bare hands at a mound of dirt and rubble.

"Under here! Under here!" she shrieked. "It fell on her! Mamma's under here!"

Elia looked wildly around and spotted a shovel leaning against the earthen wall. He grabbed it and ran, bent over, to where the children were tearing at a mixture of soil and rock covering their mother.

Working feverishly, they uncovered first a hand, then Kalyna's head. Elia dropped to his knees and pressed his ear to her face. He heard a fluttery breath, another and another.

"She's alive!" he shouted. "Dig! She's alive!"

Working more carefully now, they dug Kalyna out.

There was a large, angry bruise above her eye and one wrist was puffed to twice its size. But the greatest damage was to her right leg. Her foot was twisted in an unnatural position. When Elia tore back her pant leg, he saw the bone had snapped below her knee. The fractured bone had punctured flesh and skin and was exposed, gleaming whitely in the lamplight illuminating the room.

He swallowed hard, striving for calm.

"Olena. Bohdan." He was finally able to speak. "We're going to have to get your mother to the house. We'll have to drag her through the tunnel. After that, I can carry her. Olena, it is your responsibility to see that her leg doesn't get caught on anything. Bohdan, you take care of her hand. Understood?"

The two children, faces pale, eyes huge, nodded.

Two hours later, Kalyna regained consciousness.

Elia, seated beside her bed, heard her moan. He bent over her. She opened pain-filled eyes and looked around. At Bohdan, huddled in a corner of the room, at Olena at the foot of the bed, at Elia.

"Shit," she groaned. Her eyelids drooped. "Goddamn shit."

"Kalyna." Elia touched her shoulder. "Listen. Tell me where there's a doctor. I'll go get him."

She moved her head from side to side. "What doctor? There is no doctor."

"You . . . there has to be . . . you need . . ." Elia stammered.

She raised herself on her elbows, her face gray and shiny with perspiration. At the sight of her leg and protruding bone she fell back and cursed.

It was a startling stream of profanity. Elia fluttered over her helplessly. She reached up, finally, and grasped his arm.

"Listen to me," she gritted. "Get two sticks, flat ones about two feet long. You're going to set my leg." She closed her eyes, panting with the effort it had taken.

Elia found wood and fashioned two splints, tore a pillow case in strips. He brought them to her and laid them on the bed. But he could not bring himself to touch her leg.

"I'll hurt you," he protested.

"What hurt?" she gasped. "You think it tickles now?"

"Kalyna . . ."

"It has to be done." She moaned and bit her lip. "Goddamn you, I'd do it myself, except for my hand. Bohdan—" She gestured to the corner where her son crouched. "Get the vodka."

The boy scurried away, returning with a dusty bottle of clear liquid. Kalyna took it from him, tilted it, and swallowed twice. She passed the bottle to Elia.

"Pour some over my leg," she instructed. "Then put the bone back in place."

Elia, bottle in hand, stared glassily at the leg.

"Please, Kalyna. I can't do it," he pleaded. "I swear, I cannot do it."

She raised herself on her elbows once more. Her eyes were wild. Beads of sweat broke out on her forehead.

"Idiot! Coward! Asshole!" she screamed. "Do you want me to be a cripple the rest of my life? You can do it. You have to do it. There isn't anyb—"

She slumped back in mid-word, her head twisted at a crazy angle. Bohdan shrieked once, covered his face.

Olena dashed around the bed. She jerked her mother's arm and Kalyna's head rolled heavily, the whites of her eyes gleaming under half-shut lids. Olena wailed, a thin, animal keening.

"It's all right! She's all right!" Elia shouted, his nerves leaping at the eerie sound. "Olena! Stop! I need your help."

He took the hysterical girl in his arms and held her close. She sobbed convulsively, hiccupped, and was still.

"All right, now." Elia knelt to face her. Forcing a normal tone of voice, he continued. "Go and get hot water and some clean towels. Your mamma is going to need a bath. And find her a nightgown. Can you do that?"

Olena nodded. She rewarded him with a timorous, teary smile and hurried from the room. Bohdan, peering through his fingers, saw her leave. He jumped up and scurried after her.

Left alone, Elia drew a long, shaky breath. He clenched his teeth till his jaw ached and cleansed Kalyna's leg with vodka.

Sweating, trembling, and praying Kalyna would not regain her senses, he worked the broken bone back into position, set the splints and bound them firmly with cloth strips.

Olena returned with a basin of hot water, towels, and a bar of yellow soap. Together, they stripped and bathed Kalyna and pulled a clean nightgown over her bruised head and swollen hand.

When Kalyna was as comfortable as they could make her, Olena disappeared. She was back quickly, balancing a pot of borsch and a loaf of black bread. Bohdan followed with bowls and spoons.

The evening wore on and they clung together beside Kalyna's bed. Bohdan slept, his head on Elia's knee. Olena fought sleep as long as she could, curled like a kitten on the floor.

Several times during the night Kalyna moaned but did not waken. Elia slept fitfully.

In the morning, with Olena's help, he prepared a pot of hot kasha and they all breakfasted around Kalyna's bed. She was in great pain, her face chalky, her eyes smudged and dull. For her children's benefit, she smiled often, but she ate little.

When they had eaten, Kalyna sent Olena and Bohdan off to do their chores. She asked Elia to sit with her. Once alone, she dropped all pretense at cheerfulness and explained the accident.

There had always been a small root cellar beneath the hillock, dug by her father. When news of the German invasion reached her in early summer, she and the children extended the root cellar into a room measuring almost ten feet in diameter and five feet high at the dome.

They dug in secret, dragging the earth, sack by sack, to the ploughed field over which Elia had crawled.

In September, they hid half the harvest away. Kalyna had been carving out a passage through which to drive the cow, when a section of the roof collapsed.

"I was careless." Her mouth twisted angrily. "I was trying to work too fast. Too many interruptions. Savitskys. Germans. They'll be back, those Nazis. The cow has to be hidden."

"Where is it now?"

"In the woods. Bohdan knows where. He can show you." She plucked at the coverlet.

"Elia . . ." she began and hesitated. When she spoke again, there was a trace of belligerence in her voice.

"I'll make you a bargain, Elia," she said. "I know you want only to go to Lvov and find Anna. If you go, the Germans will take everything and my children will starve. If you stay until I can work again, or until Ivan and Dimitri come home, I'll give you Taras's papers and his clothes."

"Kalyna, I couldn't . . ."

"If you go, I'll send the Germans after you."

Elia stiffened. He studied her face. Her lips were set, two spots of color burned on her cheeks. She would not meet his eyes.

"Could you do that, Kalyna?" he asked.

Her pugnaciousness collapsed.

"No." She grimaced ruefully. "But I thought it would be better if you believed I could. I'd give you the papers anyway. You wouldn't go a mile without them."

Elia took her hand in his and smiled down at her.

"Before you threw the Germans at me, I was about to say I couldn't leave as long as you and Olena and Bohdan needed me."

Her eyes filled with tears. She turned her face away to hide them from him.

"My boys could be home tomorrow."

"Tomorrow. Or next week."

"Or next week," she repeated and added softly, "Thank you."

Elia pressed her hand. "Sleep, Kalyna," he said. "Sleep and get well. I'll be here."

Thus began the winter Elia learned the skills that would later save his life.

Although fit, he was not a strong man. The extent of his physical activity had been in walking to and from class. He had been a city dweller. Food was purchased, fuel delivered. He had never handled an ax, a cookstove, or an animal.

Awkward and uncertain in the beginning, he soon began to take a self-conscious pride in his capabilities.

He worked from sunup to sundown, trailed by Bohdan, who attached himself to Elia like an adoring puppy. Together they cut saplings and reinforced the root cellar ceiling. He completed the passageway for the cow and constructed a movable screen of scrub and branches to hide the opening. By the time the snow fell, he had laid in a store of firewood for the winter.

Instructed from her bed by Kalyna, he slaughtered her three pigs and ground the meat for smoked sausage to hang in the root cellar. With Olena's help, he put down two crocks of sauerkraut. He learned to make butter and cheese and bake bread, to milk the cow and feed the chickens.

He became very fond of the two farm dogs, though at first he had feared them. They took their jobs seriously. Twice, at their warning, he and the cow hid in the root cellar, the first time when the Savitskys came and were told the nephew from Poltava had recovered and returned home, and later when a platoon of German soldiers marched down the road. From them, Kalyna learned they were recruiting for labor camps in Germany.

Then winter set in and they were as isolated as though they lived on the far side of the moon.

In January, Kalyna was moving around on crutches Elia made for her. For Ukrainian Christmas Eve, she prepared a traditional feast. The next day, on the seventh, they celebrated Elia's thirty-second birthday.

Winter deepened, and Elia spent his days on repairs to the house and barn. He discovered neither Kalyna nor the children could read and began teaching them.

Each night, Kalyna prayed for the safe return of her sons. Elia prayed with her, hoping they would return before he left for Lvov in the spring.

March turned into the severest month of the long winter and it was early April before Elia began his preparations for the 450-kilometer trek to Lvov.

He had never before been in such fine condition. He had gained weight, mainly muscle. Kalyna found it necessary to alter Taras's clothing, adding width in the shoulders, length to the trouser legs.

Boots were a problem.

Taras's were too small. Kalyna produced an old pair of her husband's and they were much too large. After puzzling over them, Elia took them apart and rebuilt a pair for himself. They were odd looking but sturdy and comfortable.

At last, on the twenty-first day of April, the time came for him to leave.

Kalyna packed a canvas sack with bread, dried sausage, and boiled eggs. She added nuts, dried apples, and a thick slab of heavy honey cake.

And she turned Taras's papers over to Elia.

"There. Now you're my son. My Jewish son." She grinned her gap-toothed smile. "You keep your pants on, you hear?"

Elia's laughter caught in his throat. He pulled her to him and kissed the top of her head.

"Thank you, Kalyna" was all he could manage.

She hugged him tightly, then drew away.

"It is I who thank you, Elia." She wiped her eyes on her apron. "We'll miss you. When it's all over, you'll come back with Anna. Promise."

"I promise." He crouched and kissed Olena. She clung to him shyly, then turned and ran into the house.

Bohdan, fighting tears, walked with him until a turn in the road hid the farmhouse from view. Elia sent him back, watching until the boy was out of sight.

At Zhitomir, the first town on his route, he learned the Nazi's recruiting methods consisted of snatching able-bodied men and women off the streets and shipping them to Germany.

For the next six weeks, until he reached Lvov, he avoided settlements and traveled only by night.

Chapter 12

I arrived in Lvov early in June." Elia stroked the locket "And I walked those last miles scarcely touching the ground."

His gaze was fixed past me, his head tilted quizzically. I turned, expecting to see a customer.

"Hi, Mum." Jenny smiled tentatively from across the table. We were in a period of uneasy truce, both on polite behavior, each wary of the other.

"Hi, honey. What a nice surprise. Come around. I want you to meet Mr. Strohan."

Jenny sidled past Cia, who was serving one of our regulars, a man who collected carnival glass and haunted flea markets in search of the rarer pieces. She patted Cia's bottom as she passed and Cia grinned at her.

I glanced at Elia. He was watching Jenny, his eyes oddly puzzled.

There is an instant affinity between certain people when they meet, a sort of mysterious kinship that leaps the barriers of age or race or color. It's as though the body cells of one recognize those of the other, perhaps from some past life.

Whatever it is, it's the only thing that half convinces me there's something to the theory of reincarnation. And, whatever it is, I watched it happen between Jenny and Elia.

He took her hand in his. His head dipped in a courtly nod and he smiled that heart-catching smile at her.

"Jenny, my dear, seeing you makes me wish I was fifty years younger than I am."

Jenny returned the smile impishly.

"And seeing you makes me wish your were too," she said.

He tilted his head at her, his eyes blue with delight.

"Are you flirting with me?"

"Of course."

He blinked, then threw back his head and laughed. It was a full-throated laugh, youthful and infectious. I found myself joining him. Cia too.

"Hey, Jen. What the hell?"

Rick Lawrence stood on the far side of the table, his hands thrust in the rear pockets of tight white jeans.

"Hey, come on, eh?" He tossed his head to get the thick, blond fall of hair from his eyes. "You said we'd only be here a sec. Let's go."

"Keep your shirt on," Jenny said, but she withdrew her hand from Elia's and turned to leave. "Mum? I came by to tell you I won't be home for supper. Okay?"

I nodded and pressed myself against the wall to let her pass. She bent and pecked my cheek as she slid by.

"Okay, clown." She hooked her arm in Rick's. "Let's go."

They slouched away. At the mall doors, Jenny paused. She spoke to Rick and hurried back.

"Elia?" She leaned across the table. I was startled at her easy use of his given name but he seemed not to notice. "I have to know. Did you get to Lvov?"

He nodded. "I got there."

"And . . . ?" she prompted.

"They were gone. Anna, her mother, and her sister. They

had left for Warsaw in May. A neighbor told me they went
to stay with an aunt in Warsaw."

"Oh." She reached and touched his hand. "I'm sorry.
What did you do?"

Elia shrugged. "What else? I went to Warsaw."

Chapter 13

The headaches began the day after Elia left Lvov.

Following along the Lublin-Tomaszow railroad line, he had covered almost forty-five kilometers in a day and a half, sleeping in a barn and breakfasting on a raw egg and some young cabbage plants stolen from the unsuspecting farmer. He was hungry, but not savagely so, and his spirits lifted to meet the sun-drenched beauty of the June day.

Without warning, a knife stabbed behind his left eye. His stomach heaved with shock and emptied itself, leaving him on hands and knees, shivering and sweating.

He crawled into a patch of weeds by the side of the track and curled into a fetal ball, waiting for the excruciating pain to pass. Hours later, when it has settled to a dull throb, he rose to his feet and walked the five remaining kilometers to the town of Rava-Russkaya.

In Rava-Russkaya, after asking around, he struck a bargain with a Polish farmer named Stanislaw Wisnioski. He would give Wisnioski a week's work in exchange for his keep and a three-day supply of food to carry away when he left.

It was at Wisnioski's farm, some thirteen kilometers from town, that Elia first heard of Belzec. Wisnioski, a bibulously talkative man, had made several references to "the goings-on at Belzec" in a curiously oblique manner.

"Belzec?" Elia finally asked. The evening meal was finished and they were seated at the kitchen table. Wisnioski was well into his nightly habit of drinking himself into insensibility. "What is Belzec?"

"Stanislaw!" His wife turned from her washing up, her eyes warning. She was a grim, plain-featured woman, as taciturn as her husband was garrulous.

"Shut up, old woman." Wisnioski's hand flapped at her and dropped to Elia's shoulder. "This is my friend Taras I'm talking to here."

He hunched himself around his bottle and lowered his voice.

"You want to know what Belzec is? I'll tell you. Maybe the Germans call it a Konzentrationslager. But I'll tell you what it really is." His eyes narrowed. "It's a Vernichtungslager."

"Extermination?" Elia translated. "Extermination camp?"

Wisnioski's head dipped loosely.

"I don't understand. Extermination camp?" Elia looked from one Wisnioski to the other. "What is an extermination camp?"

Mrs. Wisnioski turned and left the kitchen, her mouth set thinly. Her husband leaned forward, his face a foot from Elia's. He drew an index finger across his throat.

"Everybody," he said. His breath was foul. Elia drew back. "Everybody," Wisnioski repeated.

Chilled, Elia pressed fingers to his throbbing temples. "How do you know this?" he asked.

"How do I know?" Wisnioski sprayed spittle, voice rising. He raised his arm, finger pointed to the window. "Five kilometers from here I wouldn't know?"

He lifted his glass and gulped noisily.

"The trains," he said. "Since March, the trains. Maybe fifty cars each. And every car packed with people, a hundred, maybe two hundred. Like sardines, they're packed. Sometimes two, three trains a day. And they go away empty. I've seen them." He stabbed his chest. "Me. I've seen them. They go away empty."

"But how do you know they . . . how do you know it's a . . . a Vernichtungslager?"

"Because I know." Wisnioski's expression was sly. "Never mind. I have ways. My cousin . . . never mind. I know."

"You know. Your cousin knows." Elia's skull was pounding with every heartbeat. "And you do nothing?"

Wisnioski reared back unsteadily.

"I do nothing? You say I do nothing?" he roared. "What can I do? You tell me. What can I do?"

Elia shook his head, nauseous with pain, unable to answer.

"I do nothing? What do you expect me to do?" Wisnioski raised his glass to his lips. He drank deeply and shuddered. His eyes filled with drunken tears, spilling and leaking down his seamed cheeks. "You tell me. What do you expect me to do? What's a poor old farmer supposed to do? What can anybody do? I have a farm to . . . I have an old woman . . ."

His chin dropped to his chest. His mumbled words became unintelligible.

Under a ceiling of pain, Elia left the kitchen and crawled into his bed.

Two days later he left, his canvas bag filled with food.

Mrs. Wisnioski was a dour woman but not a stingy one.

Chapter 14

*H*is progress was slow now.

The weather had turned unbearably hot. In the vast blue and cloudless sky, the sun glared down like a huge, malevolent eye. Tree leaves, with no breath to stir them, hung limply. Even the birds were silent.

Ahead, heat waves turned the railroad bed into a shimmering, swimming miasma. Sun rays, glancing off steel rails, stabbed like knives into his eyes.

After the first day, he traveled by night, more now to escape the relentless sun than for the sake of safety. He slept through the day, tortured by nightmares he could never remember on awakening.

On the fourth day, the sound of an approaching train pulled him, sweating and trembling, from his chaotic dreams. Hidden by the bushes, he watched it pass and counted the cars.

There were forty-five, each with an armed soldier hunched like a bird of prey on top. He wondered if this was one of the trains of which Wisnioski had spoken and tried to imagine two hundred living bodies packed into each car. In the oppressive heat he could not see how any would survive.

His mind refused to accept the possibility and yet, when

the second train passed a few hours later, he shut his eyes and covered his ears until the earth was still once more.

The following day, he reached the village of Szczebrzeszyn. He skirted the town and cut away from the railroad to follow the Wieprz River. The going was pleasanter now and he easily covered twenty kilometers each night.

He was able to bathe in the river, he slept without dreaming and his headaches, which had become almost constant, abated. Forced by the heat to discard the greater portion of his food supply, he ate sparingly of what was left. He felt better than he had since leaving Lvov and his principal worry as he approached the village of Krasnystaw was how to replace his boots. The pair he had rebuilt were falling apart.

He was met with a sight that drove all thoughts of boots from his mind.

Hanging from poles alongside the road were four bodies, one a young woman, the other three men. From each was suspended a placard inscribed, "I WAS A PARTISAN."

Sick with shock, Elia turned away from the village. He hid until night fell, lying prone in a field planted with beets. As soon as darkness fell he found a barn, crawled into a mound of hay, and, head pounding, fell into a fitful sleep.

Pressure on his throat wakened him.

At first he thought the sensation was part of his nightmare and tried to turn his head. The pressure became a sharp pain. He opened his eyes.

Pinkish predawn light illuminated the barn. Standing above him, legs straddling his body, was a woman. She held a pitchfork firmly in both hands, pressing the tines against his throat. Beneath the brightly printed scarf binding her graying hair, her eyes were black and cold.

"Don't move," she said in Polish. "Don't move or I will kill you."

Without taking her eyes from him, she emitted a series of short, sharp whistles.

Elia heard pounding footsteps enter the barn. A thickset

man appeared in his line of vision and bent over him, studying his face.

The man's lips tightened under his luxuriant gray mustache. Under equally shaggy brows, his small eyes viewed Elia with sharp distrust. Elia stared back wordlessly.

The man straightened and took the fork from the woman's hands. He stepped back, holding the pitchfork like a weapon, the long, lethal tines pointed into Elia's stomach.

"All right. Get up. Slowly." His voice was guttural. "Get up and put your hands on your head."

Elia obeyed silently.

"Who are you? What are you doing here?"

Elia removed a hand from his head to reach into his pocket. The tines moved closer and he hastily replaced his hand.

"My papers are in my pocket," he said carefully. "My name is Taras Zaleschuk."

The man jerked his head at the woman. She approached Elia cautiously. Reaching into his pocket, she removed the leather folder she found there and opened it. She glanced up from her inspection of the papers inside, her eyes narrow with suspicion.

"Kiev? You're from Kiev?"

Elia nodded.

"What are you doing here?" It was the man who spoke. "What are you doing in my barn?"

"I'm on my way to Warsaw," Elia explained. "My wife is there. I hid in your barn." He turned his eyes from one to the other. "I did no harm. I took nothing."

The two exchanged glances. For a minute, neither spoke. Elia waited, his heart pounding in his ears. At last the man seemed to reach a decision.

"Tie him to the post," he growled at the woman. "We'll wait until Stefan comes."

The woman's face set angrily. She glared at the man, making no effort to move.

"Do it!" he roared.

Muttering to herself, the woman obeyed, binding Elia's wrists tighter than was necessary, kicking his feet roughly into a position where she could pass the rope around his ankles.

For the entire day, Elia sat trussed like a chicken. The stocky man came to the barn twice, once with a thin cabbage soup he fed to Elia, spoonful by spoonful, once with a dipper of cold water. When Elia thanked him, he merely grunted and left.

The night was white with moonlight when he returned. He freed Elia's legs and led him across a moon-washed yard to a large farmhouse.

The woman was seated at a kitchen table. She turned hostile eyes on Elia as he entered and spoke to a tall, lean man standing near the window.

"See? I told you."

The thin man nodded. He dropped the window curtain and moved to face Elia.

"Untie his hands," he instructed. "He isn't armed."

As the mustached man loosened his wrists, Elia studied the stranger.

He had spoken with an air of quiet authority, as though accustomed to being obeyed. His eyes, fastened on Elia, were steady, an opaque, almost colorless gray. He matched Elia in height and Elia guessed him to be close to himself in age.

"So you're Taras Zaleschuk. From Kiev."

Elia hesitated. On an impulse he didn't understand, he shook his head.

"No."

The woman snorted triumphantly and began to speak. The thin man silenced her with a wave of his hand.

"Your papers?"

Elia rubbed his wrists to restore the circulation in his hands. "They're a dead man's papers," he said. "They were given to me by his mother."

The gray eyes flickered but the thin man merely nodded. "Go on," he said.

"My name is Elia Strohan. I am from Kiev, that part is true." Elia hesitated, then added. "I'm a Jew."

The woman leaped to her feet.

"A Jew?" she sneered. "You don't look like a Jew to me."

Elia shrugged. "What does a Jew look like to you?"

There was a glimmer of amusement in the thin man's eyes, but he said nothing.

The woman circled the table.

"You look like a German," she spat. "Look at him," she urged the others. Eyes. Hair. Nose. That's no Yid nose."

The thin man touched her shoulder gently.

"Give the man a chance, Jadwiga." He turned to Elia. "Have you eaten?"

Elia shook his head.

"Fix something, would you, Jadwiga? Please?" The thin man gestured toward the table. "Sit down, Elia Strohan. Let's all sit down. I'm hungry too."

The three men sat. Jadwiga, throwing dark glances, bustled about. She laid out plates and cutlery, a loaf of dark bread and a platter of cabbage rolls. She slammed a bowl of sour cream in the center of the table, then seated herself.

"Jadwiga. Kazimir." The thin man introduced the two to Elia. "I'm Stefan. Last names don't matter."

He began to eat, smiling at Elia. "Now tell us. How does a Jew from Kiev end up in a Polish barn?"

As they ate, Elia related the events of the past months, omitting nothing. Stefan listened closely, his face expressionless. When Elia finished, Stefan was silent, his eyes thoughtful. The others waited.

"A language teacher," Stefan said at last. "Tell me. Do you speak German?"

"Yes."

"Fluently?" There was a tiny note of excitement in Stefan's voice. "Well enough to fool a German, do you think?"

Elia nodded. "I think so."

For a moment Stefan did not speak. Then he smiled at Elia.

"Please. Don't be offended," he said courteously. "I must speak to my friends alone. Jadwiga will show you to the cellar. Wait there, please. I promise it won't be for long."

Elia followed Jadwiga to a small storeroom off the kitchen. She kicked aside a braided rug and raised a trapdoor set in the floor. Elia descended a narrow ladder into a small earthen room furnished with a table, a chair, and a hay-strewn cot.

The trapdoor dropped back into place with a thud that made Elia wince. In pitch-darkness, he felt for the chair, found it, and sat down to wait.

He could hear Jadwiga's angry voice and Stefan's quiet intonations but could not make out what was being said. Once or twice Kazimir spoke gruffly. After a while, Elia dozed.

He woke with a start when the trapdoor lifted.

"Come up," Kazimir grunted.

Elia climbed the ladder and followed Kazimir to the kitchen, blinking at the light.

"Please," Stefan said. "Sit down."

Elia sat, trying to read their faces. Other than Jadwiga's frown, which he was beginning to believe was permanent, their expressions told him nothing.

Stefan turned cool eyes on Elia.

"Jadwiga would like to turn you over to the Gestapo," he said dispassionately. "She believes, by doing so, we can buy credit with them for us."

Jadwiga opened her mouth to speak. Stefan cut her off with a restraining hand.

"I have other ideas," he continued. "But they may depend on you agreeing to do what we ask."

To Elia, the threat was implicit. He could not keep the bitterness from his voice.

"Do I have a choice?" he said.

Stefan's brows lifted.

"Of course you have a choice," he said. "We are not presenting you with an either-or-else situation. We are not Nazis."

Elia sighed. "All I want is to go to Warsaw. I want nothing from you. I only wish to be allowed to leave and be on my way."

"Understandable." Stefan nodded. His face hardened and an edge crept into his words. "But do you have any idea how naive you are? Have you any idea at all of how lucky you've been to have come this far? And it is luck, I assure you. The luck that protects children and fools. Once protected. No longer. Have you any idea what your chances are of reaching Warsaw?"

"I'll take my chances," Elia retorted, his face flushing with the first stirrings of anger.

"And end up in a labor camp in Germany," Stefan said dryly. "If you're lucky. And you won't be lucky. One minute after we met, you told me you are a Jew. One minute!"

He leaned forward, his index finger inches from Elia's nose. His voice turned harsh.

"Open your eyes, Jew! How could you live through Babi Yar and not understand? Babi Yar was no isolated incident. When Hitler vowed to eliminate the Jews from the face of Europe, they were not idle words. They'll do it, the Nazis. They're doing it now. They're turning Poland into a slaughterhouse. And it's lambs like you who are the first to die."

For seconds his words hung in the air between them. Then Stefan fell back in his chair and passed a weary hand across his eyes.

"Our proposition is this," he stated, as calmly as though his outburst had not occurred. "Help us and we will see you safely to Warsaw."

He turned his glance on Elia and waited.

"What do you want me to do?" Elia asked.

Stefan smiled.

"Good," he said. He pushed back his chair and rose to his feet. "There are arrangements to be made. You will stay here until I return."

"Here?" Jadwiga bounded angrily from her chair. "You're leaving him here?"

"Where else?" For the first time there was irritation in Stefan's attitude toward the woman. "And why not?"

"Why not? Because he'll run like a rabbit the moment we take our eyes off him!"

Stefan sighed. "Elia?" he said, questioning.

"I'll stay. You have my word."

"*Ptah!*" Jadwiga spat. "The word of a Jew?"

"Enough, Jadwiga!" Stefan's words were sharp, his face cold.

Jadwiga met his eyes defiantly. Then her bravado faltered and she turned away, muttering to herself.

Stefan held out his hand to Elia.

"I'll be back as quickly as possible," he promised. "A week, no more."

He clasped Kazimir's hand briefly, touched Jadwiga's arm as he passed, and was gone.

That night, and for the following five nights, Elia slept in the cellar. Each day, he worked with Jadwiga and Kazimir in the fields. When evening came, they returned to the house and ate a silent meal together.

He noted, with grim amusement, that he was never out of sight of one or the other of his hosts and that the trapdoor to the cellar was locked each night after he descended the ladder.

On the seventh night, he was awakened by the sound of the bolt sliding in the trapdoor. The door lifted and Kazimir poked his head in the opening.

"Come," he said and disappeared.

Neither he nor Jadwiga were in sight when Elia entered the kitchen. Stefan was seated at the table, finishing a bowl of soup. He pushed the bowl aside.

"Now." He smiled at Elia. "We talk. Please, sit down."

When Elia was seated, Stefan placed his hands, palms down, on the table.

"This is what we require of you," he said without preamble. "There are ten children in the barn loft. Jadwiga has given them food. They will sleep till morning. Then you and Kazimir will take them to Krasnik."

Before Elia could ask, he offered the information.

"Krasnik is a village seventy-five kilometers west."

"Excuse me," Elia raised a restraining hand. "I am not objecting, you understand. But why do you need me to do this?"

"Because you speak German. I do not. Nor does Kazimir."

"I still don't . . ." Elia began.

Stefan did not wait for him to finish.

"Let me explain." Stefan pressed his hands together. The two index fingers pointed at Elia.

"You and Kazimir will play soldier. We've obtained German uniforms and guns. You will be a corporal, Kazimir a private. The children will be your prisoners. You will march them to Krasnik. As your prisoners. So you see, it is essential that one of you speaks German."

Elia shook his head. "Is such a charade necessary? Won't we attract attention?"

"Attract attention?" Stefan's lips twisted. "This is a common sight nowadays. Necessary? Yes. The three youngest of the children, two girls and a boy, are the children of the woman you saw, the woman they hung. Five are Jews. We've been moving them from place to place since April. The other two are my sons."

"Why are . . ." Elia began. Stefan overrode him.

"When you return," he continued, "we will keep our part of the bargain. Kazimir will take you as far as Kock. He will leave you there. One of our people will take you to Zelechow. Somebody else will take you from Zelechow to Gora. You may have to wait in Gora a day, perhaps two, but there'll be somebody to take you to Warsaw. It's only about thirty kilometers. You can make it on your own from Gora, if it proves necessary."

"Our people. We. Somebody." Elia frowned. "Who are all these people. And who are 'we'?"

Stefan's face closed.

"No," Elia protested. "If I'm to put my safety into their hands, I at least have the right to know who they are."

Stefan studied Elia silently. He appeared to come to a decision and the grim lines around his mouth relaxed.

"First, forget rights. You have no rights." The words were harsh but they were spoken mildly. "There are no rights now. Only survival. That may seem an exaggeration, but it is not, believe me, Elia."

He paused, then continued, his eyes intent on Elia.

"There is an underground resistance network in Poland. I'm telling you this because you must not question the people who help you on your way. They're risking their lives. Literally. They live with fear of betrayal, deliberate or unintentional. Anyone asking too many questions . . . *phut.* You understand?"

"I understand. And you're part of it? Kazimir? Jadwiga?"

Stefan nodded.

"You mustn't mind Jadwiga," he said kindly. "There is anger burning in her nothing will appease. Her husband and her two sons were shot by the Germans, in reprisal for acts of sabotage. She hates Germans with a passion."

"And Jews," Elia couldn't help adding.

"Well . . . anti-Semitism . . ." Stefan shrugged. "There are many like her. It's a fact of life. Besides, it can be useful.

The children will wear the yellow star Jews are compelled to wear. You won't be interfered with by the Jadwigas. They're happy to see them go."

"You said her husband was shot. Kazimir isn't her husband?"

"Her brother." Stefan leaned forward on his elbow. "Now. Is there anything else?" For the first time his smile was without strain. "Ask now or forever hold your peace."

Elia smiled back, liking the man.

"There is something I'd like to know," he said.

"If I can tell you, I will."

"Don't you mean, you will if you choose to."

"Touché." Stefan laughed. "What is it you want to know?"

"Belzec," Elia said. "Wisnioski's story. Is it true?"

The laughter fled from Stefan's eyes. He nodded bleakly.

"They're really extermat—" Elia stumbled over the word. "Exterminating people? By the trainload?"

"Not just Belzec. There are other places." Tension returned in Stefan's face. "I'll tell you what we know. Some is based on rumor, most on fact."

He raised his hand, ticking off fingers as he spoke.

"Belzec. It's an extermination camp, straight and simple. It has no other purpose. It began operating at the start of the year. They're killing ten thousand people a day there. Mostly Jews, but Poles as well."

Elia paled. "Ten thousand . . ."

"Majdanek," Stefan continued. "In April the entire Lublin ghetto was sent there. They're killing them, several thousand each day."

He held up two fingers.

"Belzec and Majdanek, these are fact. We know this. Now rumor. We've heard of a camp called Chelmno in western Poland, near Lodz. We've been told they're killing a thousand a day there. From all reports, it's the same as Belzec. A camp with the sole purpose of killing. Also, there is Auschwitz, near Krakow, but that appears to be a labor camp, although we've been told it is an extermination camp as well."

He had four fingers raised.

"Now there's news of a new camp, Sobibor, near Wlodowa, where they're using gas to kill. And we've heard rumors of another camp north of Warsaw, near Sokolow. An extermination camp named Treblinka."

Elia had listened with mounting horror. Before he could speak, Kazimir appeared in the kitchen doorway.

"It's time," he said. He dropped a pair of boots and a German uniform on the chair beside Elia and turned to leave.

"Kazimir?" Stefan stopped him at the door. "Would you go to the barn and waken Petra and Natalka? Ask them to come here."

Kazimir nodded and disappeared. Stefan rose and went to the window. He drew the curtain back. Dawn was breaking. The eastern sky was flushed a pale apricot.

Elia donned the uniform and boots. They were an excellent fit and he wondered if he would be permitted to keep the boots.

Stefan turned from the brightening window. His eyes widened.

"Good God," he exclaimed. "Jadwiga was right. You're the model of an ideal German soldier. You'd fool Hitler."

"A dubious compliment."

"Isn't it," Stefan smiled.

He glanced out the window and turned back to Elia.

"Petra and Natalka will be here in a moment," he said. "They're the oldest and the only ones aware you and Kazimir are not Germans. The others are very young. We can't take the risk of them giving you away. You must never speak anything but German in front of them."

"I'll remember," Elia assured him.

"Natalka is seventeen. She's a Jewess and a very clever girl." A shadow crossed Stefan's face. "Her parents were dear friends. They died at Majdanek."

He glanced out the window once more.

"Here they come," he said. "The boy, Petra, is my son. He's fifteen, but he's very quick and resourceful. He speaks German, by the way."

The kitchen door opened and a slender, dark-haired young woman entered, followed by a tall boy, very apparently Stefan's son. Both newcomers registered an instant of shock on seeing Elia. The boy laughed nervously. The girl stared, her eyes huge in her pale, pretty face.

Stefan introduced Elia and the two relaxed somewhat.

"Natalka and I have been talking." Petra glanced at his father, eyebrows raised.

Stefan nodded and Petra turned to Elia.

"Please don't be offended, but we've decided you must leave the children entirely to us, to me and Natalka. Don't speak to them. Don't smile at them. Don't give them anything."

"If they're tired," the girl chimed in, "or hurt, please don't comfort them. Leave them entirely to us."

"You see, we don't want them to like you or trust you." Petra's cheeks flushed. "I'm sorry. What I mean is, we don't want them to trust that uniform."

"I understand," Elia said gravely. "And I agree."

Still distressed, the boy appealed to his father.

"It's for their own protection, Papa," he said.

"You're absolutely right." Stefan smiled at his son and the girl. "Now. Maybe you should start getting them ready?"

The two left the kitchen. Stefan and Elia stood at the window, watching them cross to the barn. Moments later, two small children emerged, each carrying a knapsack.

"So young!" he exclaimed.

"There's a younger one." Stefan pointed as a little girl

toddled out of the barn. "Her mother, the woman you saw hanging, was one of us."

He turned from the window.

"It will be a strange journey for you, Elia. For their safety, you must not permit yourself to be sympathetic."

"Will they be safer in Krasnik?"

"They won't remain in Krasnik. We're hoping to get them to Switzerland."

"Will you be here when I return?"

"No." Stefan dropped the curtain and faced Elia.

"Perhaps we'll meet again one day." He held out his hand. "Good luck. Be careful. God go with you, my friend."

Chapter 15

In later years, Elia was to remember the trek to Krasnik as an endless, sunstruck day. From dawn till dusk, the sky blazed blue and cloudless, a vast dome sealing in hot, motionless air.

The dusty road they traveled wound, unshaded, between cultivated fields, with only an occasional copse of trees to provide relief from the scorching sun. Long before noon of the first day, Elia knew he would have to restrain himself from carrying one or the other of the children.

Kazimir took the lead. He plodded steadily, setting the pace, seemingly oblivious to the heat. The children, herded into a tight unit by Petra and Natalka, followed, with Elia twenty paces behind.

In the beginning, the children marched lightheartedly, chattering among themselves and stealing glances back to where Elia sweated in his unseasonal uniform, shouldering his empty rifle. He forced himself to meet their eyes with what he hoped was an expression of menace.

Slowly, they emerged as individuals.

The eldest, after Petra and Natalka, was a boy Elia judged to be about twelve. A younger boy clung to him. They were the quietest of the group and unmistakably brothers.

Within the tight little band, they seemed to walk apart from the others.

The liveliest was a boy with oversized ears and quick, darting eyes, whom Elia named Meshik, the Ukrainian diminutive for mouse. He and a girl with tight brown braids flanked a blond boy with a slight limp to his gait. They were protective and Elia assumed they had been instructed by Petra to care for him.

The three youngest bore a family resemblance. A girl with a somber face. The five-year-old boy Elia had first seen emerging from Kazimir's barn. And the three-year-old Stefan had identified as the child of the partisan woman hung by the Germans.

She was a golden-haired cherub of a child. Her eyes were big and blue, her cheeks chubby and rose tinted, her mouth baby pink and soft. The name Chicha, a word Ukrainian children used for a flower, dropped like a penny into Elia's mind.

They met few people on the road the first day. An old man and an old woman, peasants, walked by, leading a goat on a cord. They drew together, eyes fixed ahead, as the little band passed. Elia glanced around and caught the woman staring back. She turned quickly away and they hurried on.

Later in the afternoon, a middle-aged couple passed in a horse-drawn cart. They stared coldly down at the children. The man, a red-faced farmer, nodded expressionlessly to Elia.

By then, the children were straggling. Natalka, her face flushed, her blouse dark with perspiration, was carrying Chicha. Petra had the five-year-old on his back and the sleeping boy's legs dangled, thumping Petra's thighs.

It was dusk before Kazimir called a halt beside a growth of trees.

He led the children into the woods, out of sight of the road. He dropped his knapsack and rifle at the base of a tree, sat down, dug into his pack, withdrew a parcel wrapped in a towel, and began to eat.

A short distance away, Petra herded the children into a circle and, exhausted, they collapsed. While Petra gathered leaves for a makeshift bed, Natalka fed the nodding children. Within minutes of eating, they were all asleep, huddled together and oblivious of the hungry mosquitos feeding on them.

When only Petra and Natalka were left awake, Elia called to them and went with them to talk to Kazimir.

"Can't we let them take it easier?" he asked.

Kazimir had allowed only a half-hour rest at noon and had permitted no stops on the way. If a child had to relieve himself, he had to run to catch up.

"No," Kazimir grunted, barely looking up.

Elia turned to Petra. In the brilliant moonlight the boy's skin was luminescent, eyes gleaming in the dark shadow of his eyes sockets.

Petra shook his head.

"They won't wait at Krasnik," he said. "There are others. They won't wait for us."

"I see." Elia glanced to the pale oval of Natalka's face. "And I can't help you? Carry one of them? They're so young."

"No!" Natalka's voice was sharp. "Don't touch them! Don't touch any of them!"

The words hung harshly in the air. Natalka reached out and touched Elia's sleeve.

"I'm sorry," she said. "Please. I'm sorry."

"Go to sleep," Kazimir growled. "We start before dawn. Go to sleep."

Natalka and Petra went to join the children and Elia stretched out on the ground beside Kazimir, who began snoring almost immediately.

While wondering, between the snoring, the heat, and the

ravenous insects, if he would ever sleep, Elia tumbled into oblivion.

The second day dawned hotter than the first. The children trudged mutely under the pitiless sun, eyes cast down, scratching where they had been bitten.

Petra had cut willow switches to fan away the persistent flies. For a while the children used them. Slowly, one by one, the switches had been dropped by the wayside.

Chicha had to be carried after the first hour. The blond boy's limp was more pronounced. The braided girl, a chatterer the day before, plodded in silence. Even Meshik's lively eyes were dulled.

Their road joined a wider, more traveled route and they began to meet more people, some walking, some on horseback or on horse-drawn vehicles, even an occasional truck.

Elia began to recognize there were only two reactions to his little flock. The travelers either avoided looking at the children and passed with expressionless faces, or they stared with avid curiosity. As Stefan had promised, none interfered.

It was early afternoon when the first German lorries appeared. Elia heard them approach and jumped to the road verge. The children scrambled to the ditch.

A convoy of seven heavy lorries, driven with disregard for anything on the road, thundered by, leaving the air behind them thick with the noise and dust of their passing. Without waiting for the dust to settle, Kazimir signaled the children to move.

After a second, then a third and fourth convoy passed, the children no longer leaped for the ditch but simply straggled to the weeds beside the road. Elia, whose nerves had knotted at the sight of the first convoy, began to relax. When the next lorry drew abreast he even looked up into the face of the driver. To his horror, the lorry pulled to a stop.

"Hey, corporal!" The driver, a sweating, obese man called out to him, "That's some bunch of dangerous prisoners you got there! What you gonna do with 'em? Line 'em up and shoot 'em?"

"Not me!" Elia called back. To his disgust, his voice was high and squeaky. "All I gotta do is get 'em to the next town!"

"What'd you do to pull that rotten job?" The driver grinned, exposing tobacco-stained teeth. "Screw the captain's wife?"

"Naw. The general's wife!" Elia grinned back.

The driver hooted. He shifted gears and the lorry roared away. Elia wiped away sweat not entirely due to the heat. He nodded reassurance at Kazimir's quizzical eyebrows and the little band moved on.

By late afternoon, Elia felt he had been walking this road all his life and would do so to the end of his days. The routine had become hypnotic. At the sound of the motor, take the side of the road and walk. Back on the road and walk. The side of the road and walk. Back on the . . .

He heard the sound of the motor behind him. He took to the side of the road. Saw the children move into the weeds.

His eyes recorded what he was seeing. The little lame boy was limping along the center of the road. The little lame . . .

Suddenly, his brain accepted the message his sight was sending. He dropped his rifle and ran.

He snatched the boy in his arms and rolled into the ditch as the lorry pounded by. It happened so quickly and the children's senses were so blunted by heat and fatigue that they simply stood and stared as Elia released the frightened child and rose to his feet, brushing dust from his uniform and hair.

Then Petra pulled the boy away and Kazimir shouted the only German word he knew. *"Raus!"*

When they made camp that night, Petra came to Elia. He stood stiffly at attention and spoke in German, aware of the children watching.

"I want to thank you," he said formally. "For saving my brother's life."

"The lame boy is your brother?"

Petra nodded. "Yes. He is deaf, you see. He didn't hear the motor. The two others, they were to take care of him. But they . . ." Petra shrugged. ". . . They forgot."

"They're young themselves," Elia said. "And very tired."

Petra's face hardened.

"Excuses. My father says these are not time for excuses. They were given a job to do. My father says there are no excuses when failure costs lives."

"Well," Elia said, hiding his smile at the boy's intensity. "At least this time there was no harm done."

"But there was!" Petra gestured behind him. "They think you're a hero, don't you see? And that is precisely what we cannot allow to happen."

Elia lifted his hands helplessly.

"I'm sorry," he said. "Really. I reacted without thought. Would you rather I had . . ."

"No!" Petra's face was shocked. "Of course not!"

"Then?" Elia spread his hands.

"We have been discussing it, Natalka and I. And we have decided that you must hit me with your rifle."

"What?"

"Hit me with your rifle. So that they see. I will tell them I tried to thank you. And that you said if anything else happens you will shoot us all. They'll believe me."

Elia stared at the boy, dumbfounded.

"I can't do that," he said. "I can't hit you."

"You must, don't you see? You must yell at me and hit me with your rifle." There was a gleam of humor in the boy's eyes. "Not too hard, if you don't mind. I can make it look worse."

"I . . ." Elia began, then gave up protesting. "All right. Get ready. I'll try to be gentle."

"I'm ready." Petra nodded. "Don't forget to yell at me."

"Yell? Yell what?"

"Anything. Anything will do. They don't understand."

"All right."

Elia picked up his rifle. He contorted his face into what he hoped was an expression of rage, shouted, *"Your father would be proud of you!"* and brought the rifle butt down on the boy's shoulder, holding back at point of impact.

Petra screamed. He dropped like a stone to the ground and brought his knees to his chest. He peered up at Elia.

"Now kick me," he hissed.

"You're overdoing it!" Elia shouted.

"Do it."

"Are you planning a stage career?" Elia roared.

He swung his boot and kicked the ground near Petra's chest. Petra screamed again. He scuttled away on all fours like a beaten dog. Elia turned the corners of his mouth down to hide his smile. What an actor the world was missing.

The children stared with terror-stricken eyes. Petra winked.

The third day was worse than the two before.

The children, badly bitten, tired, hot, and frightened, lagged behind Kazimir. His strident *"Raus! Raus!"* frightened them even more. Meshik and brown-braids were sullen. Chicha whined feverishly on Natalka's shoulder. Elia marveled at Natalka's courage. Frail herself, she carried the little one without complaint or respite.

The sun was slanting low in the sky when Elia saw, twenty yards ahead, a figure dart out of the woods, wave, then vanish into the trees.

It happened so quickly that Elia, dulled by the heat, was not sure he had seen anything until Kazimir left the road and entered the woods where the figure had disappeared. The children, strung out like weary ducklings, stumbled after him.

After the sun-bleached heat of the road, it was a relief to walk under the dappled shade of the trees. They followed a narrow path worn into the underbrush and emerged into a clearing.

It was like stepping from an empty corridor into a crowded room. In addition to Kazimir and the children, there were men moving purposefully about. The children seemed smaller than ever.

Elia was barely into the clearing when a bundle of clothing was thrust into his arms by a young man with a work cap pulled low on his forehead.

"Put these on," he instructed Elia. "Give us the uniform."

He took the rifle from Elia's grasp and turned away. Elia clutched at his arm.

"Can I keep the boots? Please?"

Dark eyes under the cap glanced down.

"Ask the Princess." The man shrugged off Elia's hand.

"Wait! The Princess?"

The man gestured across the clearing and hurried away.

Stripping off the uniform, Elia picked out the only woman among the strangers.

She was in her sixties at least, slim and gray-haired. She held the lame boy clasped in her arms and listened intently to Petra, who was talking and gesturing with youthful animation.

She laughed once, a full-throated sound of delight, and met Elia's eyes across the clearing. Her head dipped in greeting. Buttoning the faded shirt he had been given and carrying the uniform he had discarded, Elia made his way across the clearing to where she sat. She smiled up at him around the blond head of Petra's little brother.

"I was told to ask you." Elia raised a foot. "May I keep the boots?"

She shook her head.

"No. I'm sorry," she said in German. Elia felt a pang of guilt. He had forgotten the charade.

Her eyes forgave him.

"It's for your own safety," she went on. "If you are

stopped for any reason and the boots are found on you, you'll be shot. It would be assumed you had killed a German soldier for them. You were given others?"

Elia held up the mismatched pair he had been given. The right boot was of felt, the left of cracked leather. She looked ruefully at them.

"Not as pretty," she granted, smiling. "But safer. Wear them. Others can be arranged for later."

Suddenly, there was a perceptible change in the atmosphere of the clearing. Orders were called out in heavy, male voices. Movement was more purposeful. The young man in the work cap appeared beside Elia. He took the uniform and gestured for the boots.

Elia bent, stripped them off, and pulled on the new pair. The felt boot fit, the leather boot was large but not uncomfortable. They would have to do.

When he straightened, the children were leaving the clearing, the younger ones carried in the arms of men wearing rough country clothes. Petra turned and waved, whether to him or to the woman beside him, Elia wasn't sure. He raised his hand in farewell.

The clearing was suddenly empty. Only Elia, Kazimir, the man in the work cap, and the gray-haired princess remained.

"Come." She placed her hand on Elia's arm. "You've earned your dinner."

"To the children." The princess raised her glass. "And to their safe passage."

They were seated at a pine table in the kitchen of a sprawling farmhouse, less than five minutes from the clearing.

A stout, silent woman had laid out an excellent meal of chicken, cooked with vegetables in a savory cream sauce. She had placed a bottle of red wine on the table, wished them good night, and taken herself to some distant part of the house.

They had eaten hungrily, until nothing was left in the tureen centering the table. They raised their glasses and drank to the children. The wine was deliciously dry.

"So." She rested her elbows on the table, wineglass held gracefully in both hands. She smiled at Elia over the rim. "Tell me your name."

Elia felt himself drawn into the gray eyes.

They were widely spaced, with deep lines radiating from the corners of her lids. Wrinkles crossed her forehead and bracketed her mouth. Strands of hair had pulled free from her braid and hung untidily about her face. There was a smudge on a nose just a little too thin, a little too long. But her smile was luminous, distracting from any imperfection.

"Elia. My name is Elia Strohan."

"I am Elizabeta." She reached a slender hand across to Elia, gesturing with the wineglass in her other hand. "And this fine fellow is Mirko."

With his cap removed, Mirko was not as young as Elia had guessed. His hairline had receded until only a fringe of black hair, sprinkled with gray, remained above his ears. He nodded to Elia and turned his attention back to filling a blackened pipe with tobacco.

"Elizabeta." Elia repeated her name. "Mirko called you Princess. Are you?"

She chuckled, tilting her head at him.

"Of course! Poland is full of princesses. Didn't you know?"

"No." Elia smiled at her. "How would I?"

"Oh?" Her brows lifted delicately. "You're not Polish?"

"No."

"But you speak Polish. And German." She studied him, then said, "Parlez-vous français?"

Elia nodded. "Oui."

"Fascinating! Bon. Nous parlons en français, oui?"

"If you like," Elia answered her in French. "But won't the others find it rude?"

"The others? You mean . . ." She tilted her head at Mirko and Kazimir. "Mirko is accustomed to being ignored. As for Kazimir, he wouldn't be interested even if he could understand."

She set her empty wineglass aside and cupped her chin in her hands.

"Now." She smiled. "Tell me why you're here, in Poland."

They talked for almost an hour, until Kazimir rose from his chair and grunted at Elia.

"Sleep now. We leave early in the morning."

When Elia woke, the whitewashed walls in the room in which he had slept were rosy with early sun. He turned in his cot and glanced at the big bed where Kazimir and Mirko had stretched out, fully clothed, the night before. The bed was empty.

A flutter of panic forced him awake. He slid from the cot, dressed quickly, and went in search of the others.

Kazimir sat in the kitchen, dabbing at a plateful of eggs and sausage with a chunk of bread.

"Eat," Kazimir gestured, the bread dripping golden egg yolk. "We leave soon."

"The others? Elizabeta? Mirko?" Elia sat down. He was served immediately by the silent old farm woman. "Have they gone?"

Chewing noisily, Kazimir pointed a greasy thumb at the door leading from the kitchen.

"Outside," he mumbled. "Eat now."

Elia obeyed.

When he had finished, the old woman removed his plate and replaced it with a napkin-tied bundle.

"Food." Kazimir, already on his feet, explained. "Bring it."

He bent, picked up a knapsack, slung it over his shoulder, and left the kitchen. Elia followed him.

They crossed the kitchen yard to a large stone barn. Kazimir rapped twice on a heavy door made of wooden planks bleached to a silvery gray. The door opened an inch or two, then swung wide and Elia followed Kasimir inside.

After the brightness outside, the interior of the barn was black as night, the air heavy with the smell of hay and manure and an oily odor Elia did not immediately identify. As his vision adjusted to the dim light, the shape occupying the bulk of space in the barn became an automobile.

Beyond the car were two strangers, a man and a woman deep in quiet conversation. In the hushed barn atmosphere, their voices hummed like flies at a window, no word distinguishable. The woman gestured, barked an impatient *"Enough."* The man nodded.

He strode to the rear wall of the barn, lifted a crossbar, and pushed. Two great doors swung wide and the dusky barn filled with light. The car motor fired and caught. The car rumbled across the wooden floor of the barn and passed through the sunlit rectangle, leaving a cloud of dancing dust motes behind.

The car rolled to a halt. Mirko stepped out from behind the wheel, resplendent in a uniform tailored in a shade of deep maroon that matched the color of the car. In place of his work cap, a chauffeur's visored hat rode low on his forehead. Smoked glasses, hiding his eyes, gave him a faint air of menace.

But it was the woman Elia gaped at. Elizabeta? Elia found it difficult to relate this woman to his dinner companion of the previous evening.

She wore a soft pink silk dress printed with roses. Her hair was coiffed in a chic French roll. A tiny hat of pink straw and roses, drowning in a cloud of veiling, was tilted over her brow. Pearls glowed at her ears and throat. On her hands were immaculate white kid gloves, on her feet, slim white pumps.

She was every inch an aristocrat, graceful and elegant.

And, in that setting, as out of place as an orchid in a turnip patch.

"Come, Elia," she called, laughter in her voice at his dumbfounded expression. "We're ready to leave. Ride with me."

In the plush rear seat of the car, she waited until Mirko had driven out of the farmyard, then turned to Elia.

"We have only a minute or two." She spoke in German, her eyes grave behind the misty veil. "I want to thank you for saving my grandson. Petra told me what you did."

"Petra?" Elia was startled at her choice of languages. "The lame boy? They're your grandsons?"

She nodded. "Stefan is my son."

"Then why . . ." Elia frowned, perplexed. "You speak German. Petra speaks German. Surely Stefan . . ."

"Of course he does. So why did he need you?" Her nose wrinkled in mock distaste. "My son Stefan has what my American friends call a tin ear. His accent is laughable."

"I see." Elia frowned past Kazimir, seated beside Mirko, to the road ahead. Questions tumbled in his mind.

Elizabeta placed a gloved hand over Elia's.

"Ask anything you like." She smiled.

Elia gestured at the car, at Mirko.

"All this . . ." He left the sentence unfinished.

Her eyes gleamed amusement. "It all turns into a pumpkin at midnight, my dear. And Mirko into a little white mouse. Isn't that how the story goes?"

As she spoke, the car slowed and came to a halt.

"We're at the crossroads, Princess." Mirko spoke into the rearview mirror.

"So. We part company here." Elizabeta smiled at Elia as Kazimir stepped from the car, shouldered his knapsack, and started down the road without a farewell or a backward glance.

Elia picked up the napkin-tied bundle and stepped out onto the road. The car began to move.

"Wait." Elizabeta instructed Mirko. She leaned to the open window and called to Elia. When he bent to look at her, he saw the smile had fled from her eyes.

"Listen, mon ami." She spoke in deadly earnest. "You told me too much, too easily, last night. Without knowing who or what I am. Very trusting. And very foolish."

"Stefan said almost the same."

"And he was right. It's open season on Jews in Poland now. Be careful. Trust nobody. Promise?"

Elia nodded. She settled back in the car and blew a kiss with a gloved hand.

"Au revoir, Elia. Find Anna. Be happy."

Elia watched the car pull away, turn left, and disappear around a curve in the road.

Then he hurried to catch up with Kazimir.

Chapter 16

*E*lia gazed pensively down the mall.

Only a handful of customers now dawdled from one booth to the next. Some of the vendors were clearing their tables in a leisurely fashion, chatting to one another. A half hour remained before the flea market normally closed, but neither Cia nor I had any inclination to begin the tedious job of packing up.

"Was she really a princess?" I asked Elia.

"I don't know."

"Do you believe she was?"

"Yes. I do. You know, walking back to Krasnystaw with Kazimir, I had time to think. I realized I had told her everything. She had told me nothing."

"That makes her a princess?"

Elia smiled. "I suppose not. But it does make her a very clever woman."

"What about the children?" Cia asked. "Do you know if they made it to Switzerland?"

"No. I never heard of them again."

"The others? Stefan? Kazimir?"

"Nothing." Elia rose to his feet and stood, leaning on his cane. "There were so many loose ends then. People met and parted and were lost to each other. Not dead. Just lost."

I took his hand and pressed it. "We'll find her, Elia."

He looked down at me. His eyes cleared and he smiled that incredibly tender smile.

"I suppose if she's to be found, you two will find her." He touched Cia's shoulder. "Dopobachynia, my friends."

"Dopobachynia," we echoed and watched him leave.

He nodded to Ros and Mike as he passed their table and they paused in their packing to wave to him.

I turned to Cia.

"Dammit. I keep trying to remember when we bought the locket. Or where. And I can't even *remember buying* the damn thing. Can you?"

"Not a clue."

"Tell the truth. Do you think we'll find her?"

"You want the truth?" Cia picked up a vase and thumped it into a packing box. "I think we've got a better chance of finding a snowball in hell. All we can do is knock on doors till we run out of doors to knock on."

Chapter 17

I knocked on seven doors the next day.

Nothing.

In the evening we targeted Ile Bizard, an island suburb. It was my turn to drive, Cia's to ring doorbells.

With each *"No, sorry,"* she grew quieter. Crossing the bridge off the island, she slumped down in the passenger seat and stared glumly ahead. When we arrived at her house, she made no move to leave the car.

"Cheer up," I said. "There's always tomorrow."

She turned her head and looked at me.

"Liz," she said heavily, "if you were Anna, would you ever sell that locket?"

My heart actually thumped. I stared at her in dismay, aware of what was coming.

"Face it, Liz. It's not a pretty piece of jewelry. The only reason that locket would show up in a garage sale is because it wasn't important to anybody but Anna." She hesitated, then said the words. "Maybe Anna is dead."

"No!" I protested. "We'll find her. I know we will. We just have to keep trying."

Cia slipped from the car. She leaned her head into the open window and gave me a one-sided smile.

"Ooookay, kiddo," she said. "I'll pick you up tomorrow."

On Tuesday I covered six places in Pointe Claire during the day and four in the evening with Cia. Wednesday, I had a dozen radio commercials to write and didn't get out during the day. We ticked off five addresses in the evening. Thursday's total was seven. And still nothing.

On Friday morning the phone rang at six-thirty. Cia's voice came thinly across the wire.

"Liz? I'm at the airport. My father's had a stroke. I'm sorry, but you'll have to do the flea market alone this weekend."

"Good God, Cia, don't worry about the stupid flea market! I'm sorry about your father. Is it bad?"

"I don't know how bad. My mother was incoherent. I won't know till I get there. I'll call you. Sorry about Sunday."

"Forget it, Cia. Just concentrate on your family. I'll get Jenny to help me on Sunday."

"Okay. Listen, I've gotta run. I'll call you Sunday night."

She hung up.

I shopped for groceries and managed to cross three nearby addresses off my list. When I returned home, Jenny was sunning herself on the patio, her skin glistening with oil, her head tilted back to catch every slanting ray.

I warned myself against mother-type remarks about skin cancer and prepared a pitcher of iced tea. The tinkling ice cubes lured Jenny into the kitchen.

"How'd it go today?" I asked, handing her a glass of tea.

She shrugged. "The usual," she said, and crunched an ice cube.

"Are you doing anything important on Sunday?"

Quick suspicion flared in her eyes. "Why?"

I explained about Cia. "So I'll need your help with the flea market on Sunday."

"Me?" She gaped at me as though I'd suggested she join a church choir. "At the flea market?"

"You don't have to stay all day. I'll load my car. You can follow me over in your car, help me set up, and then you can go."

"Can't you do it alone?"

"I can't do it alone in the morning. The dealers and pickers are there first thing and if I want to sell to them I have to be set up and ready."

"So leave early."

"The doors don't open till eight-thirty," I said patiently, pushing down a rising bubble of anger. "I have to unload the car, set up the tables, and unpack before nine o'clock and I can't do it alone. I need your help."

She looked at me with that stony expression borrowed from Rick and his gang of morons.

"Sorry," she said. "Flea marketing isn't my thing."

The bubble surfaced and burst.

"Thing?" I shouted. "Thing? You think flea marketing is my *thing*? The flea market puts food on this table, puts the food in that insolent mouth of yours!"

"I pay you . . ."

"What you pay doesn't cover the electric bill for the ten showers you take every day." I screamed. "It doesn't pay for the power you use to wash your one-at-a-time goddam pair of jeans, much less everything else you get around here."

"So what?" she sneered. "You have to provide those things till I'm eighteen anyway."

"I have to what?" I was so taken aback the words came out in a normal tone.

"Rick says parents have to give their kids everything until they're eighteen. Legally, he says, you owe . . ."

"Now you listen to me." I overrode her, cold with rage. "I do not give one single damn what Rick the Prick has to say. I need your help. You can help me on Sunday morning or you can spend the day packing. I mean it. Help or get out."

I pushed my chair back and left the kitchen, hating her almost as much as I hated myself.

Chapter 18

On Sunday morning, early, I brewed a pot of coffee, not sure if Jenny would be down to drink any of it. I hadn't seen her the previous day.

I had spent the morning on a buying tour of Saturday garage sales, the afternoon washing, pricing, and packing the things I had bought, and the evening alone.

She came downstairs dressed in white jeans and a pink cotton shirt, knotted at the waist. Her cheeks were rosy with sun. The sprinkling of freckles she hates made her look younger than she would have liked.

"Hi, Mum." She gave me a quick smile. "Any coffee left?"

Does anybody understand a seventeen-year-old? As though Friday had never been, Jenny cheerfully helped me load my car and followed me to the flea market. Once there, she took over.

"Go visiting," she ordered when the tables had been set up. "I'll unpack and arrange the junk. You'll just get in my way. Go for a walk. And hey, bring coffee when you come back."

I stopped at the Hennessys' table and gave Ros one of the Polaroid shots of the locket.

"No luck?" she asked.

"None. We must have covered thirty places during the week."

"Well, I'll show this around this week." She tucked the photo in her bag. "Who knows? Someone might recognize it."

I stopped to chat at Danny Garette's table. He asked about Elia. And about Anna. He hadn't been in for several weeks and I wondered where he had heard about them.

"Ros and Mike told me out at Lachute. The story's making the round of the flea markets. Everybody's intrigued, even some of the customers. I hear you've been looking. Any luck?"

"None so far."

"Anything I can do to help?"

"You can show this around, if you will."

I gave him a copy of the Polaroid picture and went on to the deli for coffee.

"Hey, you find her yet?" Tony asked, fitting lids onto Styrofoam cups.

"Not yet."

On my way back to our table, three other vendors and two of our regular customers asked the same question.

Jenny was standing behind the table, open-mouthed.

"What was *that?*" She tilted her head down the mall aisle.

I turned to see. "What was what?"

"That . . . that creature you just spoke to! There! The one with the yellow chicken feathers!"

"Oh. That's Tootie Frootie."

"Tootie? That's her real name?"

"We don't know what her real name is. We just thought she's a bit of a fruitcake."

Tootie was shod in knee-high kid boots from the fifties, the needle toes curling like jester's slippers. Above the boots her thin legs were encased in purple mesh hose, her flat buttocks in mauve satin shorts.

She wore a black tube top shot with silver threads, and, coiled around her throat, long ends wafting behind her, was a boa of feathers dyed a sulfurous yellow. Her wig, a glossy shade of caramel this week, was carefully tousled above a sagging, seventy-year-old face.

"Wow." Jenny breathed. "Does she always look like that?"

"Not really. She went a little overboard this week. She didn't look so far out last Sunday. Lace picture hat with cabbage roses. A beaded chiffon dress that must have been gorgeous on somebody back in 1929. Nostalgic, sort of."

"She comes in every week?" Jenny's eyes were following Tootie's spectacular progress down the mall.

"She's a regular. She comes every week."

"Does she ever buy anything?"

"Junk jewelry. Kinky hats. She bought the chicken feathers from Ros last week. I guess they inspired her."

Tootie turned the corner and Jenny turned to me, shaking her head. "That's pathetic," she said.

"Pathetic? I don't know about pathetic. She's having fun. And you must admit, she breaks the monotony."

"What monotony? There were seven people here, all at once, all grabbing."

"Those were pickers. They run around picking for dealers. Did they buy anything?"

"Sixty bucks' worth." Jenny sipped her coffee, her eyebrows puckering. "Something else. A man came and stood at the table and stared at me. I mean, he didn't even look at the junk. He just stood there and stared at me. Really spooky."

"What did he look like?"

"Look like?" She pondered. "A sad basset hound?"

I laughed. The description was apt. "That's Old Lonesome. He's just looking for someone to talk to."

"Why didn't he say something? I'd have talked to him."

"Oh, no. He never speaks first."

"Cripes. Is everybody around here crazy?"

"No crazier than thee and me." I dropped my empty cup into the trash. "We have a couple of oddballs, but most of the people who come in are as sane as we are. If that's any criterion."

Jenny's eyes lit up suddenly and I turned to see what had caused the change.

Elia had come through the doors. He caught sight of Jenny and his face broke out in a delighted smile.

She went out to meet him, hooked her hand through his arm, brought him around the table, and seated him in the chair she had vacated.

There was a sudden influx of customers. When the flurry passed, I turned in on Jenny and Elia.

"I? A pied piper?" Elia was saying. "Hardly. Kazimir had that role. I merely brought up the rear."

"Did they keep their promise? Did Kazimir take you to Warsaw?"

"To Kock only. He handed me over like a sack of potatoes and left without saying goodbye."

"What a strange man he must have been."

Elia shook his head.

"He was a careful man. They all were, the ones who saw me safely to Warsaw."

"What were they like, the others?"

"Very much like Kazimir. Silent. Secretive. They fed me. They gave me a place to sleep. They walked with me every step of the way. They even supplied me with new boots. But they never said a word more than was necessary. Eat. Sleep. Go. Stay. Wait. I was passed from hand to hand by people whose names I never learned."

"But they did get you to Warsaw."

"They did."

Elia looked at Jenny and his eyes softened.

"The last one was a girl, not much older than you are now. She picked me up on the outskirts of Warsaw and left me in Lazienki Park with directions to the home of Anna's aunt."

Chapter 19

Elia had met Sophie and Wasyl Kusiewicz, Anna's aunt and uncle, only once and briefly.

He remembered Sophie as an older version of her sister, Anna's mother. He had a dim recollection of Wasyl, a minor official in the Warsaw municipal government, as a very fat man with a loud voice and an overbearing manner.

He didn't recognize the man who responded to his knock. Has he mistaken the street?

"Is this the home of Wasyl Kusiewicz?" he asked.

"I'm Wasyl Kusiewicz." The voice was the same, overloud. But the man eyeing Elia suspiciously had half the girth Elia remembered. "What do you want?"

"I'm Elia. Elia Strohan. Is Anna here?"

The man's head reared back. His eyes turned ugly. He glanced up and down the street, then glared at Elia.

"What is this? Some kind of joke?"

"A joke?" Elia shook his head, puzzled. "No. I'm looking for Anna. My wife."

"Elia Strohan is dead." Kusiewicz said harshly.

He began to close the door.

"No! Wait!" Elia reached out a restraining hand. "I am Elia Strohan. Believe me. If Anna is here . . . please . . ."

A nerve in Kusiewicz's cheek jumped and for one insane

moment Elia thought the man was winking at him. But the door closed an inch further.

"Listen to me." Elia used his weight to prevent the door shutting in his face. "If Anna . . ."

"Sophie!" Kusiewicz shouted over his shoulder. "Sophie! Come here!"

They waited in silent confrontation. The nerve in Kusiewicz's cheek jumped repeatedly. His eyes, fastened on Elia's face, twitched uneasily.

Behind Kusiewicz, Elia heard Sophie's timid voice.

"What is it, Wasyl?"

Kusiewicz moved his bulk aside and the gap in the doorway was filled by a woman Elia would never have recognized.

Sophie had been thin, now she was gaunt. The left side of her face was like melted wax, her eyelid obscuring the pupil of her left eye. Her mouth sagged. Her right brow frowned as she searched Elia's face.

"Elia?" Only the right corner of her mouth moved. "Elia Strohan? Is it you?"

"Yes, Mrs. Kusiewicz. It's me. Is Anna here?"

As her husband had done, she glanced quickly up and down the street. She crossed herself, her lips moving silently.

"Come in." She shuffled backward. "Quickly."

Elia followed her to an overfurnished parlor. Wasyl, his broad face unreadable, hulked near the door, chewing on his thumbnail. Sophie lowered herself into a chair and indicated the seat facing her.

Elia shook his head impatiently. "Anna . . ." he began.

"She told us you were dead," Sophie interrupted. "She told us the Germans killed all the Jews in Kiev."

"She?" Elia frowned, bewildered. "Anna?"

"No, no! Not Anna." Sophie's hand clawed the air. "The girl who came with them. Lesia."

"Lesia? Lesia Boyko? She's here?"

"None of them are here," Sophie said. "They were . . ."

"They have a place not far from here." Wasyl's booming voice cut her short. He moved across the room and dropped a heavy hand on his wife's shoulder.

"They were crowded here with us," he said. "They took a place for themselves, not far from here."

Sophie stiffened. "Wasyl . . ." Her thin voice quavered.

"They're not far from here," Wasyl repeated. His mouth smiled at Elia. "The phone, well, you know. They have no phone. I'll go there and bring Anna back."

Elia felt his heart lift.

"I'll go with you," he said eagerly.

"No!" Wasyl's retort was sharp. "You can't . . . we can't leave Sophie by herself. She's had a stroke, you know. You wait here with her."

"Wasyl," Sophie said, her head trembling with agitation. "Wasyl. Listen to me. Let Elia go. Let him go . . . alone."

"Nonsense. He'll get lost. He doesn't know the city." Wasyl squeezed his wife's shoulder. "Make him a nice cup of tea. Make him at home. I won't be gone for long."

When he had gone, Elia turned to Sophie. She was hunched in her chair, one bony hand rubbing the other. She stared at the floor, her lips set in a pained line.

"Are you all right?" Elia asked.

Her head nodded. "I'm all right. I'm all right."

"Please. Tell me about Anna. The baby?"

"The baby. The baby. It was a girl. You have a little daughter."

"I have a daughter." Elia tasted the word. "A daughter." Tell me about her. Is she like Anna? What is her name?"

"Elianna," Sophie said to the floor. "Anna named her after the two of you. Elianna."

"Is Anna all right? Was it hard for her?"

For a moment Sophie didn't answer. Then her head reared up. Her ruined face contorted, her one good eye blazed.

"Get out of here, Elia," she cried. "Get out of here. You must leave. Quickly! Now!"

Elia stared at her, aghast, wondering if the woman had taken leave of her senses. She bent forward in her chair, her nails scrabbling the wooden chair arms.

"Go!" she said hoarsely. "For God's sake. *Go!*"

"Go?" Elia sat, frozen. "But Anna . . ."

"Anna! Anna isn't here!" Sophie's voice was a thin wail. "None of them are here! My sister. My nieces. Lesia. The Germans took them, don't you understand?"

"Took them? Took them where?" Elia's throat had closed. He had difficulty speaking.

"To the labor camps. Somewhere in Germany. We don't know where. It was only three weeks ago. We haven't heard." She began to sob. "Nothing. Nothing. We've heard nothing."

Elia had the strange sensation that his body functions had ground to a halt.

He could see Sophie's quivering shoulders but could not hear the sounds of her weeping. He could feel the blood draining from his heart, the juices from his stomach. His arms and legs had turned to hollow lead and his brain seemed to lie thick and inert inside his skull.

A mist was forming behind his eyes when, abruptly, his imperious lungs demanded air. He drew a deep, shuddering breath. Flooded with oxygen, his brain stirred and he remembered Wasyl.

"Your husband. Where did he go?"

"He's giving you to the Gestapo." Sophie could not look at Elia. "He's gone to get them."

"But why?" Elia asked her quietly.

"Why?" She raised her tear-stained face. "Because they told him he must? Because he's a frightened man? Because he hates Jews? Who knows why? What does it matter why? Go before he returns. For the love of heaven, go!"

Elia pushed himself out of the chair and walked heavily

past the weeping woman. At the parlor door, he turned.

"My daughter. Elianna. Where is she?"

"A German couple has taken her."

"A German couple? The Germans have my child?"

"No, no! It's not what you think," Sophia cried. "These are old friends. They're good people. They're Germans, not Nazis. Anna arranged it. They'll be good to Elianna. They'll take care of her until the war is over. Now go, Elia. Please. You must go now."

"Will you be all right? Wasyl . . ."

"I'll tell him you left. How could I stop you?"

Elia slid back the parlor door. "Thank you, Sophie," he said. She nodded, pressing her hands to her mouth.

Elia crossed the foyer and opened the door leading to the street. Wasyl was on the step, his hand raised to turn the latch.

With him were two men in the black uniform of the SS.

Chapter 20

O h, Elia! No!"

Jenny had been listening to Elia as raptly as she had once listened to bedtime stories. Her eyes were round with compassion, her voice aching.

"Who were they? The men in black?"

"Secret state police. The Gestapo."

"Oh, Elia. If only you had left earlier." Jenny's distress was very real. Elia took her hand in his.

"*If,*" he said. "If I had left earlier. If I had arrived in Warsaw three weeks earlier. Anna would still have been there. 'If' is a terrible word."

"What happened? What did the Gestapo do to you?"

"They dragged me down to the rail terminus at Umschlagplatz and stuffed me into a cattle car."

Jenny blinked. "That fast?" she said.

Elia nodded. "That fast."

"I've heard about the trains." Jenny bent forward, her face intent. "Were they as bad as they say?"

"As bad?" Elia shook his head. "They were worse."

"Tell me about it," Jenny said. "Make me understand what it was like."

Elia eyed her quizzically. "Understand? Why do you use that word? 'Understand.'"

"Because it happened to you." Jenny said.

Elia nodded. "I see," he said. He released Jenny's hand and folded his hands on top of his cane.

"There were close to two hundred of us packed into that one boxcar," he said. "Men. Women. Children. Old people. No water, no toilet facilities. We were in that car for eighteen hours."

"Eighteen *hours!*" Jenny stared. "Where were you going that took eighteen hours?"

"Most of the time, nowhere. Most of the time we were shunted onto sidings, not moving at all. You must remember, this was in August. It was unbearably hot. The air in that car was foul. The stench . . ." Elia paused.

"What?" Jenny urged. "What?"

"There was a little girl, a child, not more than four years old, clinging to her father's leg. She raised her arms and in her little voice, she said," *"Pick me up, Papa. It stinks down here."*

Elia's gaze turned inward.

"Those words," he said. "Suddenly, I was nine years old again, in Nathan Goretsky's backyard. It was Easter weekend and Nathan had forgotten to hide his cart. The Jew-baiters had wrecked it."

"The *what?*" Jenny interrupted.

Elia, brought back to the present, blinked at her.

"Every Christian holiday, the Jews hid themselves," he explained. "Hoodlums rampaged through the Jewish sections, destroying whatever they found."

"Hoodlums?" Jenny's voice rose. "Ukrainians?"

Elia nodded and Jenny turned accusing eyes on me. I raised protesting palms.

"Not me. Not in this life."

Elia smiled. "Hoodlums, Jenny, hoodlums who happened to be Ukrainians. There are hoodlums in every culture, every country, not just the Ukraine. They wrecked Goretsky's cart. He cursed them, cursed himself, cursed the world. God too.

He raised his fist and yelled, *"Damn you, up there! Don't you know it stinks down here?"*

Elia leaned forward on his cane.

"At that moment," he continued, "it began to rain. Fat, wet raindrops. Goretsky pointed that bony finger of his at me. *"You see! You see!"* he yelled, as though he had proved something to me. *"Even God pisses on us!"*

Jenny's delighted laugh turned heads in the mall. Across from us, Mike and Ros smiled at the infectious sound.

"That's what I did, there in that stinking car," Elia said. "I began to laugh. Because, suddenly, I understood why Goretsky had laughed that day at Babi Yar. His eternal pessimism had been a joke among his friends. Now the joke was on them and it was enough to make him die laughing."

The merriment had fled from Jenny's face.

"It's not a very funny joke," she said.

"No." Elia agreed. "But I couldn't stop laughing. My trousers were wet with urine. The child had vomited on her father and on me. The old man pressed against me was either unconscious or dead, still standing. It was impossible for him to slide to the floor."

"Gross." It was Jenny's word for ultimate disgust. "That's really gross. And you were laughing?"

Elia's lips twisted.

"Maybe it was the ghost of Goretsky, laughing at me. Because, in spite of what I had seen at Babi Yar, I was trying to make myself believe, as most on that train believed, that we were being resettled."

"Resettled?" Jenny frowned.

"That's what we had been told. We were being moved out of Warsaw for resettlement."

"Did you believe it?"

"For a split second when the cattle car doors were rolled back. I saw blue skies, green trees, a train station planted with flowers."

Elia shook his head.

"Then I saw men with whips and the SS with guns lined along the platform and I knew, wherever we were, it was not for resettlement."

"Where were you?"

"Treblinka. We had arrived at Treblinka."

Chapter 21

The old man was indeed dead, his eyes milky, his jaw hanging. Elia lowered him gently to the floorboards of the cattle car.

At the open doors, the guards he had glimpsed were shouting, using their whips on the car's terrified occupants. Those in front leaped out, screaming with panic. Behind Elia, the pressure of those pushing to reach fresh air propelled, him forward.

He dropped from the car to the platform below and was immediately engulfed in the crowd being herded through a gap in a barbed wire fence. The leather whips rose and fell indiscriminately. The noise and turmoil was unbearable.

Inside the fenced area, Elia found himself in a yard flanked on both sides by wooden barracks. Atop each of the buildings were uniformed men with machine guns at the ready. Threatened from above, trapped and beaten below, the crowd milled in frightened confusion.

"Move! Men to the right!" the guards bawled, snapping their whips. "Women and children to the left! Move!"

A ragged queue formed, carrying Elia along to the right. Ahead he could hear phrases being shouted repeatedly, but he couldn't make out their meaning.

And then he could. Fear filled his chest with ice water.

"Strip! Tie your shoes together! Take along your money and documents!" The instructions were repeated over and over.

From far in front, reassuring word filtered back, passed from one man to the next. They were being sent to showers, to bathe and be disinfected.

Elia froze.

In that instant he knew that what Stefan had said was true. He was a lamb. All these panicked people were lambs, led to slaughter, believing the lie because the reality was beyond human capacity to imagine.

The mass of men flowed around him, jostling him, jarring him. He was barely aware of their movement. The scab that had formed over the memory of Babi Yar had cracked wide open.

His mind, which for months had refused recollection of that day, reeled with nightmarish glimpses of the dead he had not permitted himself to mourn. His parents. Orest. The boy whose mangled corpse he had used and discarded.

He was struck from behind, a savage blow that sent him sprawling. Around him, men scattered, fleeing the brutal whip.

"Get up!" The guard lashed out with his boot. "Get up and keep moving."

Elia scrabbled away on all fours. The guard turned his attention to the others.

"Move!" The whip rose and fell. "Keep moving!"

Forcing himself erect, Elia melted into the milling crowd, commanding his brain to think, his eyes to see.

To his right was a group of fully clothed men, hurriedly stacking bundles. He detached himself from the herd and began a slow tack toward them, buttoning his shirt as he drifted.

He was halted two feet from the barbed wire by a black-uniformed SS guard.

They faced one another silently.

The guard's eyes slid past Elia to the naked men beyond, then back to Elia. His expression was unreadable.

"Come," he growled.

He led Elia back to the open square where the train stood, doors yawning emptily.

The square was littered. Parcels and suitcases had been smashed open, their contents scattered. Strewn as carelessly were hundreds of corpses.

Shuddering with nausea, Elia stared down at the body of a woman, her skull crushed; at the swollen face of a young man with dead eyes staring at the calm blue sky.

Corpses were stacked like cordwood, their stench overpowering, the hot summer air foul with the smell. Men, clad in ragged clothing, ran back and forth, carrying the corpses, dragging bodies tied with ropes.

The SS guard halted one of them with his whip butt.

"You," he said.

The man stopped in his tracks, chest heaving.

He was short and thin, his hair a tangled mass of black curls. Above his deep-set eyes was a scab-encrusted bruise. His hands clenched a length of rope.

"Use him." The guard jerked a thumb at Elia. He turned and strode away, his whip tapping his dusty boot.

For the space of a heartbeat the little man sagged in relief. Then he bent and looped the rope under the arms of the dead young woman lying naked at his feet.

Elia knelt to help.

"What place is this?" he asked hoarsely.

"Treblinka." The man's dark eyes darted wildly about. He hunched down, his head averted.

"Don't talk," he muttered. "Keep moving."

For the rest of the day they ran in tandem, dragging corpses to an open pit almost a quarter of a kilometer away.

Elia soon lost count of the trips they made back and forth, of the bodies they dragged and threw into a mass grave. They ran in the burning sunlight, under the whips of the guards.

A second train arrived. The square swarmed with people beaten out of the packed cars. The gruesome stacks of bodies were renewed.

At dusk the work was stopped. With blows from whips and rifle butts, the guards drove the exhausted men to a barrack far to the left of the two Elia had seen earlier.

Inside, the air was vile. Elia, aware only of a burning thirst and a physical weariness beyond anything he had ever known, stretched out on the earthen floor and slept.

He was awakened before dawn by the moaning and stirring of the men surrounding him. A hand clutched his shoulder and shook him, not gently.

"Get up," an urgent voice prodded. "You must get up."

Elia opened his eyes.

His partner of the previous day bent over him, his face inches away, his eyes luminous in the semidarkness.

"My name is Aaron. Aaron Lipsky," he said. "If you don't get up, you'll be shot. Get up."

Elia staggered to his feet and followed Aaron out of the barrack. At the door, a rifle butt struck him in the small of the back and he lurched foward, bent double.

"Stand up!" Aaron hissed. "They'll think you can't work. You'll be shot. Stand up!"

With an effort of will, Elia straightened. They hurried to join the others.

Close to five hundred men were lined up outside, some gaunt to the point of emaciation, others merely pathetically thin, their garments filthy, their faces seamy with dirt. They stood erect, enduring blows from the whips and rifles of the shouting guards.

"Listen," Aaron muttered beside Elia. "Keep your head down. Protect your face. Stay on your feet. Don't fall."

Time passed. To Elia, light-headed with hunger and

thirst, five minutes or three hours could have elapsed before the red ball of the sun rose in a cloudless sky, promising another day of unrelenting heat.

He was distantly aware of a shouted command. His skin absorbed the increased tension around him but his mind hovered dreamily above the heads of the massed men. Then Aaron delivered a sharp kick to his ankle and his reverie snapped.

At a signal from an SS officer, a squad of guards began a random beating of the helpless men. When a man collapsed, he was shot.

Elia, his arm numbed from a rifle blow, gritted his teeth. From the corner of his eye, he saw Aaron stagger but remain erect. Shots rang out. Then, abruptly, the beating stopped.

The men remaining were split into work groups. To Elia's intense relief, he and Aaron were assigned to the same corpse detail.

Aaron caught the expression on Elia's face and his mouth twisted with grim humor.

"Listen, sonny boy," he muttered as they ran together. "I am not your mother. I can't wet-nurse you."

His eyes were in constant motion, checking the proximity of the watchful guards.

"Wake up," he grunted. "You have maybe five minutes to learn how to stay alive."

Chapter 22

*E*lia's voice broke.

He bent his head and pinched the bridge of his nose with trembling fingers.

Jenny looked at me in consternation. With instinctive delicacy, she silently covered his other hand with her own.

My own reaction was one of confused shock.

Until now, Elia had spoken of the past in an almost academic fashion, as though relating historical facts in a classroom. This is what happened, this is how it happened.

Until now, I don't think I ever consciously understood that everything he had been telling us was real, had happened to *him,* to the old man now seated beside me, struggling to control emotions he may have considered long buried.

He raised his head and smiled apologetically, first at Jenny, then at me.

"Delayed reaction." His voice was fragile. "I suppose, eventually, we all deteriorate into maudlin old fools."

"Hey." Impulsively, Jenny leaned forward and kissed his cheek. "You're entitled."

"I'm entitled." Elia pushed himself to his feet. "But at this late date, donetchka, it's far too exhausting."

He turned to me.

"Nu, Liz. Dopobachynia."

"Dopobachynia, Elia. You'll be back next week?"

"Of course."

We watched him leave. He leaned more heavily on his cane than ordinarily. At the door, he turned and waved.

"What does 'donetchka' mean?" Jenny asked, waving back.

"Daughter. It's the diminutive of daughter."

"And 'dopobachynia'? Is that goodbye?"

"Not literally. If you translate, it means to re-see. It's like the French 'au revoir' or the German 'auf wiedersehen.' Until we meet again."

Jenny's face wore an expression of elaborate patience.

"Good old Mum," she said. "Always telling you more than you want to know."

Chapter 23

Cia phoned early Monday morning.

"He's holding his own." Her voice was pitched low. "It's my mother I'm worried about. She's coming apart. The doctor has given us sedatives for her but she's fighting them. I've been up all night. She's just now fallen asleep."

"How are you doing?"

"Me? Christ, I feel as though I've been put through a meat grinder."

Cia's voice caught, then strengthened.

"Listen, Liz. I can't leave now. Would you call the bank and tell them I won't be in this week? Explain why. I'd do it myself, but I'm dead and it's too early to call them."

"Of course I'll call. Go to bed. You're going to need your strength. You'll be able to cope better rested."

"I know. Thanks, Liz. I'll call at the end of the week."

"Yes. Take care, Cia."

I hung up and went mechanically through the motions of preparing breakfast. Jenny, normally a morning chatterer, was silent and preoccupied. She had come home in the small hours and there were mauve smudges under her eyes. I was mildly surprised to find I had no interest in ragging at her. She finished her coffee, pecked me on the cheek, and left.

I decided to search for Anna in the Beaconsfield area and

selected addresses from the garage sale ads. There were fourteen in the section north of the highway. With luck I could
check them all out in one day.

By noon I had covered only five.

At one house, the new homeowner directed me next door,
where a gaunt, thin-lipped redhead informed me her previous
neighbors had moved west and proceeded to describe their
scandalous lifestyle in lurid detail. I escaped when her phone
rang.

I had lunch at the nearest shopping center and returned
to the area. There was no answer to my ring at the eighth
and ninth houses on my list. I marked them for a return call.

The tenth house struck a responsive chord. I remembered
it as the place where Cia and I had purchased two large boxes
of expensive articles, all dirt cheap. We had come to the con-
clusion we were the beneficiaries of a spiteful divorce.

A young woman responded to my knock. She glanced at
the locket and shook her head.

"We just moved in. But the people next door were good
friends with the previous owners." She pointed out the house
on the left. "They might be able to help you."

The woman next door, a very pregnant blonde with an
upper lip too short to cover prominent teeth, peered near-
sightedly at the locket. She handed it back to me.

"No. It wasn't Peggy's. I knew all her stuff."

"Thank you. I'm sorry to have bothered . . ."

"Were you at the garage sale?" Her eyes filled with mist.
"Wasn't that the saddest thing ever? Poor Ron. And that
poor, darling baby."

Baby? I remembered now. There had been a child. A silent, solemn two-year-old.

"Yes," I said. "We wondered . . ."

"She died. Peggy." The mist became liquid and spilled
over. She pulled a tissue from her pocket and dabbed at her
eyes. "My God. Look at me. Three months and I still bawl
when I think of it."

"I'm sorry . . ."

"It was all so damn sad, you know? They had everything going for them. Ron had a fabulous job. The house. The baby. And they were crazy about each other. I mean, the perfect couple, you know?"

She blew her nose and dabbed at her streaming eyes.

"Then they found out Peg had cancer. Twenty-nine years old! And, omigod, it took her a whole year to die. That's what the garage sale stuff was. Ron kept buying her things she'd never get to use. All the stuff he sold for peanuts because he couldn't stand the sight of it after she died."

She was crying now, snuffling into a ball of wet tissue. I dug in my bag for a fresh piece. She took it absently and crumpled it in her hand.

"Look. I'm sorry. I just . . ."

She ran into the house, leaving the door open. I pulled it shut and went back to my car.

I did the last four addresses on my list, but I don't remember much about them. I was on familiar streets before I realized I had driven home.

The phone was ringing when I let myself into the house. Jenny would be eating dinner with Rick.

I threw together a wok meal for myself and ate in front of the TV set, not tasting, not seeing. My mind was totally absorbed with trying to sort out my own feelings.

The illness of Cia's father; the poignant story of the Beaconsfield couple; neither had aroused the usual quick spark of sympathy in me.

Cia's father, if it came to that, would die in a clean hospital bed after the best care medical science could provide. There would be an elaborate funeral, well attended by family and friends. His wife, after a time, would pick up the threads of her life. Perhaps even marry again.

How could that compare with the death of the old man who had died, braced erect in a cattle car, dragged like a rotten log and thrown into a mass grave, unacknowledged, unmourned?

Or how reconcile the young woman dying, surrounded by love and luxury, with the death of another young woman who had been thrown away like garbage, nude and faceless?

I couldn't get Elia out of my mind. His pain-filled words, *"I wanted to see her face just once more,"* haunted me.

I cleared my desk, sorted out the garage sale ads by district, and prepared a schedule.

Twelve calls a day, minimum. If possible, more. Together with return calls, there were 110 addresses still to visit. I could cover them all in two weeks.

By Saturday, I had made only seventeen calls.

A client had phoned with an assignment; a brochure and a series of newspaper advertisements for a retirement complex. A quick glance at my bank balance canceled out any impulse I may have had to refuse the job. I decided to approach the campaign as a series of interviews with some of the tenants.

By the time I was through talking to those selected for me, I was seething with impatience at these coddled seniors in their plush apartments. Their complaints about children who visited too infrequently, elevator operators with long hair, cleaning maids smelling of perspiration, activities organizers planning boring outings—all seemed churlish and petty in my state of mind.

I delivered the completed copy early on Saturday and made the rounds of new garage sales. And it was at one of those sales that I realized how completely Elia's story had come to affect me.

It was a gem of a sale for any flea market vendor.

An old aunt had died, leaving her possessions to be sold by a family with no sense of their value as collectibles. Pink Depression glass, an entire dinner set. Carnival glass. Thin Bohemian stemware. Discontinued Royal Doulton's, a dozen of them. A pair of Murano glass lamps. A collection of carved ivory animal figures. Silver, linens, books, and some elegant, small pieces of Victorian furniture.

Two vendors I knew were there when I arrived, both as avid as I should have been, but wasn't.

Waiting to pay for my selections, I found myself staring down at the Art Deco charger in my hand, a lovely twenties piece in the form of a peacock. The neck and head formed a graceful handle. The spread tail, all blues and greens and bronzes, fanned out in a scalloped shape. It was unchipped, unscratched, and priced at six dollars. I knew I would get at least ten times that from any of the antique dealers.

Yet all I could think was how senseless it all was.

Things. Buying things, some old, some beautiful, some even functional. All trivial.

Selling things to people who collected as though the acquisition gave importance and purpose to their lives.

Things. I was sated with *things*.

My imagination had become a prisoner of Treblinka and everything else was lacking in substance.

Chapter 24

Aaron was wrong when he said I had five minutes to learn to stay alive."

Elia sat as he always did on Sunday, his back straight, his cane resting between his knees, the locket in his hand. Jenny sat with him, nibbling on a bagel and sipping coffee.

With no urging on my part, she had risen early. She had loaded my car while I prepared our lunches.

"Make enough for Elia," she had said.

"He never eats lunch."

"He will today. I want to hear all about that place. Treblinka."

"Staying alive wasn't really something that could be learned," Elia continued. "It was more a matter of luck than anything else. And it was luck that threw me together with Aaron Lipsky."

"What was he like? Aaron." Jenny tilted her cup, drained the coffee, and dropped the paper cup into the bag we used for garbage. "Bring him to life for me."

Elia smiled at her, a smile so sweetly sad my throat tightened.

"Do you know the term 'kindred spirits'?" he asked.

"I think so," Jenny's brows drew together. "It means the

two of you were sort of on the same wavelength, doesn't it?"

"Wavelength," Elia nodded. "I suppose that's what we were. We never had to explain ourselves to one another."

"Was he from Kiev too?"

Elia shook his head. "Aaron was from Warsaw. In the beginning, that's what he talked about. Warsaw. The Warsaw ghetto. He was determined someone—if not him, then me—someone must survive to tell the world what happened there. I was to listen and remember. And then, through many long nights, when sleep was impossible, we would talk to one another. We became closer than friends, closer than brothers. I came to know his life as well as I knew my own."

Elia reached out and touched Jenny's cheek with a gentle finger.

"So, donetchka," he said. "Let me try to bring Aaron to life for you."

Chapter 25

Aaron Lipsky was the sixth of seven children of Joseph, a Warsaw tailor, and Miriam, daughter of Moses Skolnick, a butcher.

From her kitchen, where she spent her days, Miriam ruled her family with a tart tongue and a wooden spoon. Her children were nagged, slapped, kissed, and praised. And all were put to work as soon as they were able to understand directions. The boys delivered to Joseph's customers or worked as helpers in Moses Skolnick's shop. The girls basted and stitched for their father.

The oldest boy, Nathan, became a tailor with his father. David, the secondborn, was apprenticed to his grandfather. Esther and Sadie, the two elder daughters, went to work in a shirt factory.

All lived at home and all contributed to the household, so that when Samuel, the third son, was ready there would be money to fulfill Miriam's plans for the rest of her family.

"Samuel will be a lawyer. Aaron will be a doctor. Rachel will be a teacher."

No one questioned her decisions.

"When Samuel is earning, Nathan and David can marry and start their own families. When Aaron is a doctor, Esther and Sadie can marry. Samuel and Aaron pay for Rachel's education. And Rachel will repay us by supervising the education of my grandchildren."

It had gone as Miriam had planned, principally because she knew her children very well.

Jews were discriminated against in Warsaw universities, but Samuel, the analytical, argumentative son, had the high academic standing and the tenacity to force acceptance. When he graduated, Nathan and David married and set up homes of their own.

Aaron was the most physically aggressive of the family. He was born competitor, a natural athlete. He gained a certain fame as a track star in the Jewish school he attended, and this, combined with above-average marks, won him entrance to the university.

At age thirty, Aaron married Leah Prokosh, a girl he had loved since his teens. As if to make up for their late start, they produced two children in two years. The first, a girl they named Sarah, immediately wound her baby fingers around Aaron. Then came Noah, a bright, beautiful boy who filled Aaron with a love so intense it awed him.

On September 1, 1939, when Aaron was forty years old, Hitler's armies invaded Poland. Warsaw fell.

Early in October, barbed wire barriers were erected to enclose the streets of the Jewish quarter. In November, news of a decree forcing all Jews to relocate into the ghetto spread through the community.

At Miriam's urging, the Lipskys immediately purchased an old house in the designated area. Once again, the family was under one roof. Only David was missing. He, his wife, and her family had died in a massive bombing raid on the eve of Rosh Hashanah.

The house was small. And where once there had been nine Lipskys, there were now twenty-four.

"Papa and I will have the dining room," Miriam informed her assembled family. "Aaron and Leah and the children will take the living room."

"But that's the largest room," Esther protested. "There are only four of them. Sadie and Max have three children. Why shouldn't they have the living room?"

"Because Aaron is a doctor." Of all her children, only Esther, contrary from childhood, could try Miriam's patience. "Do you expect his patients should schlepp their sick bodies up and down the stairs?"

Esther's mouth tightened but she kept silent.

"Rachel," Miriam turned to her youngest. "Since you're not married, you have a room to yourself, the little storage room by the kitchen. Nathan and Ruth, for you, the bigger bedroom upstairs. Samuel and Ida, the smaller bedroom."

She turned to the mild-mannered carpenter married to her Sadie and her eyes softened.

"Maxie. The attic. Do you think you could maybe put up a partition?"

"Sure, Mama." Max nodded.

"Good. You and Sadie take one side, Esther and Benjamin the other." She scanned the faces of her family. "Agreed?"

All nodded, Samuel with his customary shrug, Leah with her eyes on Aaron, Esther sourly.

"What choice do we have?" she complained. "But we'll be at each other's throats. Wait and see."

"We won't have time for such nonsense," Miriam snapped. "We work. Aaron doctors. Rachel teaches. And Samuel, as long as people live skin to skin, there'll be work for lawyers. Max will carpenter, and Benjamin, a rabbi everybody needs. The barbarians won't be here forever. Meanwhile, we have children to raise." She slanted a hard look at Esther. "We will control our tongues. We will stick together. We will survive."

Esther's mouth opened. Before she could speak there was a knock on the door to the street. Everyone froze.

They had all heard stories of people being dragged from

their homes in the night, never to be seen again. It was long past the curfew imposed by the Germans. No Jew would risk the streets at this time of night.

"I'll go." Nathan's chair scraped. He slid back the bolt and opened the door.

A boy, heavily muffled against the cold, stood in the doorway. Nathan, after a quick glance up and down the street, pulled him into the light and closed the door.

The boy removed his wool hat, revealing a mane of red curls. He twisted the cap in his hands, his eyes leaping from one face to another.

"Please, excuse me. I don't mean to bother you." He was shaking visibly. "My name is Daniel Zylenberg. They told me there was a doctor here."

"I'm a doctor." Aaron rose from the table. "What's the problem?"

"My father. He . . ." The boy's eyes fastened on Aaron's face. "It's not far. Please. Will you come?"

"I'll get my bag."

Hugging the buildings, Aaron followed the boy to a row of flats a block away. With hands that shook, Daniel unlocked the street door and darted up a dark flight of stairs, with Aaron stumbling after him.

Opening a door at the landing, Daniel waited in the stream of light from inside the flat. When Aaron had entered, he quickly closed and bolted the door.

Aaron found himself in a room serving as kitchen, living room, and bedroom. Four children, all with Daniel's cap of red curls, stared at him from a mattress on the floor. Somewhere, a woman was crying, her sobs rising and falling eerily.

"In here." Daniel plucked at Aaron's sleeve and led him to an adjoining room.

The man on the bed was unrecognizable.

His hair was matted with blood, his face so swollen his eyes were slits in battered flesh. One arm was twisted under him, the other broken between the wrist and elbow. He lay so still in his wrappings of torn and bloody clothing that Aaron thought he was dead.

Probing for a pulse, Aaron looked at the woman across the bed from where he stood.

She was seated on a stool. Her eyes were empty, the irises like black holes in her skull. She bent her forehead to her knees with each piercing cry, raising her head for breath to scream again. She was in shock, and Aaron knew she would be no help to him.

His fingers had picked up a steady heartbeat. He turned to the boy.

"Get water," he instructed. "Hot, if you can. And bring clean clothes."

As soon as Daniel was gone, Aaron circled the bed. He bent over the keening woman and slapped her cheek sharply. She was abruptly silent, then she sighed. Her head fell back against the wall and she stared at the ceiling with unseeing eyes. Aaron pulled a blanket from the bed and spread it over her, tucking it around her shoulders.

Daniel returned, balancing a basin of hot water, clean towels slung over his arm.

"What happened here?" Aaron soaked a towel and began gently cleansing the bloodied head. "Who did this?"

"The Germans. The Schaarfuehrers." Daniel set the basin on a chest of drawers. He squeezed out a fresh towel and handed it to Aaron.

"They came here?"

"No. On the street. Papa didn't get out of their way quickly enough."

Aaron reached for his bag. He had located the head wound. He swabbed it with alcohol.

"How did he get here?" he asked. "He couldn't have walked."

"Some neighbors saw. They waited and carried him home."

"And just left him? Like this?"

"They were afraid the Germans would come back." Daniel stared down at the gaping cut. "He wasn't doing anything. He was just walking home."

Aaron glanced up at the boy's white face.

"Listen, Daniel. I'm going to put stitches in this cut. Maybe you should go to the other room."

"I'll stay."

"As you like."

Aaron worked for ten minutes, closing the cut and applying a bandage. When he finished, he eyed the boy narrowly. Daniel's fists were clenched tightly but a tinge of color had returned to his cheeks.

"You're all right?"

The boy nodded.

"Do you think you can help me?"

"Yes."

"Good. Here's what we have to do. We must get his arm back into the shoulder socket. Do you think you can hold him while I do it?"

Daniel's face paled but he nodded.

Half an hour later, his broken arm set, the unconscious man was dressed in clean nightclothes. Aaron shook out a handful of pills and gave them to Daniel.

"When your father wakens he'll be in pain. Give him two of these. Give him two more when he needs them. I'll come back tomorrow."

Daniel nodded, his eyes searching Aaron's. "Is he . . . will he be all right?"

"He'll be sick for a while. But he'll be all right."

Tears welled in Daniel's eyes. They spilled over and he began to cry wrenchingly. Aaron pulled the boy to him and held the thin, young body close until the sobs dwindled to an occasional shuddering sigh.

Across the room the woman was asleep, breathing heavily.

"Leave your mother as she is," he told Daniel. "She'll be all right too."

The boy's head lifted and Aaron smiled down at the tear-streaked face.

"How old are you, Daniel?"

"Fourteen."

"Only fourteen? You're a good boy. Many adults wouldn't have done as well as you did tonight. Your father will be very proud of you."

Daniel's face flushed at the praise. "I'm going to be a doctor someday," he said.

"And you'll be a good one." Aaron reached for his coat and bag.

In the outer room, the four children were asleep on their mattress, curled together like puppies. Daniel bent and adjusted their blanket, covering the rounded rump of his younger brother, then unbolted the door leading to the hall. He poked his head out and peered left and right. Satisfied, he nodded to Aaron.

"I'll be back tomorrow," Aaron whispered. He patted the boy's thin shoulder. "Get some sleep. Your mother will need you in the morning."

Daniel opened his mouth to speak. His eyes, focused beyond Aaron, widened. Aaron turned quickly.

Across the narrow hallway, a door had opened silently. For a moment, Aaron could see only a head silhouetted against the dim light of the room beyond. The door swung wider. A bearded young man emerged. He clutched at Aaron's arm.

"Doctor?" he whispered. "Are you the doctor?"

"Yes." Aaron's attempt to free his arm only tightened the man's grip.

"My wife. Come." The man backed, tugging at Aaron. "It's too soon. Something is wrong. Please come."

Aaron permitted himself to be dragged through the door and into the flat beyond.

He was in a small, windowless room dominated by three cots. On the cot nearest lay an old woman, her mouth gaping toothlessly, her eyes closed.

On the second, a young woman in obvious labor writhed and whimpered, her hands knotted into fists under her chin. Her face was wet with sweat, her lips pulled back from her teeth in an agonized grimace.

"Get water and towels," Aaron shed his coat and rolled up his sleeves. "Hot water, if you can. Wash your hands. I'll need your help."

The man did not stir. Aaron, bending over the woman, glanced up impatiently.

"What's your name?" Aaron demanded sharply.

"Moshe." The man was shivering uncontrollably.

"Well, Moshe. Move. We're going to need water and we're going to need clean towels. Get them."

Moshe wrung his hands helplessly. His eyes darted around the room, avoiding the suffering mound on the cot.

"We have no water." Moshe's voice was high and strained. Then, to Aaron's astonishment, he began to sob, great tears rolling unchecked down his cheeks into his beard.

Aaron sighed.

"All right, Moshe," he said gently. "Go across the hall and ask the boy for water. Go. And wake the old woman. She can help."

Moshe shook his head. "Mama. I tried to wake her. She's sick. Let her sleep."

"So. Get Daniel. Get water."

Aaron opened the door and pushed Moshe through, closing it after. He felt for a pulse in the old woman.

There was none. The old woman was dead. Aaron pulled the quilt over the gray head and returned to the cot where the young woman strained and gasped.

It was a difficult birth, requiring all Aaron's skill. He was aware of Daniel's presence, of Daniel wiping the woman's face, holding her hand. Not till he held the newborn infant in his hands did it occur to him to look for Moshe.

He stood beside the cot on which his mother lay, swaying back and forth, head lowered, eyes closed, lips moving in silent prayer.

"Mazel tov, Moshe," Aaron announced. "You have a son."

Moshe raised his head. "My mother is dead," he said.

"Your wife and your son are alive," Aaron said. "And they need care. Have you friends, relatives who can come?"

"No one." Moshe shook his head. "We're not from here. We know nobody."

"Where are you from?"

"From Plonsk. We arrived two days ago."

"Two days ago? How did you get here? There are no trains for Jews."

"We walked. Mama. Sima. Me. We walked. The Germans drove the Jews from Plonsk. We walked. How else?"

"Walked?" Aaron looked down at the young mother. "This woman, in her condition, walked fifty kilometers in the dead winter?"

"How else?" Moshe repeated. He stared down at his son with dull eyes. The baby mewed feebly and Moshe nodded.

"Yes, cry," he said bitterly. "Your *baba* is dead. Better we should all be dead. Cry. You have a right."

Aaron turned away, stifling an angry remark. He laid the baby beside its mother. She opened her eyes and drew the infant to her warmth. Aaron brushed the wet strands of hair from her forehead.

"Rest," he said. "I'll come tomorrow."

The sky was paling in the east when Aaron let himself into the room where Leah and the children slept. He undressed quietly, tiptoeing so as not to waken them, and slipped under the covers beside Leah. She stirred.

"Aaron?" she whispered. "What time is it?"

"Very late. Or very early. Go back to sleep."

"Are you all right?"

"Tired. Cold. But all right."

"Come closer. I'll warm you."

Aaron slept until noon. It was the last time he was to get more than a three-hour stretch of uninterrupted sleep.

Chapter 26

"A aron. Aaron, wake up."

With a feeling that the words had been repeated over and over again, Aaron struggled up through black layers of sleep, pulling his leaden body back to consciousness. He forced his eyes, gritty with weariness, to open. He made out Leah's dim form bending over him.

"What time is it?" he whispered.

"Just after midnight."

Aaron groaned. He had slept less than an hour. He rubbed his burning eyes with the heels of his hands and sat upright.

"What is it? What's the matter."

"It's Papa." Leah's voice was thick with emotion. "Mama says you should come."

Aaron slipped quickly from the warm bed and donned the robe Leah held for him. He followed her groggily through the door to the dining room, where his parents slept.

Candlelight muted the rose pattern of the wallpaper and softened the outlines of the shabby furniture. Miriam sat beside the bed where his father lay, her hands clasped, her head bowed.

"Mama." Aaron touched her shoulder. She raised her head and gazed dry-eyed at her son.

"Let me," Aaron said softly. Miriam rose to make room for him.

Aaron rested his fingers on Joseph's fragile wrist. The pulse was arrhythmic and thready. It ceased, then resumed, weaker than before.

Aaron shook his head.

"He's slipping away," he said. "Mama, I think you should wake the others. Leah? Have we any tea? Would you make some?"

Leah nodded and the two women left.

Aaron took his father's hand in his own. The old man's hand was skeletal, the skin like parchment. A year in the ghetto had melted the flesh from his bones. Never robust, he had suffered more than the others from the ghetto climate of hunger and tension. His first heart attack had ended his working days. A second had left him bedridden.

Aaron looked down on the dying man through a mist of tears. Throughout his entire life he had seen his quiet, self-effacing father angry only once.

Shortly after their move to the ghetto, Aaron had returned home to find Adam Czerniakow seated with the family around the table in the communal kitchen.

His acquaintance with Czerniakow was slight. He was aware that Adam Czerniakow was one of the more dedicated of the community leaders, but the man's presence in the house roused a sense of foreboding in Aaron.

In each of Poland's cities, the Nazi had forced Jews into ghetto and commanded the city elders to form a council to act as representative of the community. The councils were required to carry out orders, collect taxes, and provide labor forces from the ghetto for German industry.

Adam Czerniakow was chairman of the Warsaw ghetto's Jewish council, the Judenrat, and he wanted Samuel as a member.

"You already have your council." Aaron frowned. "Why do you need my brother?"

Czerniakow shook his head.

"Seven members are gone, escaped from Poland," he said. "And we must have twenty-four."

"Why?" Miriam spoke up. "Why twenty-four?"

"Because the Germans say twenty-four. We must have those twenty-four members." Czerniakow scanned the faces around him and recognized the resistance there.

"Listen to me," he pleaded. "Do you think I volunteered? What kind of council would the Nazis appoint if Jews refuse to serve? Poles? Germans? Who would speak for us then?"

He turned and spoke directly to Samuel.

"You are a lawyer, an educated man. Can a bricklayer negotiate with the Germans as well as you? Represent our interests as well as you? Men like you, don't they have a responsibility?"

Samuel's gaze wavered. He glanced at Miriam, and for the first time he could remember, Aaron saw irresolution on his mother's face.

"Well . . ." Miriam said uncertainly. "If what you say is so . . . an obligation . . ."

"*No!*"

All heads swiveled to the upper end of the table, where Joseph sat in his customary place. His face was flushed, his hands knotted into fists.

"No," he repeated. "I forbid it."

The startled expressions on the faces surrounding him deepened the red in his cheeks. He raised an apologetic palm.

"Forgive me, Samuel," he said. "You are a grown man. I have no right. Only listen. Please."

He leaned foward, hands clasped tightly.

"When that man came for Max, I said nothing . . ."

"What man?" Czerniakow interjected. He turned on Samuel. "Who is Max?"

"Max Woloshen." Samuel gestured at Sadie. "My sister's husband. Szerynski came to recruit him for his ghetto police force, his Jewish police force."

"I see." Czerniakow frowned. "But it's not the same. The Judenrat . . ."

"The same! The same!" Joseph interrupted angrily. "Duty! Obligation! Responsibility! Max believed! And he was shot in the street like a dog!"

Joseph paused, fighting for breath. Aaron pushed back his chair but the old man waved him back.

"What happened?" Czerniakow looked from one face to another. "Who shot him?"

"Two German soldiers," Aaron said. "They were teasing a young girl, fifteen, maybe sixteen. Maybe they meant no harm. Who knows? She was pretty."

Aaron sighed, his eyes on Sadie.

"But she was also a courier for the underground paper. She had half a dozen copies of the *Yugn-shtime* under her coat. Max asked them to leave her alone. They laughed at him, ordered her to strip. Of course, they found the papers. They shot her. Then they shot Max."

Czerniakow shook his head silently. He glanced down the length of the table at Sadie. "I'm sorry," he said. "But the Judenrat . . ."

"The Judenrat do as they're told!" Joseph interrupted angrily. "The Germans say give us two thousand Jews for the labor camps, you give them two thousand Jews!"

"Better to give them two thousand workers than have them snatch our people off the street!" Czerniakow retorted.

"And they still snatch people off the street! They still drag them out of their homes in the middle of the night!"

Czerniakow bent forward to speak but Joseph raised his hands, silencing him.

"No. Let me say what I must say." Two spots of color burned on Joseph's pale cheeks. He turned deliberately away from Czerniakow and addressed his son.

"I ask only that you should listen, Samuel. Then I will close my mouth and Mr. Czerniakow can sing you his song. Only, first listen. Will you?"

Samuel nodded. "Of course, Papa."

"Thank you," Joseph acknowledged gravely. "So. You are now on the council. The Germans demand three thousand Jews by ten o'clock Friday morning. A list is made up. And Nathan's name is on the list."

Joseph paused for the space of a heartbeat. He glanced obliquely at Nathan.

"So tell me, Samuel. Do you give them your brother? Or do you erase his name and put another. And whose name do you put instead? Whose father or husband or son will you give to them in exchange for your brother?"

Samuel shook his head but remained silent.

"And when a man comes to you," Joseph continued, "and says, take my name off the list and I will give you food for your children. Will you do it? Will you say to yourself, just this once because my children are hungry. And when they are hungry again, what then? How soon will it be easy to sell a Jew for a loaf of bread?"

"Unfair!" Czerniakow cried out angrily. "Pardon me, Mr. Lipsky, but what you say is unfair. Unfair to me. Unfair to the Judenrat."

He bent forward, white-faced.

"You talk to me of lists? Listen to me, Mr. Lipsky. We crawl to the Germans, begging for more food, more fuel, more medical supplies, and are refused. Every day, refugees pour into the ghetto from the countryside. We beg for more space and are refused. The sanitation system is breaking down. We beg for repair materials and are refused. Soon we will be begging for water to drink. And you talk to me of lists?"

Joseph had endured the outburst with downcast eyes. He sighed heavily.

"If I have offended you, Mr. Czerniakow, I apologize. You are a good man and I meant no disrespect to you." He raised his eyes to meet Czerniakow's angry gaze. "But I know what I know and I will say what I must say."

The steely determination in his voice was totally uncharacteristic of him. Aaron, surprised, glanced at his mother. Her face wore a small, secret smile.

"It is your decision, Samuel." Joseph spoke as though he and Samuel were the only people in the room.

"But this I know, Samuel. Jews are not saints. We have our share of opportunists and thieves. And I tell you this, my son. The time will come when the Judenrat and the ghetto police will be feared as much as the Germans are."

Chapter 27

You were right, Papa, Aaron spoke silently to the still, white face on the pillow. If Samuel had listened . . .

"Aaron."

Aaron raised his head. His mother stood in the doorway. He was suddenly, shockingly, aware of her changed appearance.

The plump, bustling mother he had known had vanished. Her hair, once a brisk salt-and-pepper, was a lifeless gray. The frayed sweater she wore was tied around her waist with a length of green cord. The rolled sleeves exposed bony, chapped hands, knuckles swollen with arthritis. On her feet was a pair of felt boots that had belonged to his father.

"There's tea, Aaron." Miriam shuffled to where he sat. "I'll stay with him. Go. Have your tea."

The other family members were seated around the kitchen table, on which a single candle burned. Months had passed since they had all been together. As Aaron sipped his tea he studied the shadowy faces and his heart filled with sorrow for his mother.

She had married, given birth to children, fought with them and for them, and seen them grow to maturity. Now, life was destroying her family, one by one, before her eyes.

The face of Nathan, her firstborn, was an unhealthy yellow above the black of his beard. He coughed continuously, a harsh, dry sound that grated on the ears. Beside him, his wife Ruth looked gaunt and ill. Both worked from dawn till dark, building barrack roof sections for the German army.

David. Aaron closed his eyes and tried to recall David's face. David, who had died in the bombing of Warsaw, who had never known the ghetto. It startled Aaron that, for the moment, he could not remember what David looked like.

Esther. Querulous, plain-faced Esther. Together with her husband and son, she had left the house one morning and never returned. The Lipskys might never have known what became of them if Daniel Zylenberg had not recognized Esther and Benjamin and come to report what he had seen.

"There was a Purim service at the soup kitchen on Zamenhof Street," Daniel said, his eyes locked on Aaron. "They were there, your sister and the rabbi. I was on guard outside. Watching for the Germans, you know?"

Aaron nodded.

"They came. Five of them. I ran in to warn them, the people inside, and so everybody left then. And the German soldiers, they stopped the rabbi and pushed him back and forth between them, you know. They threw away his hat. They pulled his beard. And one of them, he took his bayonet and started chopping off the rabbi's beard. And he missed . . . sometimes he missed. And the Rabbi's face was all bloody."

Daniel drew a shuddering sigh.

"Your sister," he resumed. "They made her watch. And her son, your nephew . . ."

"Moishe."

"And Moishe went crazy. He attacked the soldier who was hurting his father. The soldier . . ." Daniel blinked rapidly. "The soldier beat Moishe with his rifle butt. On the head. On Moishe's head."

Daniel stopped. Aaron waited until the boy had regained control of his emotions.

"Then?"

"Then your sister, she tried to stop them and they beat her too. Then they took them away. The rabbi, he carried Moishe. Maybe Moishe was dead. I don't know."

In the days that followed, both Aaron and Samuel made careful inquiries, trying to learn where Esther and her family were being held. Their efforts were fruitless. Esther, her husband, and her twelve-year-old son had vanished.

"Aaron?" Sadie touched his elbow. "More tea?"

Aaron nodded. He studied his sister as she filled his glass from the heavy pewter samovar.

Since her husband's death, Sadie had changed from the prettiest and liveliest of the Lipsky sisters to a pale ghost of herself.

Her marriage to Max had been truly happy. They were two sides to the same coin. With Max gone, she was less than whole and even the loss of her eldest son to a labor camp had not penetrated the vagueness into which she had escaped. Her two younger children were left to the care of Miriam. Sadie seemed oblivious to their existence.

The glass filled, Sadie turned the samovar spigot, shutting off the flow of amber liquid. Her hands circled the warm glass. She sat motionless, her face bemused. Ida, seated next to her, gently removed the glass from Sadie's unresisting grasp and passed it to Aaron.

Ida. Samuel's wife. Once so pampered, so envied. Aaron closed his eyes, recalling her past elegance. Now she labored in a German boot factory, not knowing if Samuel was alive or dead.

Against his father's wishes, in spite of his mother's angry warnings, Samuel had joined the Judenrat council.

Chapter 28

Construction of a wall surrounding the ghetto began in the summer of 1940. By November, over half a million people were locked into the dirty, crowded quarter, under threat of death should they attempt to leave.

In the beginning, the Judenrat fought hard for better conditions. Public kitchens were set up for the hungry. Hospitals and homes for the aged and the orphans of the ghetto were maintained with money the Judenrat diverted, at great risk, from German authorities. Shelter and aid was provided for the refugees who continued to pour into the ghetto, driven from outlying districts.

Samuel served on one committee after another, begging concessions from the Germans, arguing for greater effort from the splintering Judenrat members.

Aaron saw him rarely. In the brief glimpses he had of Samuel during that period he had recognized the signs of strain on his brother. But it wasn't until one late night in December, when he returned home to find Samuel alone in the darkened kitchen, that Aaron realized how close to breaking Samuel was.

"Aaron?" There was a note of apology in Samuel's voice. "I'm sorry. I have to talk to you. I know it's late. You're tired . . ."

"Hey. Samuel. Come on. This is me." Aaron pushed back his desperate need for sleep and seated himself across the table from Samuel. "So. Tell me."

Samuel's mouth relaxed in a half smile.

"Good old Aaron," he said. "Papa's features. Mama's chutzpah."

It was an old family game. Aaron picked up his cue.

"Good old Samuel. Zeyde Skolnick, two hundred pounds ago."

The reference to their grandfather was suddenly painful to both men. For a moment they were silent, remembering the portly butcher who had been Miriam's father. Then Aaron, feeling sleep threatening to engulf him, roused himself.

"What is it, Samuel. What's wrong?"

"What's wrong? What's wrong is the Judenrat has become the Judenverrat." Samuel's mouth twisted. "Did you know that's what we're called in the ghetto? Betrayers. Betrayers of the Jews."

Aaron nodded. "I've heard it."

"Has Papa? Mama?"

"Mama, of course. Papa? He hears nothing. His hearing is gone. Didn't you know?"

"No," Samuel said, his voice heavy with anguish. "I didn't know. I've been so . . . oh God, Aaron. He was right. Papa was right. But I believed. I truly believed in what we were doing. I really thought we . . ."

Samuel's eyes closed.

"We set up a labor registry. And now the Judenrat takes bribes from anybody who can pay for a substitute. So it's the people who have nothing who are sent to the labor camps. And if they resist, the Judenrat, the Judenrat, kidnap them off the streets to fill the quota."

Samuel's eyes opened. Their expression was bitter.

"The Judenrat staff, my God, Aaron. Uncles, aunts, sons, brothers, cousins. Every member has ten relatives he wants to protect. So he puts them on the staff, where they are exempt from deportation. Maybe you can't blame them. Do you blame them, Aaron?"

Aaron's weary mind could offer no reply. Samuel seemed to expect none.

"The stealing," he continued. "Food. Money from taxes. The jewelry and gold people give for bribes to the Germans. It's all in the hands of the Judenrat. And it disappears, a little bit here, a little bit there. The members steal to buy themselves a little extra comfort. Not all of them steal. But many do."

"You?"

"Not me." Samuel shook his head. "Not yet."

"Not yet?" Aaron rubbed his burning eyes. "So what do you want from me, Samuel? Permission to steal too? You want my blessing?"

There was no flicker of anger in Samuel's gaze. A year ago, Aaron thought, he'd have blistered my ears for words like those.

"Moses Fradkin approached me today. He said he knows you."

Aaron grimaced. "I treated one of his employees. Did you know he uses children to do his smuggling? They sneak out of the ghetto at night and barter. If they can. Steal, when they can. Children! Some never make it back. This is your Moses Fradkin. What did he want with you?"

"He offered me anything I want. Flour. Chickens. Winter clothing. Even coal."

"In exchange for what?"

"For Yudelovitz's flat. It's bigger. And it has a cellar with a rear entrance."

"Is it available?"

"It is if I put Yudelovitz and his family on the next labor contingent."

Aaron felt a chill.

"I see," he said carefully. "What did you tell him?"

Samuel's gaze shifted and focused on the darkened window behind Aaron.

"If I say no, Fradkin will go to one of the other council members. Yudelovitz will still be sent away. Fradkin will still get the flat."

Samuel's face was bleak.

"I thought of Mama," he said, "trying to make meals of potatoes and cabbage, trying to stay clean without soap, trying to stay warm without fuel. And I thought of Ida," Samuel's voice thickened. "My beautiful Ida, growing thinner and paler every day."

Samuel's eyes returned to Aaron. There was anger in them.

"And what's so special about Yudelovitz anyway? Why should he be spared? If others have to go, why not him? Why should I care about Yudelovitz? I don't even know the man."

Aaron sat mute, his jaw clamped, his head pounding. He was suddenly aware of his utter exhaustion. He forced his attention back to Samuel.

"I said no to Fradkin," Samuel said. "But next time, Aaron, next time I know I'll say yes."

"So." Aaron sighed heavily. "You've made up your mind. What do you want from me, Samuel?"

"I don't know. I thought maybe just talking . . ."

"Fradkin's proposal can't be the first you've had. There must have been others."

"At first, yes. Then . . ." Samuel spread his empty hands. "I suppose the word got around. Who was approachable and who was not."

"And now you plan to be approachable," Aaron stated flatly.

Samuel's eyelids flickered. When he spoke there was anguish mixed with the anger in his voice.

"Who do I owe, Aaron? My family? The people I love? Do I let them go hungry, when with one word . . . Or do I owe the Yudelovitzes? Do I owe them? People I don't even know?"

"Samuel," Aaron shook his head. "King Solomon I'm not. What can I tell you? Other than to consider alternatives."

"Alternatives? What alternatives do I have? On the one hand, my children starve. On the other, Papa's prediction comes true. I sell Jews for bread."

"On the third hand." Aaron pressed his thumbs to his throbbing temples, "you could resign from the committee entirely."

The following day, Samuel withdrew from the Judenrat.

The day after, he was arrested by the Gestapo. Not even Adam Czerniakow was able to learn where he was taken.

Aaron raised his glass to his lips. The tea was cold. He realized he had dozed and wondered how long. The others were somnolent. Only Leah and Rachel were fully awake, talking together in hushed tones.

Although schools had been forbidden by the German authorities, both Leah and Rachel taught in classes set up in the ghetto.

The komplets, consisting of ten or twelve children each, were conducted in shops, in cellars, in kitchens; wherever they could be operated in secrecy. Leah had younger children in her cellar komplety. Rachel instructed teenagers at a public soup kitchen.

Leah sensed Aaron's gaze. She raised her head to meet his eyes and her pinched face softened. Then her glance flicked past him. She pushed her chair back and rose to her feet, her hand reaching out.

Miriam had emerged from the room in which her husband lay. She held herself rigidly, her arms clasped across her breast.

"He's gone," she said dully. "Papa is dead."

Chapter 29

Aaron pulled back the curtains to admit the pale dawn light and opened his journal. It was the third one he had filled and he would deliver it, as he had done the others, to his sister Rachel.

Rachel, in turn, would place it in the hands of Emanuel Ringelblum at the next secret meeting of the Oneg Shabbat.

"It's people like you we need." Rachel had come to Aaron shortly after the death of their father. "You're everywhere in the ghetto. People talk to you. You see things. You must keep a record."

"A record? For what? For whom?"

"For the Oneg Shabbat," Rachel explained. "It's a group Emanuel has organized to record the ghetto under occupation. We're setting up secret archives. We want diaries, journals, photographs, documents, anything like that. Someday the world has to know what is happening here."

"You're a member of this Oneg Shabbat?"

"From the beginning."

"It's dangerous, what you're doing. Does Mama know?"

Rachel shook her head. "The fewer people knowing who we are, the better. Will you help, Aaron?"

"What do you want me to do?"

"Keep a ledger. Names. Dates. And Aaron, keep the ledger hidden away, even from Leah."

Little Sarah moaned in her sleep. Aaron rose quickly, closing the journal, and went to check on her.

She was curled in a fetal position, her legs drawn up, her hands pressed against the cramping in her abdomen. Although the air was heavy with summer heat, her skin was clammy and cold. Aaron gathered the sheet she had kicked off in the night and covered her gently.

On the next cot, Noah lay sprawled, his arms flung wide in an attitude of flight. He was painfully thin, his knees and elbows knobby and scaly-skinned. His head, shaved against lice, glistened with perspiration. Aaron bent and kissed the boy's pale cheek. Noah stirred, murmured unintelligibly, and slept again.

Leah lay on her stomach in the double bed, her face buried in the pillow, her arms straight by her sides.

Aaron looked at the curled fingers of her roughened hands, at the tangle of her lusterless hair, at the telltale red stain on her faded nightgown. She smelled faintly sour and Aaron felt a surge of helpless rage.

She had always been a fastidious woman, prim in her femininity. Now, without water to bathe, with no sanitary necessities, with no privacy at all, he knew how her dignity suffered. He turned away, knowing if she should waken she would hate her defenselessness.

He returned to the window. The sun had not fully risen. It was too early to go to Walynska Street, where Rachel now lived.

He opened the journal to the first page and read what he had written there.

January 17, 1942.
It is exactly a year ago today that Papa died. Today, I amputated the gangrenous toes of an eleven-year-

old boy. He is one of the refugee children who beg in the streets. Will he survive? I don't know. They cling so hard to life, these pitiful children. Every morning we find a few, frozen to death. Whole families live in the streets, refugees with no place to go. Many die of sickness and starvation. In summer, the stench is unbearable. In winter, they freeze stiff. It horrifies me that I can think this thought: at least in winter they don't stink.

Aaron turned the pages quickly. A name caught his eye and he stopped to read.

March 23, 1942.
I talked with a man named Isadore Schanzer today. He told me the rumors we've been hearing are true. His cousin, whom he called me to treat, is from Lublin. He says he escaped from a camp at Belzec where Jews are being gassed by the thousands. We heard the same stories earlier this year about a place called Chelmno. Are the stories true?

Isadore Schanzer, Aaron thought. A smuggler, and clever. Why didn't I think of him? Perhaps he can get medicines for Sarah. What can I trade?

Aaron's fingers had been idly leafing the ledger pages. Daniel Zylenberg's name leaped up at him.

May 23, 1942.
Last night Daniel Zylenberg's family disappeared in one of the Nazi's midnight raids. Daniel was with me on a call. He will live with us now, taking over Rachel's old room. There are rumors that we will be deported from the ghetto. Adam Czerniakow told me he has been ordered to provide the German Transerstelle with population statistics. He worries that the order

may be the first step to deportation. If so, deportation to where?

Aaron's heart lurched. Was it possible there could be a connection between the Belzec and Chelmno rumors and the deportations? His hands shook as he scrabbled through the pages, searching for entries of the past two weeks.

July 22, 1942.
The ghetto was surrounded by police this morning. The deportation rumors are true. Freight cars were brought to the railroad siding and the Judenrat were instructed to deliver six thousand Jews for resettlement today. Adam Czerniakow is trying to get exemptions for some of the children. Poor Adam. His wife has been taken hostage. She will be shot if anything goes wrong with the resettlement process.

July 24, 1942.
Adam Czerniakow committed suicide last night. Six thousand Jews were deported yesterday, another six thousand today. The SS are patrolling the ghetto. The shops have closed and extra guards have been called in to stop the smuggling. We were hungry before. Now we will starve.

July 29, 1942.
Ida and her two children and Sadie and her two boys have gone. The Germans asked for voluntary resettlement. They give free bread and marmalade to those volunteering. Mama, Rachel, and I tried to persuade them not to go. Nathan and Ruth stayed. Leah looks at me with hungry eyes. Would she have gone if Sarah wasn't sick?

July 30, 1942.
Thousands more have gone. We are told when the ghetto is less crowded the resettlement will end. We

have been told families can work together in factories
in the new place. We are told the resettlement is for
our own good. We are told anyone with a work permit can stay in the ghetto. One rumor seems to cancel
out the other. Ten thousand people left on the freight
cars today. No one can tell us where the resettlement
camps are located. Why?

Aaron stared out the window, his thoughts spinning. The
sun had risen in a cloudless sky, promising another hot day.
    The stories of gassings at Chelmno, at Belzec . . .
    What you are thinking is monstrous, Aaron told himself.
Ten thousand people? Every day? Impossible. Nevertheless . . .
    He picked up the journal and thrust it under his shirt.
First to Rachel. Then to Isadore Schanzer's. And this time I'll
listen to the cousin from Lublin. This time I have questions
to ask.
    Breathing shallowly, Aaron hurried along streets already
fetid in the heat. He turned into Wolynska Street and stopped
dead in his tracks.
    The street was in chaos. People, milling and wailing, were
being pushed and clubbed onto waiting trucks. The Jewish
police were everywhere. German Sipo troops were stationed
with guns at every side street.
    Aaron slowed his pace to avoid being conspicuous. He
had reached the entrance to Rachel's building when he was
stopped by a Lithuanian soldier of the auxiliary police force.
    "That way." The Lithuanian prodded Aaron with his
club. "On the truck. Move."
    "I'm a doctor," Aaron protested. "I have papers. Work
papers."
    His face impassive, the Lithuanian raised his club and
brought it down on Aaron's head.
    The sky went black. Aaron was dimly aware of being
lifted and thrown onto the flat bed of a truck, of being

yanked to his feet, of being held erect by other bodies pressing against him.

The truck began to move.

His consciousness flickered. One moment he was clearly
aware he had suffered a concussion, the next he lost all sense
of time and place and rode the waves of pain in his skull.

The truck came to a halt.

Aaron's vision cleared briefly and he recognized the Umschlagplatz, the two adjoining squares where the Jewish hospital had been located.

The area swarmed with shouting, screaming, sweating
humanity. The din stabbed viciously into Aaron's brain. He
closed his eyes and allowed himself to be herded from the
truck. Stumbling blindly, he crossed the square.

At the entrance to the second square, SS officers and Jewish police pushed and prodded the amorphous throng into
open freight cars drawn up on an adjacent railroad siding.
Nauseous and barely conscious, Aaron was carried with
them.

He surfaced momentarily, vibrating to the pounding of
wheels under his feet, then slipped back into oblivion.

Suddenly he found himself in brilliant sunlight, every
nerve screaming, eyes leaping to take in his surroundings.

Behind him, the gaping freight car doors. Ahead, an endless line of plodding people. Beside him, a group of men lifting bales and boxes and piling them fifty feet away. Without
reasoning why, Aaron snatched up a suitcase and ran with
the group.

Back and forth. Aaron willed himself to run mindlessly.
The lines of men and women vanished. Another train arrived.
Half the human cargo were corpses. Doing as the men
around him were doing, Aaron unloaded bodies from the
cars.

Late in the afternoon, a wave of dizziness swept over him.
He braced against the freight car wall to stop from pitching
to the platform below.

"Move, you fool." The hoarse whisper came from behind. "Move, or they'll shoot you."

Aaron turned. He stared down at the bald head of a man
tugging at the arms of a hugely obese woman.

"Take her legs," the bald man hissed.

Aaron bent and grasped the thick ankles.

"What is this place?" Aaron asked as they dragged the
body to the doorway.

"Treblinka." The man's lips barely moved. "Don't talk.
Just keep moving."

Chapter 30

Aaron stumbled through the next two days, directed and protected by the bald man, Chaim. By the third day, the mists and double vision had disappeared.

Even before he could see them clearly, Aaron knew the fate of the passengers arriving on the trains.

"Don't look at them," Chaim had advised, whispering in the stillness of the nightime barrack. "For the sake of your sanity, don't look. Keep your eyes on the ground. Keep your eyes on the dead or you'll be one of them."

On the fourth day, the first train arrived at eight in the morning. Aaron, running with downcast eyes, heard his name called, the shrill cry penetrating the noisome square. He peered up from under his brows.

Running toward him, arms outstretched and face alight, was his brother Nathan. There was a sudden chatter of machine-gun fire. Where Nathan's eye had been a black flower bloomed and gouted bright red blood.

Aaron's limbs froze. A kick from Chaim sent him back into motion, dragging at the rope knotted around a dead woman's waist.

That night, seated on the sandy ground of the hot, airless barrack, Chaim berated Aaron.

"If you want to die, make it easy on yourself. Hang yourself, like that bookkeeper Hershke did last night. I told you, *don't look*. Work. Keep moving. And don't expect me to watch out for you. It's all I can do to care for myself."

"He was my brother." Aaron's throat was tight with pain. "That man was my brother, Nathan."

Chaim sighed. He reached out and placed a sympathetic hand on Aaron's shoulder.

"Yes," he said. The word echoed with grief. "Yes."

For a moment he was silent.

"We were brought here from Miedzyrzecz," he said, his voice soft in the gloom. "My father, my sister, my wife, and our two boys. Two weeks ago? Three? Days mean nothing here. The women were sent one way. My father, my boys, and I were sent to the men's line. I was pulled from the line and told to get dressed."

Chaim's hand dropped from Aaron's shoulder.

"I never saw them again."

They sat in the silent darkness.

"How do you live," Aaron said finally. "How do you live with the pain?"

To his astonishment, Chaim chuckled. It was a bitter sound.

"Are you sure we're alive?" he asked. "Maybe we died and went to hell? Could hell be hotter than it was under that sun today? Could the stink be worse? We're knee-deep in shit and pus and blood. We're hungry and thirsty. If we stop running, the best we can expect is a whip across our backs."

He leaned his head against the barrack wall and grinned sourly into the night.

"Tell me, Aaron," he said. "If you had to invent hell, what would you add?"

Next morning, Chaim was assigned to sorting bundles and Aaron worked alone. That night, returning to the barrack, he looked for Chaim. There was no sign of him.

When morning came and Chaim still was missing, Aaron

knew he was dead. The men sorting bundles were at greatest risk. If caught pilfering food from the packages, they were shot. Aaron could only guess at Chaim's fate.

He stumbled into the red dawn, numbed and not caring if he lived or died that day.

The first train of the day arrived early, enveloped in a stench that made the air unbreathable. Three thousand people had passed the hot, sultry night in airless cattle cars. Less than a third had survived.

Aaron ran back and forth, from ramp to station square, dragging body after body, stacking them like cordwood. The train pulled away and he was teamed with another man, hauling the corpses to the burial pit. He ran, incurious as to his partner's identity.

A second train drew in. Car after car, it disgorged its human cargo.

There was a sudden lull in the cacaphony of arrival. Inured to the normal uproar, Aaron looked up in alarm

Scores of children, wave after silent wave, poured from the cars to the ramp. Aaron gaped in horror. Then a bent and haggard old man, carrying a small boy in his arms, descended and Aaron recognized him.

Janusz Korczak had devoted his life to the children of Warsaw's Jewish orphanage. In the ghetto, he had begged and fought for them, taught and cared for them. And now, Aaron thought bitterly, that good old man will die with them.

At a gesture from Korczak, the white-faced children formed groups of four and fell in behind the old man. The long line snaked across the station square and through the gap in the barbed wire encircling the undressing sheds.

Aaron scarcely felt the whip goading him back to work. An ember of ancient anger took fire deep inside him. It grew and flamed as he ran, his mind in a frenzy. He was oblivious to the putrescent bodies, to his own thirst and hunger.

From that day Aaron determined, somehow, to keep a

journal once more and began, furtively, to search the bodies he carried for scraps of paper and writing tools.

The risks he was taking terrified him. Each time a guard glanced his way his heart threatened to leap from his breast. The day he found a diary with blank pages, his hands were trembling so violently he had difficulty knotting the rope under the arms of the body he had stolen it from.

He straightened, and ran blindly into the butt of an SS officer's whip.

"You." The man's voice was sharp.

Aaron sucked for breath, blinking away the sweat pouring from his forehead.

The SS man jerked a thumb at the blond man standing beside him.

"Use him," he ordered. He turned and strode away, tapping his boot with the butt of his whip.

Aaron released his pent breath. Shivering with reaction, he eyed Elia.

His first thought, this is a Jew?, was followed by a sudden, wrenching sense of loss. The helpless query in the blue eyes gazing into his startled up a memory of his son, of the child's first encounter with the reality of pain.

Shit. Aaron bent savagely over the corpse at his feet. An innocent. A baby. This one won't last the day.

As Elia knelt to help, Aaron experienced a moment of searing outrage.

No!

Aaron's mind rebelled against acceptance of the carnage surrounding him. Whoever this man is, whatever he is, they can't have him!

Not him. And not me.

Chapter 31

$\mathcal{T}$reblinka's fifty acres were divided into two separate and distinct camps.

Camp One contained the unloading ramp and station square where the lame and the very old were winnowed from among the arrivals. They were taken to the Lazarett, a fake hospital near the southern perimeter of the camp, and shot.

Directly facing the square, surrounded by barbed wire, were the undressing sheds from where a path, ten feet wide, led. The path took a right-angled turn in its hundred meter climb uphill to the gas chambers in Camp Two. Barbed wire fences, ten feet high and thickly interwoven with pine boughs, shielded the path from view in Camp One.

It was up this path, named "the tube" by the work-Jews, that the daily morning arrivals, naked, shaven, and screaming with fear and pain, were whipped to their deaths in the gas chambers. By noon, five thousand voices were stilled forever.

To the left of the undressing sheds, separated by barbed wire, were the work-Jew barracks and the appelplatz, the roll-call square. To the right of the undressing barracks was the sorting square and a large sorting shed. Beyond lay the burial pit for corpses from the transports.

At first Elia was only aware of his own work area—the ramp and the burial pit. Each day, he ran the same ground.

In the barrack each night, he ate food Aaron had stolen from the trains, then tumbled into deathlike sleep beside Aaron.

He knew Aaron was carrying him, shielding him, but he was unable to help himself. Methodical by nature, he was fragmented by events in which nothing made sense to him. He could find no order in what was happening around him.

Then, in mid-September, Aaron was transferred to the undressing square and Elia was sent to work in the sorting shed.

The transition was swift. One minute Elia and Aaron were running from the burial pit to the ramp. They were stopped by an SS guard and Galewski, the work-Jews' camp elder. The next minute Aaron was on his way to the undressing barracks and Elia was in the sorting shed, tying bundles.

He was stunned by his surroundings. From floor to ceiling, the shed was piled with clothing, layer upon layer. More streamed in constantly, carried in from the sorting square. It was then the turbulence in Elia's brain ebbed and he was able to think with a degree of clarity.

As he tied the never-ending stream into bundles and wrapped the bundles in sheets, he began to sense a system behind what had previously seemed utter confusion. And, as the stacks mounted higher, he began to comprehend the chilling efficiency of the Nazi killing machine.

"A Pole named Stefan told me Hitler means to kill every Jew in Europe," he said to Aaron that night.

They were seated together in the barrack, eating honey cake Aaron had stolen that morning. A rich transport had arrived, the unsuspecting passengers laden with provisions for resettlement.

"I didn't believe him," Elia continued. "I didn't see how it could be possible. How could something so enormous be done? I don't mean morally, how it could morally be done. I mean the pure mechanics of it."

Aaron's eyes gleamed in the semidarkness. He nodded, chewing vigorously, and pointed to his busy mouth.

"But it can be done, Aaron." Elia lowered his voice. "It's being done. Here. There were three trains today. Figure it out. Each train has, at minimum, twenty cars. Each car carries, at minimum, two hundred persons. Which adds up to at least three thousand per train. Aaron, ten thousand people died here today. Ten thousand!"

"Elia! For the love of God!" The words were thick.

"It takes less than two hours to kill a trainload. Less than two hours from the freight cars to the gas chambers. And the gas chambers, at most twenty-five minutes."

"Elia . . ."

"It's being done, Aaron. And we're doing it. You. Me. Without the work-Jews they couldn't . . ."

Aaron's fist clamped on Elia's wrist. He squeezed with such force, Elia's words were cut off.

"Stop right there," Aaron whispered. "You know as well as I do they could shoot every work-Jew in the camp tonight and replace them from a single transport in the morning."

"Of course I know. So what are you saying? If we don't do it, somebody else will?"

"I'm saying be glad they haven't thought of it. Yet." Aaron's voice was dry. "I'm saying it won't make a particle of difference if we do it, you and I, or some other poor damned Jew."

Aaron was silent for so long Elia thought he had fallen asleep.

"Except for one thing." Aaron picked up as though he had just finished speaking. "And I've thought about this, Elia. Treblinka started operating two months ago. I've been here almost since the beginning."

Aaron began packing the remains of their stolen food. He tied it in a shirt Elia had taken from the sorting shed.

"How many work-Jews die every day?" he continued. "Fifty? A hundred? Every night some of the old faces are gone. Every day new faces are added. Think of the turnover, Elia."

"How many of us are there?"

"I estimate between four and five hundred. That's just down here. Up in Camp Two, I don't know. But the point is, as time goes by there will be fewer and fewer who've been here since the beginning. And at least one of the few must survive to testify."

"Testify, Aaron?" Elia said bitterly. "To whom?"

"Yes! Testify! The day will come, Elia, the day of reckoning. And I mean to be here!"

Elia let his head fall back and closed his eyes wearily. He listened to the familiar night sounds of the barrack, the moans of men yearning to escape in dreamless sleep. Nearby, a man cried out from his nightmare, another wept hopelessly.

"I'll survive." Aaron spoke fiercely. "And not because I have a sense of mission, though there's that too. But you know what I feel, Elia? *Wrath.* My father used that word when we were small. It seemed such a biblical word to me then. But I feel it now. A terrible wrath. I will not permit them to take my life away from me. I will not permit it!"

Chapter 32

On the last day of September Daniel Zylenberg arrived with the first transport. Aaron pulled him, naked, out of the line in the undressing square.

"Find something to put on. Quickly. And make yourself busy," Aaron instructed and ran to find Galewski.

"I know him well," Aaron pleaded. "He's a good boy. A worker. He has character. And he has courage."

"He'll need both," Galewski sighed. He was a patrician man with infinitely sad eyes, a former engineer in Warsaw. "How old is he?"

"Seventeen."

"Seventeen." Galewski shook his head. "Keep him near you. If I can, I'll find something for him."

In the barrack, after they had been locked in for the night, Daniel ate with both hands; cheese in one, sausage in the other. He pushed food into his mouth, apologizing between bites.

"I'm sorry. I'm sorry." His eyes agonized above cheeks as round as chipmunks. "They held us in the Umschlagplatz a day and a night and gave us nothing."

"Eat, boychick," Aaron urged, patting the boy's bony shoulder. "News from home can wait five minutes."

Finally, Daniel sighed. Looking faintly green, he pushed

aside a poppy-seed cake from which he had taken only a bite.

"In my entire life I have never eaten so much," he groaned. "Is it always like this?"

Above his head, Elia and Aaron exchanged glances.

"Later." Aaron smiled at the boy. "Tell me. Leah. The children. My mother."

Daniel's face lit up.

"Like a rock, Mama," he said. "And Rachel too. And Aunt Leah. And Noah, a smuggler like you wouldn't believe."

"A smuggler? Noah?"

"Noah and me. We're a team. Noah, you wouldn't believe how smart he is. One time, a chicken even. A live chicken. Under his shirt. You should have seen. His chest was scratched like you wouldn't believe. And Noah, he said he was going to do worse to the chicken than it did to him. And Mama made chicken soup and chicken stew too, and Noah laughed the whole time he was eating that chicken."

"Noah." Aaron was stricken. "My little Noah. But he's a baby. He's just a baby."

"Noah a baby? He's eleven years old, Uncle Aaron."

"Yes. Eleven years old." Aaron rubbed his face wearily. After a moment, he asked, "And Ruth?"

"She went with Uncle Nathan. Oh, a long time ago. In August. They took the voluntary resettlement. They said they would write, but so far . . ." Daniel shrugged. "Mama thinks they're in Russia, maybe."

Aaron looked away. "Maybe," he said.

Next morning Daniel was taken from the undressing shed. Aaron passed the day vacillating between fear for the boy's safety and an optimistic faith in Galewski's promise.

But in the barrack that night, Daniel refused food. While Aaron and Elia ate, he sat silent and pale, kneading his hands together, his knuckles crackling. Finally, Aaron closed his fist over the boy's fingers.

"Tell us," he said.

"I can't." Daniel shook his head.

"Yes. You can." Aaron's voice was stern. "Where did they send you today?"

"To . . . to the tube," Daniel whispered.

"What?" Aaron's grip on Daniel's hand tightened. "What did you say?"

"They sent me to the tube. To work in the tube."

Tears slid down the boy's ashen face.

"It's terrible, Uncle Aaron. Oh God, it's so terrible. They shave them. Everybody. Men. Women. And children too. All the hair. All. And they make them run. Naked, all of them naked. They beat them with whips and make them run. Five at a time with their arms up, so."

Daniel raised his hands above his head, his arms shaking uncontrollably.

"They make them run and they . . . they shit themselves when . . . when they run and they run . . ." He was sobbing now, the sounds ripping from his throat.

"And we cleaned . . . over and over . . . we cleaned . . ."

Aaron pulled Daniel to him and held him, cradling the shivering boy. Slowly Daniel's sobs abated and he slept.

In the morning, Aaron risked a beating to seek out Galewski.

"I didn't know." Galewski's face set grimly. "I'll talk to your Kapo again."

At noon Daniel returned to the undressing square.

"Thank you, Uncle Aaron," he whispered, bending to pick up a pile of clothing.

"Not uncle," Aaron muttered back. "Just Aaron. You are no longer a child."

Chapter 33

The days grew colder as October progressed. Elia stole warmer clothing for Aaron, Daniel, and himself. The barracks were vermin-ridden and, following Aaron's rules of survival, he replenished their garments every two or three days.

"We can avoid body lice and we can keep ourselves as clean as possible," Aaron insisted. "Don't you see? The SS want to think of us as less than human. They have to see us as animals to do what they do. If we can at least look like men and not filthy dogs at roll call in the morning, they might think twice about killing us that day."

Aaron shrugged, grinning sourly.

"On the other hand, they might think a third time and shoot us anyway."

In mid-month, Daniel was sent with a detail outside the camp to forage for branches to replace those screening the tube. He returned late in the evening.

The barrack was quiet. Most of the inmates had escaped into numb sleep. Elia felt himself drifting when Daniel began to talk. The soft voice haunted the darkness.

"In the ghetto everyone was ugly. But I didn't know. I thought Mama was beautiful. And Rachel. And Chana Smilovich, I thought she was the most beautiful girl I had ever seen."

Puzzled, Elia raised himself on his elbow. He could make out a silhouette in the moonlight from the barred window. Daniel sat motionless, a blanket bulky around his shoulders.

"Then the first time I went through the wall, I couldn't believe," Daniel's voice went on. "Streets without crowds, without a single beggar lying in a doorway. I saw, listen, I saw a woman sweeping her doorstep and she was *singing!* And I saw a girl like Chana, her age. And she had a summer dress on, so pretty, so clean. And she looked at me. She looked at me, straight in my eyes."

Daniel broke off. In the silence, Elia waited.

"I had Aaron's medical bag to trade with at the market," Daniel resumed. "The market! The smell of flowers like you wouldn't believe. People. Talking and haggling and *laughing!* The red tomatoes, the orange carrots, the green beans, colors like you wouldn't believe."

Elia stirred himself. "Daniel . . ." he began.

"I crawled back through the wall and ran home," Daniel continued. "A wall, I thought. Just a wall can make such a difference? How can it be?"

"Daniel . . ." This time it was Aaron who spoke.

"No. Listen." Daniel's voice took on an urgency. "There is a barbed wire fence around the camp. And next to the fence the fields are plowed. A farm! There are farms all around the camp, did you know? The trains, all the people, the stink. And farms? Listen, I saw a boy out there. He was throwing a stick to his dog and laughing. Just a fence? How can it be?"

"Enough!" Aaron's voice was harsh. His black shape bulked between Elia and Daniel.

"Don't do this, Daniel." Aaron's tone had gentled. "Trying to find reasons for how it can be will drive you insane.

Please. Do me this. Empty your head. Work. Eat. Sleep. And for the love of God, let me sleep. All right?"

"All right. I'm sorry."

"Sorry, schmorry. Go to sleep."

A moment later Daniel's furtive whisper snatched Elia back from the brink of oblivion.

"Aaron?"

His only answer was a groan.

"Aaron, listen. I heard two of the men on the detail talking about escaping. Do you think it's possible?"

"Daniel, I swear to you, if you hadn't sold my scalpel I'd cut your tongue out. We'll talk about it. But tomorrow, tomorrow."

Chapter 34

As October waned, more and more trains began to arrive. On occasion, as many as six transports in a day delivered twenty thousand people who would die before the sun set.

Separating and bundling their possessions drove the sorting crew at a feverish pace. Each night the square was cleared. Each day a new mountain arose.

The relentless work and the unremitting atmosphere of fear that were the fabric of the camp's daily routine had deadened Elia's sensitivity to his surroundings. His mind had retreated into a protective dullness.

He ran to avoid being beaten by the Kapo of his command, a brutish former Warsaw thief and pimp. He ran to avoid being shot on the hair-trigger whim of an SS guard. At nightly roll call, he experienced his only emotion, relief that Aaron and Daniel had also survived the day.

Daniel had grown silent and withdrawn, brooding on escape. He clung to Aaron, working as closely as he dared in the undressing square throughout the day, hovering within arm's length at night.

Aaron's reaction alternated between solicitude and sharp exasperation.

"You're like a boil on the ass," he snapped. "A person can't sit down without knowing it's there."

Of the three, only Aaron preserved an edge to his mind. He had given up his journal as too risky. Instead, he stored facts in his head, talking and listening to everyone with whom he came in contact. He speculated on every rumor, even the most fanciful, as much for mental exercise as for truth.

He had become adept at stealing and hiding gold and jewelry. He traded with the Ukrainian guards, who had no access to the valuables, bartering for fresh vegetables the guards could purchase from the neighboring countryside. Enormous quantities of food arrived with each transport and what Aaron could not steal, he bought.

Trains bound for Berlin now left Treblinka crammed with the possessions of the dead.

Countless bales of human hair, destined for use as mattress stuffing, were shipped each week. Freight car after freight car pulled away, laden to overflowing with clothing, boots, rugs, linens, spectacles, tools, umbrellas, and food.

Trunks and cases were transferred from the shop where the gold-Jews registered the valuables. They contained a fortune in cash, watches, dental gold, gold coins, jewelry, and diamonds, some ferreted out of hiding places in food and clothing, some pried from the body cavities of the dead.

And still the storage sheds were glutted. Day after day the transports arrived. As November drew to a close, Daniel began once more to talk of escape.

"We have to try," he pleaded. "I can't bear to see them, Aaron. Naked, how will it be in winter? The children turn blue now. How will it be in January? Today the gas chambers motors broke down and they had to wait in the square. Hours they had to stand, naked in the cold. Why must they be naked? If they have to die, why can't they die warm?"

Aaron closed his eyes. For a moment Elia thought he

would reply in anger, but when he spoke it was as gently as to a child.

"Because naked, people are helpless. Don't you understand? If they're warm and clothed and they have to wait, if the pace stops, they might turn on the guards. They might risk being shot. They might risk the dogs. But naked, don't you see, psychologically they're reduced to nothing."

"Aaron." Daniel's whisper was anguished. "I can't bear it, Aaron."

"I know." Aaron reached out and placed his hand on the boy's shoulder. "I know."

"I'd rather be killed trying to escape than go crazy and die in the Lazarett."

"I know."

Two days later, seven men were caught in an attempt to escape. They were taken to the Lazarett and shot.

At roll call, the camp adjutant made an announcement. For every work-Jew who escaped, or tried to escape, ten others would be shot.

Daniel never spoke of escape again.

Chapter 35

As winter set in, Daniel retreated further into himself. His eyes, hollow and haunted, sank into his skull as though receding from the sights forced upon them. In his awful empathy for the throngs pouring past him into the tube, he shivered continuously.

The gas chambers were working beyond capacity. Men, women, and children were forced to wait, to stand naked in frigid temperatures, until the chambers were cleared. Often the feet of small children froze and stuck to the icy ground. Under the whips of the guards, their frantic mothers tore them loose and ran, weeping frozen tears.

Daniel wept with them.

Late in December, the fires in Camp Two began to burn.

Flames leaped high above the earthen wall and the branch-twined fence that separated the two camps, turning the barrack windows into squares of lurid brilliance.

"They're burning the corpses," rasped Saul Baratz, a man from the sorting sheds with whom Aaron had become friendly. His larynx had been damaged by a guard's rifle butt and he was unable to speak above a hoarse whisper.

"Burning the corpses?" Aaron turned his eyes from the window. "How do you know?"

"Yankel told me. He's the only one who gets to go up to Camp Two."

"Yankel Wiernik? The carpenter? He said they're burning corpses now?"

"That's what he told me. He said they're digging up the old corpses and burning them too."

"The old corpses? My God, there must be hundreds of thousands of them! Why would they . . ."

Aaron suddenly sat upright.

"Listen to me." His voice was taut with suppressed excitement. "They never do anything, the Germans, without a reason. I can understand burning the new corpses. How many bodies can you bury before you run out of space? But why dig up the old ones? Why would they dig up and burn the old corpses?"

Elia leaned foward, caught up by Aaron's mood.

"Maybe they're trying to hide what they've done?"

"Hide why? Hide from whom?" Aaron's eyes were luminous in the half-light. "Do you know what this could mean? The Allies are getting close. Maybe the Russians are advancing. What other reason could there be!"

The fires continued to burn. Day after day, a pall of sulfurous smoke and an acrid, sickish stench hung over both camps.

Each time Elia raised his eyes to the black clouds riding overhead, he experienced a precarious elation. If what Aaron suspected was true . . .

Then, deep inside, a small voice shamed him. The clouds are flesh, it whispered. The flesh of helpless men and women. The flesh of innocent children. Have you forgotten? And deeper still, a treacherous voice responded. *Yes. But they were dead anyway.*

My God. Elia closed his eyes, shutting out the leaden sky, the littered square. What have I become?

A blow, like the kick of a dray horse, shattered the thought. Elia grunted with shock and pain. He picked up a bundle and ran to the sorting shed.

"What have we become?" In the darkness of the barrack, Aaron pondered the question.

"Listen to me, Elia," he said. "Don't waste your energy on such ephemeral philosophies. Just consider yourself as an amoeba."

"Educated bastard." Saul's words slurred over a mouthful of food. "I hate educated bastards. So, what's an amoeba?"

"An amoeba? It's a single-cell animal." Aaron's voice grinned. "No feeling. No memory. All an amoeba has are the requirements for survival. A mouth hole and an asshole."

Elia's spontaneous laugh broke off abruptly.

He had forgotten laughter was a physical act, and the sudden spasm had sent an arrow of pain shooting through his bruised back. He grimaced and closed his eyes, trying to remember when last he had laughed.

From the guard's quarters, separated by barbed wire from the barrack, came loud sounds of celebration. Laughter and shouts played counterpoint to the strains of an accordion.

To Elia, there was something familiar about the tune the accordionist was playing but, until the clamor ebbed and a single tenor voice picked up the melody, he couldn't identify the song. Then it came to him.

"Aaron?" he whispered into the darkness. "Do you know what the date is?"

"I think it's January. Why?"

"It must be January the sixth. The Ukrainian guards are celebrating Christmas Eve. That's a Ukrainian Christmas carol he's singing."

"May he choke on it." Aaron's tone was dry. "So it's Christmas. So?"

"Well. So . . ." Elia felt momentarily foolish. "Tomorrow is my birthday."

"So mazel tov."

There was a creaking and stirring and Elia felt Aaron's presence beside him.

"Listen, my friend. I have a birthday gift for you," Aaron whispered, his breath warm on Elia's arm. "But you must keep it to yourself. Understood?"

Elia nodded.

"A revolt is being planned. Camp One and Camp Two. We are going to blow Treblinka straight to hell."

Elia lay rigid as the words sank in. When their meaning reached his brain he tried to sit up. Aaron pressed him down.

"How do you know this, Aaron?"

"Galewski's the chief organizer. He told me himself."

"When?"

"Soon. But tell no one. Not Saul. Not Daniel. No one."

Next day Elia worked through his birthday with feverish energy. For the first time in months he thought of Anna. To his dismay, he could not recall her face to his mind's eye. He thrust aside the memory of her as too painful. *Later.*

Neither Aaron nor Daniel were in their accustomed places at roll call that night. For seconds, Elia was only puzzled, then his stomach plummeted into the icy waters of fear.

He raised himself on his toes, searching over the heads of the men around him. His gaze slid past the whipping post twice before he realized that the man tied to it, arms upraised and buttocks bare, was Aaron.

Nearby, two Ukrainian guards held the sagging figure of Daniel between them. The boy's eyes were closed, his face the color of chalk.

Elia took an involuntary step forward. He was jerked back by a powerful hand clutching the tail of his jacket. He turned his head and sent one swift, imploring glance behind him, the most he dared.

"Daniel went berserk." Saul Baratz's harsh whisper rasped in Elia's ear. "He attacked Aaron."

Chapter 36

Elia could not credit what he had heard. Daniel attack Aaron?

Impossible. Even taking into account Daniel's mounting depression. Elia had little doubt the boy had considered suicide. The signs had been too much in evidence to ignore. But he knew Daniel would never have placed Aaron's life in jeopardy, no matter how little he valued his own.

One of the Ukrainian guards stepped forward, whip in hand. His red-rimmed eyes were bloodshot. His complexion, in spite of the stinging wind, was doughy and pale.

He raised his whip and sent it snaking across Aaron's back. Elia closed his eyes, his heart draining.

Beatings were commonplace, an almost nightly occurrence. Like the other men standing frozen and silent around him, Elia had schooled himself not to think of what was being done, not to feel, only to endure. This time there was no escape.

The whip cracked a second time. Elia's eyes flew open against his will, against his agonizing need not to see.

The lash had missed Aaron entirely. The guard raised the whip and gaped at it, a look of stupefaction spreading across his broad face. Suddenly he bent double and vomited, spewing yellow bile and undigested food.

Oh God, thank you, God. The words exploded in Elia's head. He's been celebrating. It's Christmas Day and he's had a skinful of vodka.

Then Elia saw Kurt Franz stride up to the guard and snatch the whip. His momentary elation turned to dread.

Franz, the camp adjutant, was mortally feared and hated, not only by the work-Jews, whom he terrorized, but by the most brutal of the SS guards.

With a gesture of the whip, he ordered Aaron released and Daniel tied in his place.

Every man watching counted the strokes with a dreadful helplessness. At the count of ten, Daniel had ceased to cry out. He hung by his arms, unconscious, his white skin crisscrossed with streaks of red. At the count of twenty, his back and arms had been flayed to a bloody mass. At thirty, he was obviously dead.

And still Franz continued, his legs spread and braced against the weight of the heavy whip. His face was scarlet and pouring sweat. A grimace of effort split his features in a hideous grin.

At forty, his arm began to faulter. The strokes grew slower and weaker. When he reached the count of fifty, his arm fell to his side.

He stood wavering for a moment, chest heaving, eyes blinking rapidly. Then he threw the whip in the Ukrainian guard's face and stalked away on unsteady legs.

Chapter 37

Daniel didn't attack me."

Aaron's voice was dull, his black eyes dusty, as though a light had been extinguished behind them.

Two days had passed since Daniel died, two days in which Aaron had neither spoken nor eaten. Saul and Elia had hovered over him like fearful hens, fussing as much as they dared.

"They were on the transport that morning." Aaron's gaze rested, unseeing, on the bread Elia had placed in his hands. "Leah and Mama. I didn't see them. Maybe Daniel saw them before I did, I don't know. There was a fuss, a woman refusing to undress and a guard was beating her and I looked up and it was Mama. And Leah. Leah was hitting the guard with her shoe and screaming, screaming."

The bread rolled unheeded from Aaron's fingers.

"I started to run to them and Daniel jumped me. He jumped on my back and we both went down. I tried to get him off and it was as if he'd grown ten extra arms. And then a guard clubbed him and they dragged us apart. I looked for Mama and Leah. But they were gone. They were gone."

Aaron was silent. Elia waited, but nothing more was forthcoming. He picked up the bread and replaced it in Aaron's hands.

"Eat," he said. "You must eat."

Aaron's fingers tore at the bread. He seemed oblivious to what he was doing, his hands working of their own accord. When nothing remained but a heap of crumbs, his fingers continued to knead together.

"He should have let me go." Aaron's voice was a dead monotone. "If he had done nothing. That's all he had to do. Nothing. He had no right."

Elia's eyes met Saul's. An unspoken agreement passed between them. They would carry Aaron as long as he needed them, as long as they were able.

As the days passed, Aaron grew more and more silent. He was consumed by his sense of responsibility for Daniel's death and nothing Elia or Saul could say relieved him.

He became careless of his appearance. He changed his clothing only when Elia insisted. Where once he had shaved once a day, he was clean-shaven now only when Saul forced him to sit and be shaved.

The greater risk fell on Saul. Working with Aaron, he had to watch over him and still work at a speed that would preserve his own skin. For Elia, in the sorting shed, the days were filled with dread that did not ease until the barrack doors were locked at night and he knew the other two were safe.

Then, late in January, conditions in the camp changed and Aaron became a minor problem.

Since mid-January, there had been fewer and fewer transports. As January turned to February, the trains ceased.

For the first time, the work-Jews were forced to survive on camp rations alone, a slice of stale black bread and a plate of watery soup each day. And, for the first time, Elia, Aaron, and Saul were lice-ridden. No new clothes were coming. The clothes on their backs were all they had and they worked, slept, and lived in them. The huge storage sheds were empty. Everything had been shipped away.

Each passing day increased the aura of fear in the camp. Without the transports, what use were they, the work-Jews? Without victims to herd, without possessions to be sorted, packed, and shipped, what justification was there to keep them alive? Even the SS guards, outnumbered by their starving prisoners, were on edge, ready to shoot on any provocation.

As the days turned into weeks, the men became increasingly emaciated and apathetic. Many died from lack of food. More died when typhus struck the camp.

Elia, Aaron, and Saul endured, each differently.

For Elia, hunger was less painful than the loss of communication with Aaron. He talked at length to Aaron each night, as much to preserve his own spirit as to reawaken Aaron's.

Aaron seemed neither to know nor care. He ate his rations without comment or complaint, listened to Elia without apparent comprehension. His silence was broken only in sleep. Haunted by nightmares, he cried out and wept in desolation until either Elia or Saul wakened him.

Saul simply endured. Less cerebral, more stoical, he banked his fire to an ember and endured.

March was drawing to a close when the transports began arriving once more.

The first train was the Balkans, carrying twenty thousand Jews who had equipped themselves for resettlement with a freight car of provisions.

When all were dead, the starving workers fell on the mountain of food left behind. Not even the whips could stop the desperate men.

Other transports followed. By mid-April, trains were arriving regularly once more.

And in April, Elia was sent to work in Camp Two.

Chapter 38

I was taken up to Camp Two," Elia repeated, "without a chance to say goodbye to Aaron or Saul. They came, the SS, to the sorting shed and pointed. You, you, and you. Come. And we went right away. We went . . ."

Elia's voice drifted into silence.

The flea market was quiet. There were a few noontime browsers moving from one vendor to the next, chatting to them in low voices.

Old Lonesome hesitated at our table but I only smiled at him. He moved on. I waited for Elia to continue.

"Elia?" Jenny, finally impatient, broke in on Elia's thoughts. "Can I ask you something?"

Elia's head lifted. He looked at her with clouded eyes. They cleared and he smiled at her.

"Of course."

"Why didn't they rebel? Why didn't they fight back?"

"The work-Jews?"

"No, no." Jenny shook her head. "All the people from the trains. There were more of them than there were guards. Why didn't they fight?"

Elia's smile softened.

"You would have?" he asked gently.

"I think so," Jenny said, then more positively, "Yes, I would have."

Elia nodded several times.

"Yes," he conceded. "Yes, I think you probably would have. One girl did. She was about your age. A pretty girl."

"What happened?"

"She jumped over the barbed wire fence, naked, of course, and ran toward us. One of the guards tried to stop her but she got his rifle from him. How, God only knows. She wounded one of the guards before they all went after her. She shot another guard in the arm before they got her."

Elia paused, his eyes searching Jenny's rapt face.

"They kicked her to death," he said.

Jenny's eyes widened in shock. She blinked several times before she spoke, her tone less certain.

"That was one person," she said. "But if they'd all acted together? If they'd all fought back?"

Elia's expression saddened. He sighed heavily.

"Long after, after it all became known," he said, "many wondered the same thing. To some, the people who died in the gas chambers were like sheep, allowing themselves to be led to slaughter. Have you heard that said?"

"Yes," Jenny acknowledged. "But still . . ."

"Why didn't they fight back?" Elia finished for her. He studied her thoughtfully, then reached out and took her hand.

"Suppose you were in one of those cattle cars on your way to Treblinka? Can you pretend? Can you close your eyes and imagine yourself there?"

Jenny smiled and I could see she was relieved at not having offended Elia.

"I don't even have to close my eyes," she said.

"Good." Elia patted her hand. "So now you're locked in with two hundred strangers. You know what's ahead and you try to tell them. You shout over the noise of children crying, of old people moaning. *No resettlement! Gas cham-*

bers and death! Even if you could get them to listen, they wouldn't believe."

"Why? Why wouldn't they believe me?"

"Because what you're telling them is incomprehensible. It has never happened before in the history of the world. Pogroms, internment camps, those they can believe. But to kill a trainload of people for no reason? Gassing innocent men, women, and children? Who can believe such a crazy story?"

Elia paused. He drew a deep breath and added, "Now, we can believe it. Because it has happened. But then?" He shook his head.

"All right," Jenny conceded. "That's in the cattle cars. But when they reach Treblinka?"

"When they reach Treblinka? The men with whips move in. Form lines. Move! Strip. Quickly! Delousing, the hair chopped off. So now they're bald and naked. To the showers. Schnell! Schnell! Up the tube and into the chamber. The door slams shut and locks. The gas blows in. *Then* they believe. An hour and a half too late."

"An hour and a half?" Jenny echoed, puzzled.

"Or two hours. From the opening of the cattle car doors to the closing of the gas chamber doors, maybe two hours."

Elia paused. He squeezed Jenny's hand and released it.

"So. Tell me. At which point in those two hours can three thousand strangers be organized to rebel? Old men and old women, frantic mothers and fathers, children and babies? At which moment in that noise and chaos would it be possible to convince them they outnumber the men with the whips and clubs and guns? That they can fight back?"

Jenny had paled. Her stricken gaze was locked in Elia's. For a moment they stared wordlessly at one another. Then Elia's stern face relented.

"One group fought back," he said quietly. "A transport arrived late, after we had been locked in for the night. The guards tried to handle it themselves. We heard the screams and gunfire all night. In the morning, we came out to the square littered with the dead. The people on that transport had rebelled. They were courageous people. They died fighting back. But they died all the same."

In the silence that followed, a phrase from my reading flicked through my mind and I quoted it aloud.

"The only escape was up the chimneys."

Elia tilted his head inquiringly.

"I read it somewhere," I explained. "The only escape was up the chimneys."

"Auschwitz." Elia nodded. "That was said of Auschwitz. There were no chimneys at Treblinka."

"No chimneys? But I thought . . ."

"No chimneys," Elia repeated. "No ovens. No crematoria. They did exist at places like Auschwitz. The selections. The medical experimentation." Elia's brows rose. "Is that what you were thinking?"

"Yes. I suppose I was."

Elia nodded slowly.

"Yes. That's what most people think of today. But camps like Auschwitz were quite different from Treblinka. Auschwitz was a concentration camp. There were factories at Auschwitz, producing Buna rubber. The camp inmates, those who survived the selections, worked in the factories. They were the living skeletons found when liberation came."

"Treblinka was, purely and simply, an extermination camp. Compared to the concentration camps, Treblinka was a small place. There were no factories. Nothing was produced there. The only prisoners at Treblinka were the work-Jews necessary to process the victims and their possessions."

"*Process!*" Jenny leaped on the word. "How can you say that, Elia? You make it sound like a production line, a meat factory. That's gross!"

"Yes." Elia nodded. "It is gross. But that's what it was. A production line. And what's more gross is that even we, the work-Jews, eventually thought of it that way."

Chapter 39

Camp Two began at the gas chambers.

Each of the chambers was a room, fifteen feet square and seven feet high, each equipped with a gas-pipe inlet.

The chamber floors were of baked tile, slanted slightly toward the Camp One platform doors through which the victims, five hundred to a chamber, were prodded and beaten. When the chamber was full, the hermetically sealed iron doors closed and locked. Motors pumped gas to the inflow pipe and into the chamber.

Each chamber had a door opening on Camp Two, through which the corpses were dragged. Elia was put to work at the door of one of the chambers.

When the doors were opened, the dead stood upright, pressed together, skins yellow with gas, bodies soiled with urine, excrement, and menstrual blood. Stiffened in death, it was necessary for them to be pried apart.

Babies were torn from the rigid embrace of their dead mothers. Families died together, holding hands, and Elia sweated breaking that final clasp in order to clear the chambers for the new load. He threw the bodies to the work squads, who handled them next, the crews with hammers who smashed dental gold from the jaws of the dead.

In the early days of Treblinka, the corpses had been carried immediately to the burial pits and thrown into vast communal graves. In late December, orders had come from Berlin. Bodies were to be burned, not buried. All evidence of the mass killings was to be erased.

The old graves were opened, the rotting corpses exhumed. Fires were lit, the cremating began. And it was found that the piled dead, even soaked in benzene, burned too slowly. By the time Elia arrived at Camp Two, the roasts had been devised and were in operation.

The roasts were enormous racks, constructed of used railroad rails, mounted on concrete foundations. Bodies were stacked by the hundreds, piled like cordwood onto the racks, and set afire.

The sick smell of their burning, combined with the stench from the newly opened burial trenches, made the air unbreathable. The sounds of the burning bodies, a constant sizzling and crackling, was a hideous assault on the ears.

With spring came the blue-bottle flies, their bodies iridescent as they crawled over the dead and living alike. Between the pits and the fires, the earth was slippery with maggots, squirming from their cadaver nests.

If, as Aaron had warned, Elia had five minutes in which to learn to stay alive in Camp One, he had only seconds to acquire the technique of survival in Camp Two. There was no roll call, no nightly punishment. But the abuse was more frequent, more vicious.

The majority of guards in Camp Two, many of whom never drew a sober breath, were illiterate peasants. Subjected to the same loathsome conditions as the Jews they despised, they brutalized their prisoners. The least infringement of any rule brought instant death. Working at less than a run resulted in rifle-butt beatings. Almost every worker bore the marks of repeated poundings: blackened eyes, missing teeth, bloodied heads. And since there was no opportunity to steal food to supplement the camp rations, most were in a state of near starvation.

May brought fewer transports and Elia was transferred to the burial pit detail, where long-dead bodies were being excavated.

A giant crane dropped a claw into the mass of rotted flesh and raised blue-black corpses so tightly packed it was impossible to think of them as once having been individual, living human beings. The work-Jews carried the putrescent, liquifying bodies to the fires.

Once again, Elia ran in tandem with another man, carrying between them a stretcher piled with the dead from the pit to the fire. Running. Always running.

For Elia, the days had no reality. His body performed what he demanded of it with dogged repetitiveness. But his mind was afire.

A tentative date of June 15 had been set for the uprising, planned since November in Camp One. Elia had become a member of the secret Camp Two committee. Each night, after the barrack doors were locked, the committee met in one of the upper bunks to plot and prepare for the day.

With infinite caution, they organized the theft and hiding of axes and heavy tools for use as weapons. They siphoned benzene into hidden caches for setting fires, held back gold from the mouths of the dead to be used to divert the avaricious watchtower guards.

But June passed without a signal from Camp One. "Wait" was the only word brought by the carpenter Wiernik, the sole link with the leaders in Camp One.

In Camp Two, the men alternated between terror at the risk of discovery and a hysterical impatience at the enforced delay.

There were fewer transports now. Survivors of the Warsaw ghetto uprising, pitifully thin men, women, and children, arrived and were processed. Two trainloads of men and women of the Polish underground came. A band of gypsies passed through the gas chambers and were burned.

The weather turned hot and the fire grates gave off a

terrible heat. Elia endured, drawing deep into himself, concentrating his thoughts on the coming day of deliverance.

In July, work in Camp Two was speeded up. Two additional excavators were brought in, more fire grates constructed. In mid-month, a new group was sent up from Camp One to replace the work-Jews who succumbed daily to the blistering heat, the foul air, and the brutal hours of unremitting work.

With them came Aaron. Elia scarcely recognized him.

Aaron's hair, once thick and black, now grew in tufts of dingy gray. His skin was sallow, the color of clay tinged yellow. Only his eyes were the same, and they burned with a feverish intensity.

Elia had only a moment to stretch his parched lips in a grimace of welcome before a guard's bellow threatened him back to work.

By now, three quarters of the buried corpses had been excavated and burned. The work-Jews had been set to mixing the ashes of the dead with earth to fill the empty graves. The land had already been graded and planted in lupines. Soon nothing would be left of the dead but a field of flowers.

When the barrack door was locked that night, Elia and Aaron clasped one another in joy.

"A bag of bones." Aaron stepped back and grinned. "I tell you, Elia, there were skeletons in medical school with more meat on their bones than you have."

Elia laughed.

"Aaron, I'm so happy to see you I won't even talk of pots calling kettles black. What of Saul? Is he alive?"

"Saul." Aaron shrugged eloquently. "Let me tell you. On the day God leans down and says 'That's it, mentshhayt, I'm closing the store', it will be Saul he'll be talking to."

"Saul?" Elia tried to remember back three months, a lifetime ago. "He never struck me as exceptional."

Aaron nodded.

"I know," he agreed. "Uneducated. Inarticulate. But I tell

you, Elia, I've never known anybody with such a fierce grip on life. And he bullied me, there's no other word, he *bullied* me into staying alive. If I live until the day we destroy this place, it will be because Saul Baratz kicked my ass every inch of the way."

Elia's pulses leaped. He grasped Aaron's wrist.

"When?" he whispered eagerly. "When, Aaron? What's going on down there? What are we waiting for?"

Aaron's eyes darted fearfully. "They're careful," he said, "they have to be. Even a hint. A smell. It would be over before it started. They'd slaughter us all on the least suspicion. I know only that it's soon. It has to be soon."

In the days that followed, Elia grasped the truth of Aaron's words. If Aaron was to survive, the uprising would have to come soon. Each night he burned with fever, each morning, when he wakened, he was weaker.

As July drew to a close, the weather turned scorching. Heat radiating from the roasts made work torture.

The remaining graves had been emptied, the last of the corpses were burning. And the work-Jews faced the final truth. As witnesses to the mass killings, they would never be permitted to remain alive.

Then, on the last Saturday in July, word came from Camp One. The revolt was set for late afternoon of Monday, August 2.

There could be no postponement.

Time had run out.

Chapter 40

Nóne of us slept the night before," Elia remembered, smiling into Jenny's wide eyes. "Our nerves were stretched like piano wires.

"You have to consider the condition we were in," he continued. "We were all half-starved. Many of us, like Aaron, were sick and weak. And I don't think any of us, even the most optimistic, really believed we could succeed. We'd planned carefully, done everything it was possible, under the circumstances, to do. But what did we have, after all? A few clubs and axes, some benzene to start fires with. And we were up against guards with rifles, against watchtowers manned by guards with machine guns."

"The only thing we had, really, was the element of surprise.

"The guards had become so accustomed to their awful power, you see. Every day they had watched as thousands of strong, healthy people were reduced to ashes. So why would they think they had anything to fear from a handful of scarecrows?"

Elia was silent. Then, he shook his head as though his thoughts had taken a direction he preferred not to follow.

"Watching the sun come up through the barred windows of the barrack, we all knew that before it set, many of us would be dead. We would be free or we would be dead.

"We were divided into groups of five. Each group had a specific job. My group, which included Aaron, was assigned to set fire to the barrack.

"The riskiest job was getting the guards down from the towers. We had organized gold to lure them with, they were all mad for gold. The quickest, strongest men were chosen for that. If they succeeded, our chances were better. If they failed, we were finished.

"The time for the uprising had been set for five-thirty in the afternoon. A shot would be fired in Camp One. That was the signal.

"It was hot. My God, it was hot. The day was scorching and the fires made it unbearable. I had set my mind to endure the heat when I heard a shot. It was the signal, more than an hour early."

Elia had been sitting back in his chair. Now, he leaned forward, his hands tight on the chair arms.

"We ran to do our assigned jobs. On the way, we looked up at the watchtowers. *They were empty!*"

"I think I was out of my mind for a while. In all the bedlam, the fires, the shooting, the explosions, all I get now are flashes, like old film clips. A guard dropping with an ax buried in his head. Aaron racing from the burning barrack. A work-Jew falling, his chest blown away. A guard smashing at me with the butt of his empty rifle."

Elia stroked the scar running from his lip to his chin.

"I didn't even feel it. Every second counted. We ran, Aaron and I together. We climbed the antitank barrier surrounding the camp and ran for the woods we could see in the distance. We ran through a swamp.

"We were halfway across an open field when the shooting began. They were after us with guards from another camp who had seen the fires.

"I was exhausted and Aaron was stumbling, hanging on to my sleeve. Behind us, the guards were in jeeps and coming closer, so fast, so fast. The woods were just ahead, not more than a hundred meters. I strained to keep going.

"Then Aaron fell, pulling me down with him."

Elia stopped. He took a deep, careful breath and rubbed his face with a trembling hand.

"He couldn't go on. I knew that. But I couldn't leave him. I slung him over my shoulder and ran. He was so thin it was like carrying a child.

"I ran into the woods. I ran until the trees were thick and dark and cool and I couldn't hear the sound of shooting any longer.

"I let Aaron slip to the ground and dropped beside him. It took a long time to get my breath back, to notice Aaron hadn't moved.

"There was a bullet wound in his head and another in his back. I had carried a dead man.

"I held him close for a long time, just held him. Until the woods were dark with night.

"Then I dragged him with me under a pile of brush and fell asleep."

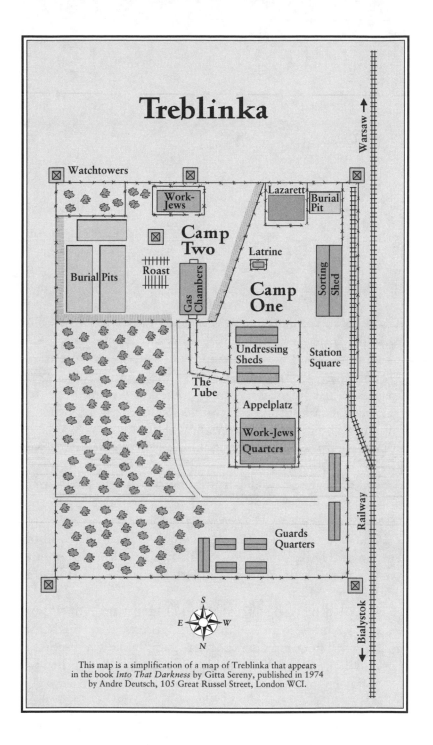

Treblinka

Warsaw →

Watchtowers

Work-Jews

Lazarett

Burial Pit

Camp Two

Latrine

Burial Pits

Roast

Gas Chambers

Camp One

Sorting Shed

Undressing Sheds

Station Square

The Tube

Appelplatz

Work-Jews Quarters

Guards Quarters

Railway

Bialystok →

S
E · W
N

This map is a simplification of a map of Treblinka that appears in the book *Into That Darkness* by Gitta Sereny, published in 1974 by Andre Deutsch, 105 Great Russel Street, London WCI.

Chapter 41

Packing and driving home from the flea market, Jenny was preoccupied and silent. I had no idea what was going on in her head.

My own head was swarming with horrifying images.

I make my living with words. To me, words evoke instant images. Which is great when it comes to writing television commercials and promotion films. As I write, a projector in my mind flashes the corresponding action.

It's a gift every competent film writer has to have. And I'm a competent writer. That's an objective statement. I gave up any false modesty about my abilities at the same time I stopped thinking writing advertising copy was a glamorous career.

Elia had taken a little over two hours to tell us about Treblinka. He had told the story simply, with no attempt to dramatize the facts. And his understatement had made it all the more real to me.

It would be arrogant to say I suffered with him. I don't believe anybody, other than those who went through that hell, can truly comprehend. There simply isn't any comparable evil in our safe lives we can use as a frame of reference.

But deep inside I was trembling with reaction to the sights

my imagination had forced me to witness. I could not escape the images in the back of my head.

"Mum!" There was annoyance in Jenny's tone. I realized she had been trying to get my attention for some time.

"I'm sorry, honey. What is it?"

"Was my father anything like Elia?"

"How do you mean?"

"Sort of warm. And sweet. You know what I mean?"

No, I thought, he wasn't. But I said, "You really like Elia, don't you?"

"I think he's . . ." She paused. "You won't laugh?"

"I won't laugh," I promised.

"Well, I have this feeling, sort of, as if we've known each other forever. As if I could walk into his heart without knocking and he'd say 'Welcome home,' You know what I mean?"

I winced inwardly at the florid imagery but I didn't laugh. Florid or not, it conveyed her feelings precisely.

"Do you suppose it's because I've never known my father and Elia's never known his daughter?"

"Could be."

We drove without speaking for a couple of blocks.

"Mum," Jenny broke the silence. "You have to find Anna."

"I'm trying, honey," I said. "I'm sure as hell trying."

Cia phoned late in the evening. Her father was dead.

"The funeral's on Wednesday." She sounded weary. "Would you call the bank for me? I'm going to bring my mother back with me. We'll be there Friday."

"Of course I'll call. Want me to meet you?"

"Thanks, but no. I hate being met. We'll grab a cab. I'll see you Saturday morning for the garage sales."

"Forget it, Cia," I protested "You don't have to . . ."

"Hey," she interrupted. "I love my mother dearly, but

my father didn't call her Sarah Heartburn for nothing. I have
to. Believe me. Any luck with the locket?"

"None."

"Maybe tomorrow."

On Monday and Tuesday I covered twenty addresses.

Driving through the affluent lakeshore suburbs with their
stone houses and manicured lawns, I had long thoughts
about life's unfairness and God's indifference and it seemed
to me that individual fates are decided purely by chance. And
that, ultimately, man had no more importance than daisies
growing at random in the fields.

Seeds carried by the winds to free and open meadows are
warmed by the sun and kissed by the rains. They germinate,
grow, bloom, and drop their seeds, season after season.

But those that fall on pastureland are stomped by cows
and eaten by sheep.

I snickered to myself. At least Jenny came by her over-
blown metaphors honestly.

On Wednesday, an agency phoned with an assignment,
a training and safety film for a cement products manufac-
turer. I was happy to get the job. It meant September expenses were assured.

But I would have to give up the search for Anna for at
least two weeks.

Chapter 42

I was sorry to hear about your father." Elia held Cia's hand in his. "Please accept my condolences."

"Thank you." Cia smiled at him.

We had gone together, Cia and I, to at least twenty garage sales the day before. I had brought her up to date on Elia's story and she had told me of her problems with her mother.

"She's furious at Dad for dying and leaving her," Cia said. "As if he had a choice. She fought with his doctor, his lawyer, and the funeral director. And me. I spent the last week biting my tongue."

"And your mother?" Elia said. "I'm sure it must be a very difficult time for her."

"My mother." Cia's mouth tightened. "Is making it a very difficult time for everybody."

"Don't be upset," Elia said gently. "It takes time."

"I'll survive." Cia changed the subject. "Liz told me you escaped from Treblinka. What did you do then?"

Elia's smile erased any hint of mockery in his reply.

"I survived," he said.

Chapter 43

Elia was roused at sunrise by the twittering and fussing of forest birds, the harsh cawing of a crow. No bird had sung at Treblinka and he lay still, his eyes closed, listening. Then he crawled from under the brush and stretched his limbs, filling his lungs with the sweet forest air.

He was hungry and thirsty. He had no idea where he was or where he was going. But he was free!

He permitted himself one brief soaring moment, then brought his spirits back to earth.

In a small clearing, he located a spot under a linden tree where digging would be easiest and he returned to the brush for Aaron.

Carrying the frail body, he was suddenly and terrifyingly overwhelmed with the sensation of being watched. Nerve ends in his back, sensitized by months of tension, sounded a strident alarm

He turned slowly, hugging Aaron close.

A white-bearded old man stood in the dappled sunlight on the far side of the clearing, a rifle cradled under his arm. At his knee, ears erect, was a large brown-and-white dog of indeterminate breed.

Elia froze, his heart thudding painfully.

"You from that place?" The old man jerked his head to the west. "Down there?"

Elia nodded.

"Your friend too?"

"Yes." The word was a hoarse croak.

"He dead?" The old man's neck stretched, cranelike.

"Yes."

"Put him down."

Elia obeyed, lowering Aaron to the ground, his eyes fixed on the old man.

"Come." The old man gestured with his rifle. He waited until Elia crossed the clearing, then spoke to the dog.

"Go, Bronia."

The dog flicked a plume of tail and disappeared into the brush. The two men followed in silence and emerged, quite unexpectedly, into a large clearing. A small log house with a sod roof, surrounded on all sides by row upon row of split and stacked firewood, stood in the middle of the clearing.

The old man plodded to a shed attached to the rear of the house. Reaching inside, he brought out two spades and handed one to Elia.

Gesturing with his rifle, he ordered Elia to follow and led the way back to the linden tree. In silence, together, they buried Aaron, then returned to the clearing.

The old man circled the house and shuffled between two rows of piled wood, Bronia trotting at his heels. Elia followed, and almost tripped over the dog when the old man halted abruptly.

He pointed to a hook driven into the end of a log, then grasped the hook and pulled. A section of logs came away, leaving an opening large enough for a man to climb through.

"Get in." The old man indicated with his thumb.

Elia hesitated. The hiding place could be a haven, or it could be a trap. He had no way of knowing what the man was planning, sanctuary or betrayal.

The old man watched Elia stolidly from under shaggy brows. His eyes were small, blue and set closely together. His beard, yellow under the walrus mustache that hid his mouth, was gray and untrimmed. It lay raggedly on his chest, the same shade of gray as the shirt that covered surprisingly brawny shoulders.

His torso and limbs were mismatched, the arms and legs short, as though designed for a smaller man. His hands, liver-spotted and corded, held the rifle loosely, the barrel pointed to the ground.

He waited. Beside him, Bronia, the dog, sat patiently, ears cocked, yellow eyes intent.

Elia finally broke the silence.

"I'm a Jew," he said.

The old man shrugged. The rifle swerved to the opening in the wood pile.

"Not the first," he said.

"You've hidden Jews? Here?"

The old man nodded.

"Hidden Jews? From the Germans?" A second nod and Elia found himself asking, "Why?"

Again the old man shrugged.

"Why?" Elia insisted.

"Yids?" The old man's shoulders lifted and fell in an expression of indifference. "Germans? Swine. Pigs from hell."

He turned his head and spat at the ground.

Elia spent the day in the woodpile, not uncomfortably. The hiding place, created by carefully arranged logs, was high enough for him to sit erect and smelled sweetly of pine needles, laid thickly as a rug on the bare earth.

Before replacing the door section, the old man had brought a chunk of coarse, black bread, a greasy, fried leg and thigh that was either chicken or hare, and an earthenware crock filled with cold tea. Elia gnawed at the tough meat, chewed on the bread, and drank the sugared tea gratefully.

He could hear and identify the sounds the old man made as he moved about the clearing, the ring of an ax splitting logs, the chunk of wood being piled.

As the day warmed and wore on, Elia dozed. He was startled to wakefulness by Bronia's barking. Moments later, her clamor was joined by the deeper baying of several dogs and the shouting of men's voices, some in German, others in Polish.

He crouched, rigid, listening.

The soldiers were hunting Treblinka escapees, combing the countryside with dogs. After checking the old man's papers and warning him anyone harboring the fugitives would be shot, they departed and silence fell on the clearing.

The old man came after night had fallen, dark and moonless. Elia heard the scraping of the door logs being removed, the word "come." He crawled through the opening.

More by sound than sight, he followed the old man through the woodpiles into the lamplit house.

The house was uncomfortably warm. The air, after the freshness of the forest, smelled of rancid fat and stale sweat. Elia's eyes adjusted to the light and he saw a wooden table set with two plates.

The old man gestured for Elia to be seated, sat down himself, and began eating immediately, slurping his food from a large spoon held like a dagger in his fist.

Elia stared down at his plate, a wide soup bowl in which, under a skim of grease, was a stew of potatoes and cabbage, interspersed with lumps of gray meat. He picked up his spoon.

Hungry as he was, the sight and smell of the food repelled him. His stomach knotted, nonplussing him. Why was his body rebelling now? He had eaten worse in Treblinka. And eaten gratefully.

The old man's eyes were on him, expressionless, spoon raised halfway to his mouth. Elia summoned a smile.

"My name is Elia Strohan," he said.

The old man nodded. "Stolinski. Mikolaj Stolinski."

"I would like to thank you, Pan Stolinski . . ."

"Mikolaj," the old man interrupted. He gestured with his spoon. "Eat."

Elia ate. To distract himself from the food, he looked around, taking in his surroundings.

The room they were in appeared to constitute the entire house. Against one wall was a huge porcelain stove, grease covered and filthy. A narrow bed, unmade, occupied a corner of the room beside a blackened stone fireplace. On opposite walls were two small, uncurtained wondows, both tightly shut. Under one window was a counter littered with dishes, rags, and an assortment of tools. Below the other window, a wood box had been constructed, ten or twelve feet long and four feet high.

An ancient rocking chair beside the fireplace, the stools on which they sat and the table at which they ate completed the furnishings.

The old man finished his meal. Without waiting for Elia, he pushed away from the table, leaving his plate. He went out into the night, returning moments later with a thin, straw mattress. He laid the mattress on the wood box and jerked his beard at Elia.

"You sleep here."

"Thank you."

The old man sat down on the cot and removed his boots. In stocking feet he crossed to the table, bent, and blew out the lamp. The room went black.

Elia heard the creaking of rope springs, the rustling of straw as the old man settled himself in his cot. Minutes later, he was snoring.

Elia groped his way to the wooden box and stretched out on the straw mattress.

The room was hot, airless, and black as pitch. For a long time he lay staring into blackness, eyes stretched wide for any glimmer of light. There was none. He let his eyelids droop and lifted them again, momentarily diverted by night so complete he could tell only by touch when his eyes were closed.

The food he had eaten lay sour and heavy on his stomach. He found it necessary to swallow constantly against cold saliva rushing into his mouth. Behind his left eye, a pinpoint of pain was building like a thunder cloud, threatening the return of the headaches he had experienced before. They had ceased without his being aware. He recalled Aaron's comment when he remarked on their passing.

"You're surprised?" Aaron's grin was feral. "Listen, oy-fele, Treblinka has cured the minor ailments of thousands of people. Permanently cured."

The discomfort in his stomach had moved up to his chest. He raised his hand to press the spot where the heaviness lay and his fingers encountered metal.

Puzzled, he traced the outlines of a circle, felt string and followed its loop around his neck.

Temples pounding, he sat up, opened his eyes and looked down. Hung on the string around his neck was an alarm clock. He recognized it and the clothes he was wearing.

He was dressed in scheissmeister Julian's clothes.

Work-Jews at Treblinka were permitted use of the latrine for a maximum of three minutes and the SS had conscripted a prisoner to act as time-guard.

For their own amusement, they had given him the title "shit-master," had forced him to grow a beard and dress as a rabbi, and had hung a large alarm clock around his neck. Julian, a gentle man from Czenstochowa, had endured their abuse and ridicule, but each night he had lain in his bunk and wept.

Elia tore at the hideous clock, but the string was too short to remove over his head and too strong to break. The harder he struggled, the tighter the noose became.

He awoke, fighting for breath, threshing wildly and sweating with nausea. His throat filled with bile, his stomach churned.

Shivering and swallowing convulsively, he rolled off the wooden box and searched in the total darkness for the door. Finally, he dropped to his hands and knees and crawled until his fingertips found the door frame.

He burst from the house. Bent double, he vomited repeatedly, everything he had eaten, over and over until nothing was left but a dry retching.

For a while he lay still, too weak to move. Reluctant to exchange the fresh night air for the confines of the house, he tottered to the lee of a woodpile and lay down there.

Sometime in the night he felt the warm, shaggy presence of Bronia. She curled up beside him. He circled her with his arm and they both slept.

Chapter 44

Breakfast was an unappetizing mess of potatoes and sausage, fried in grease.

Elia viewed his plate with a bilious eye. His body had been too long without fat for him to digest the heavy fare. He picked at the food, reluctant to offend Mikolaj.

The old man ate noisily, slurped his tea, wiped his mouth with his sleeve, and made the longest speech Elia was ever to hear from him.

"I'm taking wood to town. Won't be back until nightfall. Bronia will stay. She barks, you hide."

Elia nodded agreement. He followed Mikolaj from the house and helped the old man load an ancient wood cart. A bony mare named Halinka was led from the lean-to beside the house and stood patiently while Mikolaj harnessed her to the cart.

With a nod to Elia and a cluck of his tongue at Halinka, Mikolaj and the cart creaked across the clearing and down a rutted track into the woods.

Elia was splitting logs when Bronia sounded her first alarm. He was safely hidden by the time men's voices invaded the clearing. They spoke in Polish but were too far away for Elia to hear what was being said. He remained in the woodpile hiding place long after the men had gone.

In the late afternoon, Bronia barked again.

This time, Elia could make out the sound of two separate groups, one arriving moments before the other. They met within a stone's throw of where he crouched, scarcely daring to breathe. He could hear them clearly.

They were Poles, hunting escapees. Accompanying the first group was a guard from Treblinka whose voice Elia recognized. It was the voice of Ivan, one of the most brutal guards, whom the work-Jews had called Ivan the Terrible.

It was from the lips of Ivan the Terrible that Elia heard the outcome of Treblinka's uprising.

There had been close to eight hundred work-Jews at Treblinka. More than five hundred had died in the escape attempt. Only two hundred had succeeded.

Within hours, security troops had fanned out from the camp to a distance of five kilometers, hunting the men.

Of the two hundred who escaped, all but a handful were caught. By evening, all who were caught were dead.

Only twenty, at most thirty, work-Jews survived the revolt at Treblinka.

Elia stayed in the woodpile until after dark, when Mikolaj came to free him.

Hunched over the meal the old man had prepared, Elia told him of the day's events.

"I'm a danger to you," he concluded. "If they find me, they'll shoot you."

The old man's eyes glinted. He made an obscene gesture with his finger.

"Still," Elia said. "It would be best if I left. If you will permit me to stay tonight? I'll leave in the morning."

Mikolaj reached across the table and pinched the skin on Elia's bony wrist.

"Put some meat on you. A week."

Not if I throw up everything you cook, Elia thought. But he said, "Thank you, Mikolaj. Tell me when you want me to go and I'll leave."

Three events occurred that, more than kindness on Mikolaj's part, delayed Elia's departure.

The first concerned the matter of food.

Fat and a frying pan constituted the sum and total of the old man's culinary skills.

He used and reused the same fat to cook the meat and fish and vegetables and eggs for which he bartered a portion of his wood. As a result, in addition to the odor of the rancid fat, every meal bore the flavor of its predecessor.

After three days of witnessing fresh produce reduced to inedible garbage, Elia gave up searching for a way to take over the cooking chores without offending the old man and broached the subject directly.

"Unless you have any objection, I would like to prepare my own meals," he said.

Mikolaj's little eyes narrowed suspiciously.

"I enjoy cooking," Elia added hastily. "I'll cook for you too, if you like."

Mikolaj nodded wary agreement and Elia passed his fourth day of freedom scouring pots and pans. He discarded Mikolaj's tins filled with congealed grease in which were imbedded the corpses of a variety of crawling insects. He scrubbed the porcelain stove until it shone and prepared chicken stew as Kalyna had taught him to do, with fresh vegetables and fluffy potato dumplings.

Mikolaj returned from the village and entered the house, sniffing the air like a hound on scent. He seated himself, eyed his plate, picked up his spoon, and ate without comment.

When he finished, he gestured for more. Finally, his plate clean, the old man pushed himself from the table and belched loudly.

"Good." He brushed his mustache dry with the heel of his hand, first one side, then the other. "You cook now."

The second incident was related to Bronia.

She returned from a foray in the woods with her tail between her legs, her snout bristling with porcupine quills. To Elia's astonishment, Mikolaj ignored her predicament.

"Stupid old bitch!" was his only comment.

It took Elia the entire evening to remove the quills, pushing them through the flesh and pulling them out from inside the dog's mouth. Bronia submitted patiently, her yellow eyes fastened on Elia's face, her plumed tail flicking an occasional acknowledgment of his efforts.

Mikolaj grumbled at the lamplight, but he watched the procedure from his bed with furtive interest. When Elia, finished at last, bathed the dog's mouth with a vinegar solution, the old man's lips pursed thoughtfully.

In the morning, he removed his shirt and beckoned Elia to come close.

He raised his arm. An angry red boil bloomed in the old man's armpit, another at the nape of his neck.

Elia prepared an oatmeal poultice as he had seen Kalyna do and applied it to the boils. He recalled a remedy she had sworn by and instructed Mikolaj to dicker for cabbages on his next delivery to the village.

"I'll make sauerkraut," he said. "You'll drink the kvas, the sauerkraut juice, every morning. You'll be rid of the boils in a few weeks."

The old man looked dubious, but he hitched Halinka to the cart and left on his trip to town.

The days passed into September.

Between the poultices, the change in diet, and the kvas the cabbage produced as it fermented, Mikolaj's boils healed and vanished. Nothing more was said of Elia's departure.

Elia, gaining strength, began to venture farther from the clearing, hewing wood. Bronia had attached herself to him and he became accustomed to her following at his heels.

Though his days were filled with the peaceful forest, his nights were haunted by nightmares.

In Treblinka, he had mastered the technique survivors had to learn in order to preserve their sanity.

"Listen to me," Aaron had urged. "Don't try to reason with what you see. Let it register on your brain, but don't let it into your mind. If you accept the reality of this shithole you're done. Do you understand what I'm saying? Don't try to think!"

Now, as though resentful of the burden it had carried so long alone, Elia's brain was stirring, regurgitating the horrors it had witnessed.

His eyes had seen and his brain recorded the corpses of pregnant women being cremated. When the body gases were sufficiently heated, the women's abdomens burst open and the burning fetus inside was exposed.

In his nightmare, Elia was forced to watch the fetus squirm from the flames, eye sockets empty, charred hand reaching, imploring. And Elia, recognizing the face of Daniel, screamed aloud. He awoke, wet with the sweat of terror, his heart thundering.

At Treblinka he had seen, more than once, a man hung upside down, left suspended the entire day, beaten to death at sundown. In his nightmare, the man was his father.

At Treblinka he had seen Kurt Franz's dog, Bari, trained to attack, bring down a helpless prisoner and tear the man's genitals from his body. In his nightmare, the man was Nathan Goretsky, the baker who had died at Babi Yar.

He had seen a hundred men lined up five abreast and ordered to kneel, machine-gunned as they knelt. And in his nightmare every man bore Aaron's face.

The dead of Babi Yar and Treblinka's dead became entangled. In his nightmares, men and women who had never survived Babi Yar were tortured to death in Treblinka.

He became agonizingly aware that he, himself, was never

a victim. With the realization, a terrible sense of guilt festered in the darkest reaches of his mind.

Each night he willed himself to remain awake. Each night the hideous dreams claimed him.

Chapter 45

*E*lia went alone into the forest that day, Bronia, as usual, at his heels. Mikolaj remained behind to split the logs they had dragged into the clearing the day before.

October was drawing to a close. There was a hint of approaching winter in the air. Elia selected a stand of trees, removed the ragged jacket the old man had provided, and set to work.

Mikolaj, while slovenly in his personal habits, was meticulous in his care of the tools of his trade and the keenly honed ax bit deep into the wood with each stroke. Elia fell easily into the now familiar rhythm.

He occupied his mind estimating the number of strokes required according to trunk diameter, counting off each swing of the ax and experiencing an almost childish gratification when his guess proved correct.

He worked until the pale sun rested on the forest ridge, then cleaned the ax and gathered his belongings. Bronia had loped off in her eternal pursuit of elusive forest creatures. He knew she would follow when she heard him moving through the woods.

She met him at the edge of the clearing, tail waving in greeting, her tongue lolling from a wide, doggy grin. They were almost to the house when she growled softly, a deep rumble in her throat. She halted, ears laid flat. A ridge of hair down her back rose stiffly.

Instinctively, Elia dropped to one knee beside her. He placed a hand on her snout to silence her. Hardly daring to breathe, he waited for a recurrence of the sound that had alerted her, wondering at the same time if he should risk a dash to the woodpile hiding place.

He heard a sudden gasping cry of pain from within the house, then the savage voice of a man shouting.

"You stupid old fart! You want to die? Where is it?"

There was a moment of silence. Then the air was split by a high, animal scream of pain.

"Come on, old man! You're going to tell us in the end. Where is it hidden?"

Elia dropped on all fours. With the ax in one hand, the fingers of the other buried in Bronia's ruff, he crawled to the side of the house, dragging her with him.

Pressed against the rough logs, he tried to still his quivering nerves.

It. The man had demanded to know where *it* was hidden. Not where *he* was hidden. They were not searching for him.

Raising himself to a crouch, Elia sidled to the window. Slowly, cautiously, he stood erect and peered through.

Mikolaj lay on the bare wood floor, curled on his side, his arms wrapped into his groin. Blood matted his beard and the side of his head. His one visible eye was swollen shut.

Two men stood above him, their backs to the open door. From his vantage point, Elia could see their faces, the coarse features of peasants in their middle years.

As he watched, the taller of the two swung his boot and kicked Mikolaj, a brutal blow to the kidneys. The old man's body spasmed. He screamed hoarsely.

Lessons learned at Treblinka siezed on Elia's mind. The torment of fellow prisoners must be ignored. To interfere was to die, accomplishing nothing. Heroics produced two corpses instead of one.

He looked longingly to where the hiding place in the woodpile was located. To reach it, he would have to pass the open door. But if he moved quietly . . .

He was at the door when the blinding fury exploded in his head.

For the first time in his life, Elia acted without reason. There was no instruction from his brain. His body simply went berserk. A roar of outrage tore from his throat and he plunged into the house, ax swung high.

The taller man's head swiveled.

In the split second the ax arced toward him he recognized the face of death and his eyes bulged with horror. Then his head was severed from his body.

Blood gouted, spurted, spraying Elia as he turned on the second man, his arms retracing the arc, the ax soaring.

The shorter man gaped, white-eyed. He was helpless, frozen in shock, an expression of raw, wrenching fear on his drained features.

Suddenly, his face was the face of any of the thousands Elia had seen die in terror at Treblinka.

The frenzy left Elia all at once. His arms dropped. The ax slipped from his nerveless fingers and thudded to the floor.

The smaller man's limbs unlocked. He took a tentative step, his eyes fastened on Elia. A second step, then he plunged past Elia and out the door, running as though the hounds of hell pursued him.

Elia followed, stumbling blindly from the house. He crashed through the underbrush, heedless of thorns and brambles, until he came to the place where Aaron was buried.

He dropped to the ground, his back braced against the linden tree. He could not stop yawning. Minutes later, Bronia found him.

She crawled between his splayed legs and pressed against him, murmuring wordless comfort, burrowing her muzzle into his neck.

Resting his cheek on the dog's silky ear, Elia fell asleep.

Chapter 46

*H*e woke, chilled. Bronia was gone.

There was still light in the sky and he knew he had not slept long. His bones felt liquid, as though he had passed through an illness, as though a fever had broken, leaving him weak but strangely at peace.

I killed a man, he thought.

He looked down at his hand. Fingers loosely curled, it lay inert on the ground under which Aaron lay.

Did you hear me, Aaron?

I killed a man. And something even worse. I inspired mortal fear in another human being.

A wave of longing for Aaron's tartness, for his macabre humor, swept over Elia. He pressed his palm on the sod above the grave, needing contact, half believing Aaron might feel the weight of his hand.

This isn't the way it should have been, Aaron. We were meant to be friends for life. You and your Leah. Me and my Anna. Our children, growing up as friends. We were robbed, Aaron. We were cheated of the way it should have been.

Elia rested his head against the linden tree and gazed up at the darkening sky.

Have you met God yet, Aaron? Did you ask Him if this is what He intended?

Do this for me, Aaron. Tell Him I think He's a fraud.
Tell Him I don't believe His lies any more.

Elia's throat tightened. He closed his eyes to hold back
the hot tears springing to his eyes.

Tell Him I think He's full of shit.

Elia opened his eyes and pure joy streaked through his
veins at what he saw.

A wind had sprung up. Thirty feet away, a slim white
birch swayed, waving leafless arms to capture the random
snowflakes drifting from an opaque sky.

Anna.

Anna stepped, full-blown, into Elia's mind. Anna in a
white dress, dancing in a plum orchard.

They had gone for a day in the country. He and Anna.
Orest and Lesia. Saul and his wife, Marusia.

Orest had brought his bandura and the three girls had
danced to his music, weaving in and out under the white
foam of the blossom-laden plum trees.

Elia, stretched out on the ground beside Orest, had filled
his soul with the sight of Anna as she danced, cheeks flushed,
white petals dappling her sun-streaked hair.

She had paused, breast rising and falling, skin dewy
Bending over Orest, she had whispered in his ear, her eyes
sparkling at Elia.

Orest had nodded and begun to play a melody Elia had
recognized. It was the song of the sun, the song he thought
of as Anna's.

She had come to him, coaxing him, with her eyes and her
hands and her body, to dance with her.

He had first protested, drowsy with sun and air and the
voluptuous perfume of the flowers. But she had insisted, teasing until he rose and took her into his arms.

They had waltzed through sunlight and shadow until the
music was a faint echo in the distance. And he had made love
to her under the scented cloud of blossoms, kissing the petals
that drifted down on her soft lips.

Anna. Against the screen of his eyelids he could see every line of her face, every perfection, even the tiny mole at the corner of her mouth.

Something cold and wet touched his cheek.

Elia's eyes flew open. Bronia's snout was inches from his face.

Mikolaj bent beside her, peering at Elia with his one good eye. The left side of his face was puffed and bruised.

Elia stirred and the old man grunted.

"You're alive." He gestured with his head. "Come."

Elia followed, Bronia beside him. He hesitated at the door to the house but Mikolaj pushed him through, snorting his impatience.

There was no blood, no ax, no torso. No head. Elia looked questioningly at the old man.

"Buried him." One small blue eye glinted with cold satisfaction. "Bastard."

Over a plate of thick soup the old man had kept hot on the stove, Elia thought to ask, "What were they looking for?"

"Thought I have money." The eye narrowed. "Don't."

In the morning, Mikolaj hitched Halinka to the cart and departed for the village.

He returned with worn, warm clothing for Elia and a set of identification papers.

"Thank you, Mikolaj." Elia scanned the papers. "Jerzy Masiewicz? Who is he?"

"Dead." Mikolaj tapped his temple with his forefinger. "A fool."

Elia thanked the old man once more, smiling at the thought of how his new identity would have delighted Aaron.

Chapter 47

*T*he nightmares ended that day.

When Elia woke the next morning after a night of dreamless sleep he was wary, probing his mind gingerly. After a second night, then a third, he fell back into his old habit of dissecting and analyzing his thoughts and emotions.

Had the murder he committed ended the nightmares? Deep in his subconscious, was there a sense of having avenged the thousands of murders he had witnessed? Had the act, by the sheer violence of its nature, purged him of the guilt he felt because he, of them all, had survived?

Or had the nightmares ended because Anna had been restored to him.

He had lost Anna at Treblinka. In the beginning, thoughts of her had been too painful to endure. In the end, it had become impossible to remember her face. She had faded from the hell that was his reality, with no more substance than a character in a novel he had read in another life.

And now she had returned. He could close his eyes and recall her every expression.

Her eyes, glistening with excitement or narrowed in concentration above the violin cupped under her chin. Heavy-lidded with passion or flashing in anger.

Her mouth, pursed in thought. Her hair, the color of

wheat, flowing on the pillow beside him. The provocative swing of her hips when her mood was teasing, her determined stride when her mind was on undertakings of her own.

They had had almost two thousand days together. Each night Elia removed one of the days from his file of memory.

A winter day they had gone skating on the frozen river, she fleet, he awkward.

A rainy Sunday when, after unsuccessfully playing the opening bars of the Mendelssohn E Minor Concerto over and over, she had stormed out of the flat, returning hours later, sodden-haired. Without speaking, she had picked up her violin and played the entire first movement flawlessly.

Elia permitted himself to relive one day at a time. As winter closed in and darkness fell early he sat beside the fire each evening, lost in recalling every minute detail.

Across from him, Mikolaj rocked and honed his axes or whittled the squat wooden figures he sold in the village, as oblivious of Elia as Elia was of him.

On several occasions, Polish partisans came to the clearing. There were women among them and often children, some barely into their teens. Mikolaj fed them, gave them whatever provisions he could spare, and they moved on.

After the first such visit, during which one of the partisans questioned Elia narrowly enough to alarm him, he affected the shambling gait, the dropped chin and empty eyes of the idiot he was supposed to be. He was ignored by the groups that followed. His performance invariably produced a rusty chuckle from Mikolaj.

He never developed a fondness for the old man. Mikolaj seemed to possess most of the negative characteristics of the illiterate peasant with few of the redeeming qualities.

He was narrow-minded, mistrustful of everyone, and suspicious of every motive. He never spoke if a grunt or a gesture would suffice. He ate piggishly, belched rumblingly, and broke wind loudly. If he ever bathed, Elia never witnessed it and, in the confines of the small, sealed house, he smelled like a goat.

He treated his animals shabbily, feeding them no more than was necessary to keep them alive and working, whipping Halinka and kicking Bronia if they failed to respond at once to his commands.

As time passed, Elia assumed more of the chores and the old man took to spending several days a week in the village. Often he returned drunk, the reins loose in his hands, trusting Halinka to find her way home. On those occasions, Elia carried him to the house and put him to bed.

In the summer of 1944, when Elia had been in the forest almost a year, Mikolaj brought news that the Russians had pushed into Poland, forcing the German army westward. Six months later, in January of 1945, Warsaw was liberated.

At the first sign of spring, sad to be parting from Bronia but with no feeling toward Mikolaj save gratitude, Elia left the forest.

His only link with Anna lay in Warsaw.

Chapter 48

Warsaw was in ruins."

Elia raised his head from the locket in his hand and gazed past Cia and me, his eyes on a distant horizon.

"I couldn't find the street at first, the street where Anna's aunt and uncle lived. When I did find it, there was nothing there. Rubble where all the houses had been.

"I sat down on a pile of stones where I guessed the Kusiewiczes' house had been and tried to think what I could do. Sophie and Wasyl had been my only hope.

"They must have learned, in time, where Anna had been sent. They had known the name of the German couple who had cared for Elianna. Without them, where could I start?

"Further down the street I saw a couple, a man and a woman, clearing rubble. I went to them to ask if they knew the Kusiewiczes."

The man straightened and eyed Elia wearily. His seamed face was gray with dust.

"Sophie and Wasyl?" The woman rubbed her hands on her skirt and pointed in the direction opposite from where Elia had come. "Of course. They lived two houses over that way."

"Do you know where I can find them?"

"They're dead," the man said. "Sophie died, let's see, in 1943?" He glanced at his wife. She nodded. "A stroke. Her second. Or her third. And Wasyl was shot by the Germans."

"Wasyl? Shot? Why?"

"The street executions." The man frowned at Elia's puzzled expression. "You're not from Warsaw?"

"I only arrived yesterday."

"Mirko?" The woman placed her hand on her husband's arm. "I'll make tea. If you like . . ." She dipped her head in Elia's direction.

"Of course." The man extended his hand to Elia.

"I am Mirko Paczka," he said formally. "May I present my wife, Pauline. We would be honored if you would join us."

"I am Elia Strohan." Elia shook the proffered hand, then followed the Paczkas into the basement of their ruined house, where they lived, the two of them, alone. Their sons has died early in the war.

They told Elia what had happened to Wasyl.

"The street executions were reprisals for the activities of the underground movement," Mirko explained. "The Nazis took hostages and shot them in public executions. Wasyl was one of the hostages."

"What happened here?" Elia gestured at the street above.

"The underground fought back," Mirko said. "It lasted sixty-three days, the Warsaw uprising, before it was crushed. Then the Germans systematically destroyed the city."

"There was no need," Pauline said sadly. "Why did they destroy us? We had no arms. We weren't the underground. We were nothing."

Mirko and Pauline shook their heads at a world grown incomprehensible to them. Elia waited a moment, then asked if they had known Anna.

"The niece?" Pauline nodded. "Sophie had only one letter

from them, from her sister. They were sent, the mother, two sisters, and another girl, to a forced labor camp in Landshut. To a textile mill."

There was a sudden influx of customers. Cia and I served them quickly and returned to where Elia sat, lost in thought.
"So what did you do?" Cia demanded eagerly.
Elia smiled at her. "I went to Landshut, of course."
"Where is Landshut?" I asked.
"In Germany. Not far from Munich."

Chapter 49

*I*t sounds so easy, now, to say I went to Landshut."

Elia leaned forward in his chair, his thumb stroking the locket, and began to talk . . .

I left Warsaw on April thirteenth, the day Hitler committed suicide, though I didn't know it then. By May seventh I had gone as far as Lodz, a distance of some hundred and twenty-five kilometers.

That summer, the summer of 1945, when the war ended, was chaos. There was an endless stream of people, searching for members of their family, a friend, a fellow townsman, anyone from their past life who might have survived.

There were thousands of them. Walking, hitching on hay carts and wagons, hanging on railway coaches. Begging food, begging water. Sleeping where they could. Always moving to get a few miles closer to . . . to what? Asking everybody they met, others like themselves, *do you know . . . have you heard of . . . have you seen . . .*

There was no mail service. No telephones. And if there had been, where would they write to, who could they call? Their lives had been torn apart and scattered to the winds. There was only one way to find out if someone had survived. Keep walking. Keep looking. Keep asking.

Camps for the displaced were being set up by the Allies. Eventually there were some two hundred Displaced Persons Camps in Germany and Austria alone. People would stop at a camp, read the lists of others who had passed through, leave their own names, and move on. Many were too ill to go on and died in the DP camps. Many gave up and remained in the camps for years.

From Lodz, I walked to Gorlitz, then to Plauen, then south to Regensberg, then to Landshut, in all a distance of some three hundred kilometers. You could drive it, now, easily in a day. I was five months on the road.

I arrived in Landshut toward the end of September. And I learned that a contingent of women from the textile mills had been transferred, months before, to Grunberg, a town more than a hundred kilometers northwest of Landshut. Anna may have been one of them.

At the same time, I heard there were women from the slave labor factories at a DP camp near Linz, some fifty kilometers to the east, in the American Occupied Zone of Austria.

I was in no condition to go east, then backtrack west. I had lost sixty pounds since leaving Warsaw. I had injured my bad leg, jumping from a moving freight car. And winter was on its way.

I went east. To Linz.

The DP camp was in Leondig, a town near Linz. I was a month getting there and I arrived with a fever that turned into pneumonia.

The irony of it! To have survived so far and then to die of something as absurd as pneumonia. Outrage kept me alive.

There were two women from Grunberg at Leondig, both in pitiful condition. They had survived months of an enforced march during which two thousand women had died. Neither had known Anna.

When I was well enough, I went to the American Office of Strategic Services in Linz and asked for work. I was a bag

of bones and I hadn't much stamina, but I spoke English.
And, of course, the other languages.

They hired me, and after a week I rented a furnished
room in Linz.

During the day, I worked for the Americans. At night and
on weekends, I worked on the lists at the Jewish Committee.
The lists were names of known survivors passing through.
They were added to and revised daily.

Many brought lists from other camps and we added their
names to ours. It was while I was copying one of those lists
that a name leaped off the page at me.

Lesia Boyko was at Camp Admont, a DP center in the
British Occupation Zone, less than fifty kilometers away.

By then I had been with the OSS for several months and
I didn't hesitate to ask for a few days' leave and a travel
permit to the British Zone. The Americans were always very
kind to me, very understanding. The man I worked for drove
me to the train station.

Camp Admont was in a beautiful alpine valley. The day
I arrived, early in October, a perfect autumn day, the air was
like wine. I found Lesia in a group on a balcony, their heads
tilted to sunlight flowing down like liquid honey.

I would never have known her. If she hadn't recognized
me and called my name I would have passed her a dozen
times.

She couldn't have been more than thirty then. She looked
fifty. She was gaunt. Her hair had always been a mass of red-
gold curls. Now, it was dull and thin. Her face was skin
stretched over bone. Only her eyes were the same. Large and
green and still bright with intelligence.

She told me what had happened to her. And to Anna.

They were picked up off the street in Warsaw, on their
way home from church. Anna, her mother and sister, and
Lesia. and sent to a forced labor camp in Landshut. There,
all four worked on looms weaving parachute silk. Anna's
mother died at Landshut. Her sister hanged herself. At Grun-

berg, after they were transferred, Lesia and Anna worked on spinning machines, tying broken threads.

The winter before the war ended, with the Allied armies approaching, the Germans began marching the women westward. Lesia and Anna managed to stay together. They were liberated by the British.

Lesia was very ill. Tuberculosis from lint-laden air in the factory and the starvation diet. How she survived the death march, God only knows. And Anna had only one thought in her head. To get to Hamburg and claim Elianna.

Lesia was transferred from one camp to another after Anna left and they lost touch with one another.

Then, one day, a letter was brought to her by a Czech girl, one of the girls from Grunberg. She was searching for her husband. She had carried the letter with her from camp to camp before she found Lesia at Admont.

The letter was from Anna.

Chapter 50

*E*lia reached inside his jacket and withdrew a small leather billfold. He opened it.

Inside was a folded paper, yellow with age, the creases worn thin. He unfolded it carefully and translated the faded script for us. He read:

Dear Lesia,

I am writing, hoping this letter will find you.

I can only hope someone will know where you are now.

I have Elianna with me. The Klausens will miss her and she them. They are such good people. She is four now and speaks only German. We will teach each other. I am writing to tell you I will soon be leaving for Canada. I met a Canadian named Pierre Tremblay at the American Forces hospital where I have been working. He was with the occupation forces. He lost a leg and his eyesight and I began reading to him. He has no family, only an old aunt in Montreal who raised him. When he is ready to go home, I will go with him. He has offered marriage so that Elianna and I can go to Canada.

As I write, I realized how cold I must sound. But only Elianna matters. What happened to us must never happen to her.

I will try to get in touch with you from Montreal.

Take care of yourself until we meet again.

Your old friend,
Anna

Cia and I watched silently as he refolded the letter and replaced it in the billfold.

"And Lesia?" Cia asked when the billfold was safely back in Elia's pocket. "What happened to Lesia?"

"She died that winter." There was bitterness in Elia's words. "The Nazis were claiming victims even after the war ended, you see."

"When did you come to Canada?"

"Not until 1952. I applied as soon as I knew Anna was here. I had to wait five years for a visa."

Elia pushed himself up from his chair. He was leaning heavily on his cane, more so than usual, and I reached out to put my hand on his arm.

"Why don't you wait, Elia. We'll be packing up soon. I'll drive you home."

"Thank you, but no." He smiled. "I enjoy my walk. It is the only exercise I take."

He sidled out from behind our tables into the mall corridor and walked slowly, nodding to Mike and Ros as he passed them.

At the doors, he paused to wave, then went out into the August heat.

I turned to Cia. "Does he look well to you?"

"I don't know." Cia frowned. "He does look a little

tired." She reached under the tables and pulled out one of the cartons we use for packing.

"Let's pack up and get out of here, Liz." She made a rueful face. "I really feel guilty about leaving my mother alone for too long."

Chapter 51

I was at my desk early the next morning, working on a script for *The Romance of Concrete*.

The title was definitely not mine. The client had invented it, fallen in love with it, and was adamant about keeping it. Gentle persuasion will work nine times out of ten, but when that tenth balks you back off. It's his money.

By midafternoon I had read more about concrete than anybody would ever want to know. The front door downstairs slammed and Jenny came up the stairs to my office. She was wearing my best blouse and a smug smile.

"Guess who took me out to lunch today." She leaned in the door frame, arms akimbo, ankles crossed.

"Robert Redford." I closed the reference book I had been reading and reached for a scratch pad.

"Very funny." She tilted her head, let three seconds elapse, then said, "Elia. Elia Strohan."

"You're kidding!" I swiveled in my chair. "Really?"

"Really. I looked up and there he was. He came all the way out to the airport, just to take me to lunch."

"Well, I'll be darned." She had my total attention now. "Tell me about it."

"Let me get out of these hot clothes first."

I pushed away from the desk.

"Go ahead. I'll make iced tea. Come downstairs when you've changed."

Five minutes later, she plunked her bikinied bottom on the kitchen chair across from me and placed her handbag on the table. I waited while she gulped half the tea in her glass.

"So?" I prodded.

She dug for an ice cube and popped it into her mouth. Crunching on the cube, she reached for her purse. She brought out a blue velvet jeweler's box and handed it to me.

I snapped the box open and sucked in my breath.

A heavy gold chain lay coiled on the white satin lining. Attached to the chain was a gold locket. I lifted the chain from the box and held the locket in my hand. It was Elia's locket redesigned by an artist.

In place of the yellow bead was a large diamond, the facets shooting rainbows in the afternoon sun. A series of graduated diamonds, forming the rays, extended beyond the perimeter of the golden disc. There had to be at least sixty of them, all flashing fire.

"Push the big diamond," Jenny instructed.

I pressed and the locket sprang open. Inside, on the left, was a small portrait of the Elia we knew. The right side was empty.

I snapped the locket shut and looked at Jenny. "Surely Elia didn't give this to you. This is an expensive bauble."

Instead of answering, Jenny leaned forward on her elbows and asked me a question.

"Have you ever wondered why Elia's been telling you all about himself?"

"Once or twice, yes." I dropped the locket onto its satin bed. "As a matter of fact, I have. Do you know why?"

Jenny nodded.

"He's never told anybody what happened to him. Can you imagine all that inside you and never telling anyone? Never talking about it all your life?"

"No. I can't. So why now? Why me?"

"So you can tell Anna."

"He'll be able to tell her himself. We'll find her. We'll keep looking until we do."

"Maybe not in time. His heart. He explained it to me. He has one of those things, you know, a bubble?"

"An aneurism?"

"That's it. On the . . . the aorta?"

"Aorta. The large heart artery." I looked at Jenny in dismay. "Oh, no."

"He told me it could rupture. Just like that!" Jenny snapped her fingers. "Is that true? Could he die? Just like that?"

"I suppose it could happen. But people with an aneurism can live for years if they're careful."

I hoped what I said was true. It at least reassured Jenny. She picked up the locket.

"He had it made about fifteen years ago," she said. "If he . . . you're supposed to give it to Anna if he can't."

"What happens if we never find her?"

"He wants me to have it." Jenny sprang the locked open and traced the empty circle inside with her finger. "You have to find her, Mum. Did you look today?"

"No. I've been working on that damn concrete film all day. I'll be on it for another two weeks or so."

Jenny's eyes flew wide. "You mean you won't be looking for her for two whole weeks?"

"Honey, I can't. I have a deadline to meet."

"Can't you tell them you don't want the job?"

"You know I can't do that." My voice rose as it always does when I'm on the defensive. "I get a lot of work from this agency. If I let them down, they'll find some other free-lancer. In the second place, we need the money."

"What about Cia?"

"Cia has her hands full with her mother."

"Then nobody's looking?" Jenny's voice soared to match mine. "Mum. Elia could *die!*"

"Honey, what can . . ." I began helplessly.

"Have you got a list?" Jenny interrupted. She dropped the locket back in the case and snapped the lid shut. "Give me your list and Elia's locket. I'll go."

I dug out the street map, the lists, and the locket while Jenny went up to change. She was back in minutes, tucking a T-shirt into her jeans.

"If Rick calls, tell him I'll give him a shout when I get home." She picked up the lists. "How many of these were you doing a day?"

"Ten? Sometimes twelve."

She glanced at her watch. "It's five o'clock now. What do you bet I can't knock off a dozen by seven?"

"A dime."

"You're such a cheapskate."

She pecked my cheek and was gone.

Chapter 52

So, how many places did she cover?"

Cia and I had finished setting up, the dealers and pickers had come and gone. We were relaxing with our first cups of coffee.

"She went out after work every day. She crossed fifty addresses of the list."

"Fifty! How did she do it? We had a hell of a time doing seven a day."

"To quote her, she didn't stop to chat. What's the matter?"

Cia's eyes had drifted past me. There was a puzzled frown on her face.

"Coming down the mall," she said. Her frown deepened. "Is that who I think it is? No. It can't be."

Two women were approaching slowly. They stopped to browse at Betty's table.

The younger was one of those heavy, pugnacious women who brazen out a loaded cart in the eight-items lineup. The older woman was a typical suburban senior citizen. She was dressed in a flowery print. Her carefully sculptured hair was faintly blue. On her feet were sensible laced oxfords.

There was something tantalizingly familiar about her. She caught my eye and smiled. I returned the smile automatically, then did a double take of sheer astonishment.

"Migod, it is," I breathed as the two drifted to our table. "It's Tootie Frootie."

Tootie introduced her daughter.

"She's in town visiting with me this week. Isn't that lovely?" She placed her hand on her daughter's arm. "These are my friends, dear."

Her daughter nodded, not lifting her eyes from the assortment on our tables. She picked up a petit-point pattern china cup and saucer priced at twelve dollars.

"Is this the best you can do on this?" She looked from Cia to me. "I'm buying it for my mother."

"Oh, no, dear," Tootie protested. "It's not necessary."

"Please, Mother," her daughter said firmly. "I want to buy you something nice."

She pinned her gaze on Cia. "How much?"

"Since it's for your mother," Cia smiled at Tootie. "You can have it for ten."

The woman turned to Tootie. "There isn't something else you'd rather have, is there?"

"Oh, no, dear." Tootie snatched her hand from the gold mesh evening bag she had been stroking. "The cup and saucer are just lovely, dear."

While Cia wrapped the purchase, Tootie asked about Anna.

"Well, maybe next week," she said when I told her we were still searching. Her smile was bland. "There's always next week, isn't there."

She fluttered her fingers at us and followed her daughter down the mall.

"I'll be damned." Gazing after them, Cia chortled with delight. "So old Tootie is a closet flake."

I nodded. "Looks like it. She is old, isn't she, Cia. Funny, I don't think I ever thought of her as old before. A bit dotty. But not old."

"There's a moral in there somewhere," Cia said. "You

know, she'd much have preferred that flashy gold bag. Let's put it away and give her first go at it next Sunday."

Elia arrived moments later.

"Jenny will be by at noon to pick it up," I told him. "She thinks she can cover Ville St. Laurent this afternoon."

If Elia was surprised Jenny had taken over, he gave no indication. He simply nodded.

"You've trusted her with a valuable piece of jewelry, Elia," I said. "What is it with the two of you? Does Jenny remind you of Anna?"

He took a moment to answer.

"Not really," he said, thoughtfully. "Oh, superficially, perhaps. Blond hair. Blue eyes. But facially, no. And Anna was small, five-two at most. There was a girl, once, on Sherbrooke Street . . ."

He let the sentence die and sighed heavily.

"You can't imagine how I felt when finally I arrived in Montreal. I was in the same city with Anna at last, breathing the same air, under the same sky as she was, able to walk the same streets . . ."

Chapter 53

The first thing I did when I got off the train was run to a phone booth, to a phone directory.

There was page after page of Tremblays. Thousands of Tremblays, hundreds of P. Tremblays. There was no Strohan listed.

I found a room, applied for a telephone, and took the first night job offered me, cleaning office buildings. I had to work at night, you see. I needed the days free.

The day the phone was installed I began calling. Always the same question. Are you any relation to the Pierre Tremblay who was hospitalized in Hamburg, Germany, in 1947? Always the same answer. No.

I ran advertisements in the personal columns of all the English and French newspapers. No response.

I wrote to the Armed Forces Headquarters in Ottawa, applied to the various regimental headquarters in Montreal. The war had been over for years. They needed more information. All I had was the name. And in Montreal, the name Pierre Tremblay is as common as John Smith anywhere else. Another dead end.

I went to concerts. Maybe Anna was a violinist in some orchestra. I attended every Tremblay wedding the papers listed, every funeral. I moved from one section of the city to another, from room to room. For a while I moved every six months, searching new neighborhoods.

Every Christmas I haunted the department stores, hoping to meet her shopping. I rode streetcars, then buses. I walked the streets, looking at every woman who passed me by.

Then, one day, walking along Sherbrooke Street, I saw her across the street. She was coming through the McGill University gates, her arms laden with books.

I shouted at her but she didn't hear me. Sherbrooke is a noisy street. She couldn't hear me. She turned and began walking westward.

I ran across Sherbrooke. I didn't even hear the brakes screeching, the horns blasting. I caught up with her and clutched at her arm. I was panting for breath.

The girl—of course it wasn't Anna—the girl screamed. And screamed. But I couldn't let go of her arm. My fingers wouldn't open. My hands just wouldn't let go.

Some men, passersby, pulled me away. A police car arrived and two policemen pushed me against the fence. The girl was rubbing her arm and sobbing words about crazy old men. And I was shaking with fright.

I babbled a story. I thought the girl was my daughter. I showed them the camp tattoo on my arm. They let me go.

I went home.

I didn't go to work for three days. I lay on my bed and stared at the ceiling. Then I got up, went into the bathroom, and looked at myself in a mirror. And what I saw, for the first time, was a crazy old man.

Time had stopped for me. Stopped when I returned to the flat in Kiev and found Anna's letter. Somehow, I had assumed I would remain thirty years old until I found her again. I had assumed that, when I found her, we would be as we were before we were parted.

I imagine it was this delusion that made me think the girl on Sherbrooke Street was Anna. The girl was eighteen or nineteen years old. How could she be Anna? Anna would have been a middle-aged woman by then.

Looking in the mirror, I saw what I had become.

I was fifty-four years old. I had been in Montreal thirteen years and still wore some of the clothing I had arrived in. I owned only what could be packed in a single suitcase. To move easily.

I hadn't been to a dentist. I cut my own hair, chopping with scissors. Sometimes, I forgot to shave. I got by on very little sleep. At night I worked. By day I searched.

I put myself back together.

I got a job with the Department of Immigration, rather easily since I had the languages. I moved into an apartment. I became fascinated with the English language and took night courses. Soon I was living much as I had when I met Anna.

Every two years I moved to a different section of the city and walked, still searching, even though I had finally accepted that finding Anna lay not in my efforts but in the laps of the gods.

Chapter 54

Elia looked down the mall, a half smile on his face.

"In fairy tales," he said, "it would be the gods who sent me here. Actually, I started going to flea markets and church bazaars looking for old books."

His face lit up.

Jenny had come into the mall and was sliding around our tables. Rick had followed her through the doors. He remained in the corridor, an exaggerated expression of patience on his handsome face.

"Hi, everybody!" Jenny bent and kissed Elia's cheek. "Who has the locket?"

Elia raised his open palm and Jenny took the locket.

"We'll find her today," she smiled down at him. "I have a feeling in my bones."

"Will you be home for dinner?" I asked.

She shook her head. "We'll grab something somewhere."

"We? Is Rick going with you?"

"I bullied him into it." His eyes narrowed at the tone of my voice. "Don't wait up," she said coolly. "I'll probably be home late."

She smiled at Cia, at Elia, and sidled past me.

Rick, following her down the mall, laid a proprietary hand on her shoulder. My muscles tightened at the intimacy of the gesture. I sat down angrily and glanced at Elia.

Hc was frowning, his eyes on the door through which Jenny and Rick had exited. He felt my gaze.

"Is she fond of that boy?" he asked.

"I'm afraid so."

Elia shook his head. He seemed about to speak, then changed his mind. He stood up and smiled at us.

"Well, time to go," he said.

"Hey!" Cia cried. "You haven't finished."

Elia shrugged. "What is there to finish? I retired four years ago. I still go wherever there are people. I still look. But after all the years it's as much a matter of habit and for exercise as it is a search."

Cia shook her head. "That's not what I meant."

"Oh? What then?"

"You haven't told us how you feel."

"Feel?" Elia looked puzzled. "Then? Now?"

"Now. No bitterness toward those monsters? The SS? The guards? The Kapos?"

"Monsters?" Elia said mildly. "They weren't monsters. Only men. You can meet their counterparts every day. Scratch any ten men anywhere in the world and five would qualify."

"Do you believe that?" Cia's voice was shocked. "Do you really believe that?"

"Yes. I believe that." Elia's expression was faintly surprised, as though he found Cia's reaction unnatural. "I met many in the civil service who'd have made excellent camp guards."

"You're joking."

"Am I? Think, Cia. The world has always had little men who will do as they're told. They threw Christians to the lions in Roman times. During the Spanish Inquisition they tortured heretics. What of Stalin? Idi Amin? Who did their torturing and killing for them?"

Cia stared at him. "Are you saying we should accept mass

brutality and murder as a natural human condition? No guilt?"

"No. But feelings of guilt are not sustainable. They turn too quickly to resentment. Then to anger and hatred. And Treblinka happens again."

"So what's the answer?"

"I'm not sure there is one."

"There has to be."

"I suppose there is one. That every man, individually, will refuse to kill."

"But you don't believe that will happen."

"Ah, but I do. Not in my lifetime. Maybe not even in yours. But the seeds have been planted. Remember the sixties? The young men who refused to go to fight in Vietnam?"

"Vietnam? Do you really think the world can be changed by a few protesters?"

"Why not? Think of the effect the crucifixion of one man had on it." Elia shrugged.

Then he said, thoughtfully. "But to answer your question, how do I feel? I wonder, sometimes, if I had known that never in my life would I see Anna's face again, would I have fought so hard to survive?"

He smiled at Cia. "Any more questions?"

Cia hesitated, then asked, "Didn't you ever meet anyone else, Elia?"

For a moment I thought he wouldn't answer.

"There are people," he said at last, "people like me. How can I explain? We live as prisoners of ourselves. Locked inside. We're born not knowing the secret of reaching out, so we are condemned to sit in our prison and wait for someone with the right key. For me, if there hadn't been Anna there would never have been anybody."

He touched my shoulder. "You asked me, Liz, if Jenny was like Anna." He smiled. "When Jenny looks at me, she sees me. *Me*. Not the old man's body I'm wrapped in. And I see Anna in that look. Does that make sense to you?"

I nodded. "It does."

"Then may I leave now?" He directed the question to Cia.

Cia nodded silently. We echoed his dopobachynia and watched him make his slow way down the mall.

"In fairy tales," Cia quoted Elia sadly, "the gods would have been the ones who sent him here. You know what this tale needs, Liz? A happy ending."

Chapter 55

On Monday, Jenny came home directly from work. Seated at my desk, I could hear her quick showering, then the opening and closing of drawers in her bedroom. She came into my office, clad in panties and bra, carrying a light cotton sundress of mine and a pair of sandals.

"Hi, Mum. Sorry to interrupt. Can I wear this dress? It's too hot for jeans."

"Where are you going?"

"To look for Anna." She flapped the dress at me. "Can I wear it?"

"Sure. But if it's so hot outside why don't you wait till evening when it's cooler."

"Can't." Her head emerged from the dress fold. "There's a pool party at Tina's tonight. I won't be able to go later."

The doorbell rang. Jenny slipped her feet into the sandals. She bent to kiss my cheek and ran to answer.

"That dress needs a slip!" I called after her. "You can see right through it!"

"Who cares?" she called back from halfway down the stairs.

I heard the front door open, then Jenny's surprised exclamation.

"Rick! What are you doing here? It's only three-thirty. Why aren't you at work?"

"The hell with work." Rick's lazy drawl raised the hackles on my back. "Anyway, I quit."

"You quit your job? Are you crazy? Come on in."

The front door closed and I heard the two of them move to the living room.

"Why did you quit?" Jenny asked. "That was a good job."

"Bull," I heard Rick say. "The fuckin' floor manager was always on my case. Come on. Grab a towel. Let's go to the quarry for a dip. I've got a cold six-pack in my car."

"I can't. I'm just on my way out.'

"Where you going?"

"I told you last night. I'm going to look for Anna. Why don't you come too?"

"No way!" The indignation in Rick's voice slipped to a whine. "Aw, come on, Jen. It's too hot to go driving around. We shot yesterday looking."

"And I'll shoot today, tomorrow, and the next day, if that's what it takes." There was a momentary silence, then Jenny said reasonably, "We can swim at Tina's tonight, Rick. Look, I don't mind if you don't want to come along. Why don't you pick me up at nine?"

"I wanna swim now." Rick sounded like a petulant child.

"So go swim, for Pete's sake! You don't need me to hold your hand."

"Maybe I'll just get someone else to hold my hand."

I could feel the air chill all the way up the stairs.

"Why don't you just do that." Jenny's voice was icy.

There was another silence. When Rick broke it, he was conciliatory.

"Aw, hell, you know I wouldn't anyway. Come on, Jen. Grab a towel. Come on, babe."

There was a longer silence. My hands closed into fists. This time Jenny broke it.

"Knock it off, Rick. Look. You go to the quarry. I'll do my list and I'll see you tonight."

"I want to see you *now*. Christ, Jen. I don't get it. I thought it was you and me."

"It is," Jenny placated. "You know that."

"You have one hell of a way of showing it." Rick had caught the mollification in her words and leaped to regain advantage. "I go to all the trouble of picking up a six-pack and come all the way over to take you for a swim and you tell me you'd rather run errands for some fuckin' old kike."

I was on my feet and had taken one outraged step toward the door when something, a sense of occasion perhaps, halted me.

A few months before I'd have bet my last cent on Jenny's reaction to the insulting words. Now, I wasn't quite as certain. Balanced against her natural distaste for bigotry in any form, as well as her affection for Elia, was Rick's influence, his status as a desirable male, and her youthful desire to conform to the ethics of his crowd.

I waited, listening shamelessly.

"What did you call him?" Jenny's voice was brittle. "A fucking old kike?"

Rick's laugh was forced.

"Aw, hey, come on, Jen," he said. "I was sore. What the hell, he is old. And he is a Jew, isn't he?"

When Jenny spoke her voice was soft. I strained to hear.

"You know what my mother calls you, Rick?" she said. "She calls you Rick the Prick. How about that?"

"Your mother?" There was complete bewilderment in the words. "What the hell has . . ."

"Go swimming, Rick," Jenny interrupted. "I'm going to do my list."

I heard the click of her heels in the hallway, the sound of a door opening, then Rick's tentative voice.

"So I'll pick you up at nine, okay?"

"I'll call you later."

"Hey, Jen, look I . . ."

"I'm in a hurry, Rick," Jenny said. "I'll call you."

The door slammed. Seconds later, Rick's car pulled away, tires squealing. Then I heard Jenny leave.

I ate alone and worked late. Rick phoned at nine, again at ten and again at eleven. No word from Jenny.

It was almost midnight when I heard her car pull into the driveway. She came quietly up the stairs and went directly to her room.

"Hi, honey," I called to let her know I was still awake. "Any luck?"

"Nope," she called back.

"Rick called several times."

"Yeah. G'night, Mum."

"Good night, Jenny."

So she didn't want to talk about it.

Oh, Lord, I thought. Give me the strength to keep my effing mouth shut.

Rick phoned repeatedly for two days. Then the calls ceased. Jenny said nothing.

We saw one another only in passing. I was at my desk ten hours a day and Jenny came home only to grab a quick bite, change clothing, and sleep.

At four-thirty on Friday afternoon the phone rang. I picked it up.

"Mummy!" It was Jenny, her voice wild with excitement. "I found her! I found Anna! I'm here, sitting beside her! Come right now!"

Chapter 56

I picked Cia up at the bank and drove like a madwoman to the lakeside suburb of Dorval, to a high-rise apartment building on Lakeshore Boulevard.

Jenny opened the door to our ring. Her face was pink with excitement, her eyes sparkling.

"Elianna's here, too," she exulted. "And Mummy, wait till I tell you. You won't believe how close I came to not finding her!"

We followed her into the apartment.

Sunlight, streaming through windows overlooking the lake, filled the room with light. Two women were seated on a beige velvet couch. They rose as we entered and the younger woman crossed the room to greet us.

There could be no doubt she was Elianna. Her resemblance to her father was strong. She was tall, though not so tall as Jenny. Her blond hair was cut short and curled crisply. Her eyes were a blue-gray. And her smile was so like Elia's I felt the same quick pull his inspired in me.

"I'm Elianna. And you're Cia." She reached out her hand to Cia, then to me. "And you are obviously Jenny's mother. Please, sit down. I've made fresh tea."

We sat, Cia and I in chairs, Jenny and Anna on the couch.

I looked across at Anna and experienced a mild sense of shock.

Illogically, I had expected to see a young woman. At that moment, I understood completely Elia's pursuit of the girl on Sherbrooke Street.

What I saw was a small woman in her sixties.

Her hair was silver-gray, cut short. Her face was oval, the cheek bones high and defined. Wrinkles radiating from her blue eyes and bracketing a firm mouth were those of a woman who laughed more often than she frowned. It was a strong face that would be beautiful still when she was ninety.

The diamond locket, suspended around her neck, shot sparks on her navy dress. One hand rested in her lap and Elia's locket lay in her open palm. A chill ran through me. The index and middle fingers of the hand were missing.

"So hard to believe," she murmured. Her accent was more pronounced than Elia's. "So many years. So hard to believe."

"She's been saying that over and over." Jenny laughed. "I can hardly wait to see Elia's face! Where does he live? We checked the phone book. He's not listed. There aren't any Strohans at all. Where does he live?"

Cia and I looked at one another. It had never occurred to us to ask. On the one or two occasions we had offered to drive him home he had declined, preferring to walk.

"We don't know where he lives." I lifted my hands helplessly.

"We never thought to ask," Cia added.

"You don't know?" Jenny was aghast. "But how are we going to get in touch with him? You have to know!"

Elianna, returning with the tea tray, smiled at Jenny's agitation.

"Take it easy, Jenny," she said. She set the tray on the coffee table and seated herself, cross-legged, on the floor.

"First, tell them how you found us. We'll figure something out later."

She poured tea and served us while Jenny launched into her story.

"I went down to the older section of Beaconsfield," she began. "Down by the lake in the Gables Court area.

"At the third place I tried, the woman said they had moved in only a couple of months before. She thought the lady next door might know where the Macauleys, the people who sold them the house, had gone.

"So I went next door and the woman told me the Macauleys had retired to Florida. I figured another dead end.

"Just then, another woman came up the walkway. She saw the locket in my hand."

Jenny paused dramatically. "And that's when it happened!

"She said to me, and I quote, 'That looks very familiar to me.' Then she said, 'I know that locket. It belonged to Elianna's mother. Mrs. Anna.' "

Chapter 57

The two women invited Jenny into the house.

The older woman introduced herself as Mrs. Johnson. The younger was her daughter, Laurie.

"I think we should call Elianna first," Laurie said when Jenny had calmed down enough to tell a coherent story. "It's going to be quite a shock to Mrs. Anna."

"Please," Jenny said. "Whichever. But now!"

The excitement in her voice made Laurie smile. She picked up the phone and dialed.

"May I speak to Dr. Altman please?" she said. "It's quite important. Tell her it's Laurie Johnson."

She covered the mouthpiece with her hand. "Elianna's a doctor," she explained. "A pediatrician."

"Altman?" Jenny said. "Is that her name now?"

Laurie nodded. "She's Mrs. David Altman. He's a doctor, too. A surgeon." She snatched her hand away from the phone. "Elianna? Are you sitting down?"

She listened, then laughed.

"Yes, I do think you'd better. There's someone here who wants to speak to you. And what she has to tell you is going to knock you flat on your bottom."

She handed the receiver to Jenny.

"Elianna?" Jenny drew in a deep breath. "My name is

Jenny Cantrell and I don't know how to say this without just coming right out with it. Your father isn't dead.

"He's been looking for your mother and you since the war ended. He found the locket, the one he made for your mother in Kiev? He found it a few weeks ago on my mother's table at a flea market. My mother bought it at a garage sale. She's been trying to find your mother. Can you tell me where she is?"

There was a dead silence at the other end of the line. Then a husky voice spoke.

"Where are you now?"

"At Mrs. Johnson's. In Beaconsfield."

"Are you familiar with the big, white apartment building at the corner of Dorval Avenue? On Lakeshore Road?"

"Yes. I know the one you mean."

"I'll meet you there, in the lobby. Twenty minutes."

"So we met." Jenny and Elianna smiled at one another. "I told her about Elia. She went upstairs alone. Then she buzzed me to come up."

Cia leaned forward and replaced her empty cup on the coffee table.

"There's something I don't understand," she said, glancing from Anna to Elianna. "How did the locket come to be in a garage sale?"

It was Elianna who answered.

"My mother was the Macauleys' housekeeper for years. I grew up in their house."

She smiled at her mother. "And it was my fault the locket was lost. I took it from my mother's room to show Laurie the picture of my father. I forgot to put it back and it got misplaced somewhere in the Macauleys' house. Remember, Mama? It was the only time you ever spanked me."

"I remember." Anna touched the diamond locket on her breast. "The picture here. Is it a good likeness?"

"Not really," I said.

"Not at all!" Jenny was more vehement. "The picture in there is of a stern old man. Elia isn't like that at all. Wait, Elianna, you'll see what I mean when you meet him."

Elianna nodded, but her eyes were on her mother. Anna's head was bent low. She sat very still. Only her thumb moved, stroking the locket's yellow bead.

Abruptly, Elianna jumped to her feet.

"I should be getting back," she announced in a brisk voice. "I ran out on a patient and there are others waiting."

Jenny gaped at her.

"But what about Elia?" she cried. "What are we going to do about finding Elia?"

"I don't think there's much we can do."

Elianna avoided Jenny's wide-eyed stare. She looked at Cia, then at me, her eyes sending a message, a plea for us to follow her lead.

"We'll come to the flea market on Sunday," she said. "What time does he normally get there?"

"Around ten."

I picked up my handbag from the floor beside my chair. Cia followed suit. I gestured to Jenny.

"Come on, honey. I think Elianna's right. We'll wait until Sunday."

For a moment I thought she would argue. Her expression was changing from disbelief to one of stubborn resentment. Then, sensing an undercurrent she didn't understand, she nodded and joined us at the door.

With an obvious effort, Anna pulled herself from some far-off place. She rose to her feet and followed us.

"I am sorry. I . . ." She lifted her hands. They fell back to her sides. "Please. I . . . it is all so sudden. Please. Pardon me."

"It's all right, Mama." Elianna bent and kissed her cheek. "Everybody understands. I'll call you tonight."

We waited in silence for the elevator. I could sense Jenny's anger and impatience. Her cheeks were flushed and her lips were compressed but she said nothing.

When the doors slid shut and we began our descent, Elianna placed her hand on Jenny's arm.

"I'm sorry, Jenny. You deserve an explanation."

Her smiles included the three of us.

"There's a coffee shop in the shopping mall on Dorval Avenue," she said. "Why don't we meet there?"

Chapter 58

M y mother was always cheerful, always smiling when I was growing up," Elianna said after the waitress had served us and departed.

"I know that sounds saccharine, but it happens to be true. Except for the locket episode, I can't remember her ever losing her temper. The two Macauley boys adored her. They still do. She's godmother to one of their kids."

Elianna circled her coffee cup with both hands.

"About a year after David and I were married, she fell apart. It was as if she waited until I was safe before she let go. She tried to kill herself. You can't imagine what a shock it was, how completely out of character. We brought her to stay with us, David and I. We didn't want her to be alone.

"She was very ill. There were times when she was totally lucid, others when she seemed to be in some kind of hell. Sometimes she wept without a sound for hours. I would sit with her and just hold her hand.

"One day we were sitting in the garden, she and I, and she began to talk. Very quietly. Very calmly. I think she had to finally get it all out. To tell somebody."

Elianna pushed her cup away. She clasped her hands, her fingers tightly meshed.

"The women in the labor camps," she said, her voice low,

"particularly the young, pretty ones were . . . were preyed upon by the guards, civilian and Nazi guards both."

Elianna looked at each of us in turn. At me, at Cia and at Jenny last.

"You must remember that the women in the forced labor camps were starving. My mother watched them die, a few more every day. An extra crust of bread, an extra spoonful of fat could mean one more day of life. And all my mother could think was that she had to survive. For me.

"Her mother died for lack of food and care. Her sister hung herself. I believe my mother felt her sister's act was a judgment on her, a condemnation of what she was prepared to do in order to stay alive. After the liberation, my mother went to Hamburg. To Klausens."

"Klausens?" Jenny frowned. "What's Klausens?"

"The German couple who took me when my mother was sent to the labor camps," Elianna explained.

"Oh, yes," Jenny nodded. "I'd forgotten."

"The occupation forces weren't knights in shining armor, you know." Elianna sat back and folded her arms across her chest. "They had everything. The Klausens were the defeated Germany. They had nothing. Nothing. My mother supported them, supported us, by . . . by . . ."

Elianna's lips tightened. She let the silence fill in what she could not bring herself to say.

"After a while, she got a job as a nurse's aide in the armed forces hospital in Hamburg. She met Pierre Tremblay there."

Elianna turned to me.

"Jenny told us my mother wrote to Lesia that he had offered to marry her?"

I nodded. "So she could bring you to Canada."

"Offered." Elianna spat the word. "He offered nothing. He bargained. In exchange for his name and Canada, my mother was to . . . service . . . him."

I sucked in a shocked breath and looked at Jenny. Her face had flushed.

"Oh, God," she said. "That's so gross. I thought we were supposed to be the good guys. What a pig."

Elianna's face softened. She smiled at Jenny's youthful vehemence.

"Anyway, they were married. Pierre never made it back to Canada. He died on the boat ride home."

Nobody spoke for a moment. I remembered the reference to an aunt in Anna's letter to Lesia.

"The old aunt?" I said. "Did your mother meet her?"

"Where else could she go?" Elianna answered. "She took care of the old woman until she died, a year after we came to Montreal. Then my mother went to work for the Macauleys."

We were silent, each wrapped in our thoughts. Elianna broke the silence with a sigh.

"It's enough to break your heart," she said. "A young, beautiful, talented musician, married to a man she loved. And it was all snatched away. Even her music. She lost her fingers on a loom at Grunberg. She could no longer even play a violin. Once, when she was ill and raving, I realized she was talking to God. And, in the middle of it, she suddenly said, clear as a bell, *'I've spent my life as a whore and a servant and I curse Your name'."*

I shivered involuntarily. Elia, too, had denounced God.

"And now," Elianna said, "after everything she did to survive, after all that was done to her, she's going to meet my father again. Knowing the Anna he loved no longer exists."

She turned to Jenny. "Do you understand now?"

"No!" Jenny replied hotly. "I do *not* understand now. Because neither does the Elia she loved exist any longer. The man she is meeting survived by burning murdered Jews!"

"There's a difference," Elianna said. "When the fire dies,

a man can walk away. A woman carries her body, the scene of her shame, with her for the rest of her life."

"That's such a crock!" Jenny protested. "That's pure and unadulterated chauvinistic thinking!"

Elianna nodded. "I agree. But I know it's the way my mother is thinking."

Jenny opened her mouth, closed it. Then, frustrated, she asked plaintively, "So what's going to happen on Sunday?"

Elianna shook her head. "We'll have to wait and see."

It wasn't good enough for Jenny. She turned on me.

"Mummy!" She used the same tone as when I'd left a bedtime story dangling when she was a child.

"What's going to happen?" I fell into the old routine. "I'll tell you what's going to happen. Elia is going to see Anna as she still is. His Anna, still beautiful. And Anna will see the gentle, loving man she married. Nothing else will matter a damn."

"And they'll live happily even after," Jenny said, and smiled, misquoting as she always had.

Chapter 59

Sunday dawned hot, promising to be even hotter. The sun was a red ball hanging in the milky sky of a humid August morning.

I dragged myself downstairs, gulped cold orange juice, put coffee on to perk, and went to pack the car. Jenny was down a minute later, simmering with the excitement of a five-year-old on Christmas Eve.

She carried boxes and cartons, moving effortlessly, while I plodded in her wake, wheezing in the near-liquid air.

"There." She slammed the tailgate down. "All packed."

She pulled the damp shirt away from her breast and blew down into it. "It's going to be a stinker," she said. "Thank goodness the mall is air-conditioned."

"We'll get a crowd today."

"A . . . oh, you mean customers! Why?"

"The outdoor flea markets will be a turkish bath. The customers will all come to the mall."

"Who cares about customers!" Jenny shook her head at me. "Geez, Mum, aren't you even excited?"

"All I am right now is hot, sticky, and cranky." I could hear the phone ringing. "Would you run and get that, honey?"

It was Cia. She sounded harassed.

"I'm sorry, Liz," she said. "I should have been there an hour ago to help you pack. I'm waiting for my mother to get dressed. I told her about Anna last night, hoping she'd realize how lucky her life has been in comparison. So this morning, at the last damn minute, she decided she wants to come with me today."

"So bring her. And relax. Jenny did most of the packing anyway. We'll be leaving in about fifteen minutes."

"I wish I could say the same." Cia snarled. "But she's been in the shower for the last five minutes. I don't know when we're going to get out of here."

"Hey. Simmer down. It's too hot to get upset. Anytime you arrive is fine with me."

I hung up, feeling suddenly cheerful. And guiltily happy that Cia's problem wasn't mine. Together with the upsurge in spirits came the first tingling of anticipation.

By the time Cia and her mother arrived at nine-thirty, every vendor in the flea market was aware Anna had been found.

Pickers and dealers, normally long since departed for greener fields, were still around, chatting in groups. Most of the regulars lingered near our tables, making a show of browsing, with one eye trained on the doors. Casual customers wore puzzled expressions at the tangible air of excitement permeating the mall.

Heads swiveled when Cia ushered her mother through the doors. For a second Cia was startled, then she shook her head vigorously, laughing at the mistaken assumptions.

"My mother," she explained to Ros and Mike as she passed by them, and again to Betty after she had seated her mother behind our tables.

Her mother, an older version of Cia, but without the sharp edge of common sense and humor, smiled tremulously at me. I was serving a customer and could only give her a quick smile of greeting in return.

They came a few minutes before ten.

Anna, looking small and cool in a lettuce green cotton dress, flanked by Elianna and her husband, David.

Cia and I exchanged glances.

"Kirk Douglas," she said. "Minus the dimple."

"Right on," I agreed.

Jenny, her face incandescent, went to meet them.

Suddenly, there was no room in front of our tables. Word had passed swiftly down the mall. Danny Garrette strolled by with two of his customers.

Vendors left their tables and scurried past for a quick, smiling look at Anna. Phil Perkins and Judy Haxton. Alice. Jean-Paul and Marise. Antique dealers Shirley, Francesco, Marc, and Roberto. Customers. Nadia, buyer of Art Deco. The Pink Man, whose name we didn't know, who collected pink Depression glass. The doll lady. The Hummel man.

Tootie Frootie teetered by, bangles jangling, her wig bright orange, her blouse a splash of scarlet poppies, her black cotton skirt lying almost horizontal over layers of crinolines.

Elianna's eyes widened and a look of delighted astonishment passed between her and David.

Old Lonesome stood quietly by, smiling and nodding. The Weeper stopped, stared, and wept.

I doubt Anna was aware of the sensation she was causing. No one made any attempt to approach her. With a delicacy that surprised me, they came, they saw, they departed.

Within ten minutes, everyone who knew the story had seen Anna. The aisle was filled only with customers. And we were faced with a problem we hadn't anticipated.

There was simply no place for Anna and the two others to sit and wait for Elia. We had three folding chairs, but with three seated it was a tight squeeze. And to remain in the aisle was to be buffeted by the throng of browers moving from table to table.

I turned to Cia.

"Why don't you take everybody down to the deli for coffee," I suggested. "Jenny and I will stay here. She'll go get you when Elia arrives."

They trooped away and Jenny came behind to help me serve customers.

I wish I had a tape recording of the next five minutes. I'd play it for Jenny next time she told me how mature she was at going-on-eighteen.

"Why isn't he here, Mum? It's almost ten-thirty!"

"He's coming. Stop worrying."

I handed her a cup and saucer to wrap while I made change. The customer took her bag and departed.

"What if something's happened to him?"

"Nothing's happened to him. Don't worry. He's coming."

Another sale, a Fisher-Price toy, bought to placate a howling child.

"What if he doesn't come today?"

"He's coming, honey."

Time-out for a short discussion with a woman who wanted to pay three dollars for an alarm clock priced at eight.

"What if he decides it's too hot to come today?"

"He enjoys his walk."

"Then where is he?"

"Honey, he's com— *There he is!*"

Jenny was out from behind the table and into the aisle before the words were out of my mouth. I steadied a teetering vase and followed her more sedately.

Elia had paused inside the doors, mopping his forehead with a large white handkerchief. His face was flushed and mottled with heat, his thin hair wet and disarranged. Jenny clutched his arm and dragged him into the mall.

"We found her, Elia! She's here! Elianna too. Anna's here!" It was all coming out in a single breath. "Stay here. I'll go and get her."

She was gone, pushing her way heedlessly, leaving a startled trail behind her.

Elia looked at me, his eyes dazed and very blue.

"It's true," I assured him. "Jenny found her on Friday. We had no idea where you live or we'd have . . . why don't you have a phone?"

"To call who?" Elia drew a deep breath. "Anna," he said, "Anna."

"She's fine. And she's as beautiful as you remember, Elia. And Elianna, she looks just like you. She's a doctor. She's married. To another doctor, a man you'll like. You'll be so proud of her, Elia."

Far down the mall I could see Jenny's blond head bobbing toward us. She was taller than the people surrounding her. A momentary break in the throng gave me a brief glimpse of Anna's green dress.

"They're coming, Elia!" I was now as excited as Jenny. "I can see them."

His hand gripped my shoulder and I turned to smile.

His face had drained of color, the skin ashen. His mouth hung loose, lips rimmed white. For a split second his eyes blazed blue and agonized, then turned gray and opaque.

His hand clawed my arm and I clutched him to me, his dead weight pulling me down.

Panic-stricken, I raised my head to call to Jenny. She was only yards away. I saw her face change, her mouth open in a soundless scream. Then I sank to the floor, holding Elia in my arms.

A moment later, Anna knelt beside me, her hands reaching out. I released Elia to her and rose on quivering legs.

"Did he see her?" Jenny's fingers dug into my arm. *"Did he see her face!"*

I shook my head silently.

"No!" Jenny seemed to fold down in anguished stages. She knelt beside Elia, pounding the cold, gray marble floor with clenched fists.

"No. No. No."

Chapter 60

E lia was buried on Tuesday.

Several of the flea market vendors attended the funeral. Betty. Ros and Mike Hennessy. Danny Garrette. Tootie Frootie came, dressed in her suburban matron costume. Old Lonesome, looking more like a sad hound dog than ever.

The two Macauley boys were there, grown men with pretty wives. Jenny, Cia, and I sat with a group I assumed were friends of Elianna and David.

On Wednesday, we began location shooting of my *Romance of Concrete* script and for the balance of the week I was home only to sleep. Saturday, we edited all day and Cia did the garage sale round on her own.

The hot weather held. Once again the flea market crowd took refuge in the air-conditioned mall.

I was glad to be busy. Cia was subdued, wrestling with her mother's inability to cope with widowhood. And I was fighting a malaise compounded of physical weariness and a somber melancholy.

Jenny came into the mall as we were beginning to pack up. She carried a brown paper bag.

"We finished emptying Elia's apartment," she said. She withdrew two tissue-wrapped packages from the bag, hand-

ing one to Cia and one to me. "Anna and Elianna want you
to have these."

Cia tore the tissue away, revealing a small ivory box,
exquisitely carved. My package contained a leatherbound
copy of *Lempriere's Classical Dictionary,* published in 1894.

"No wonder he never bought anything from us." Cia's
finger traced the intricate pattern of birds and flowers.
"We've never had things like this."

"He didn't have much," Jenny said. "Mostly books. In
six languages. Elianna and David are keeping some of them."

She crumpled the paper bag and dropped it in our trash
bag.

"You're coming straight home, aren't you, Mum?"

"Yes. Why?"

"I have to talk to you. It's important. Suppose I pick up
a pizza for dinner?"

"Fine by me."

She waved to us and left. I watched her push the doors
wide and stride through.

"What d'you suppose that's all about?" I mused uneasily.

"Rick?" Cia volunteered.

"Oh, damn. I hope not."

Chapter 61

When I arrived home, the kitchen table was set. In addition to the pizza, Jenny had made a tossed salad and a pitcher of iced tea.

I showered quickly, donned a comfortable cotton caftan, and we sat down to eat.

"I quit my job," Jenny announced with no preamble. "I'm going back to school."

My initial reaction was one of gratification. My next was, omigod, where will the money come from?

To give myself time I merely nodded and asked, as casually as I could, "What brought this on?"

"Actually," Jenny toyed with her salad. "I've been thinking about it ever since I had lunch with Elia that day."

"I see," I said, though I didn't.

"He said something that really got to me. I asked him if he hated the Germans. You know what he said?"

"I can't even guess."

"He said, 'Hate? If I hate Ukrainians because of the Ukrainian guards at Treblinka, must I hate Anna? Or Kalyna? And if I hate the Poles because of people like Jadwiga, do I hate Stefan? Or Mikolaj? The Klausens were Germans. What of them? What of the Jewish Kapos at Treblinka? Some were worse than the German SS. Do I hate Jews, then?' "

Jenny dropped her fork. She pushed her salad bowl away and leaned her elbows on the table.

"He said what he hated was not being allowed the chance to screw up his own life."

I blinked, "Elia said 'screw'?"

"Why not? That's what he meant."

"I suppose." I shrugged. "Go on."

"He told me what he hated was the inhumanity that made it possible for people to rob one another of their right to live their own lives, to make their own mistakes."

Jenny leaned forward earnestly.

"He told me I had something that had been denied him and the people who survived, as he did, and the people who died. I had the opportunity to live my life without looking into the face of evil."

She let the thought hang in the air. I waited.

"And he told me," she continued, "that I had a choice they were denied. I could use my life or I could waste it. But," she paused, giving her words significance. "*I do have the choice. They never did.*"

"And that's what got to you? That's what made you decide to go back to school?"

She tapped her temple, grinning.

"Well, it sure started the old wheels grinding."

I bit my lip, hating to throw cold water on her mood, realizing I had no choice.

"I think it's great, honey." I placed my hand over hers. "I really do. We can swing school fees somehow by cutting here and there. But there's no way I can handle your car payments. Unless you can get a part-time job, your car will have to go."

Her smile widened. "But it won't," she said. "I'm to be the first beneficiary of the Elia Strohan Scholarship Fund."

"The what?"

"Well, that's what we think we'll call it."

"We? Who we? You realize I haven't the foggiest notion of what you're talking about?"

Jenny laughed. "I know. It's all just been happening. And I haven't seen you all week."

"What's all been happening?" I sat back, exasperated. "Indulge me. Start at the beginning."

Jenny raised her index finger. "One question, okay?"

I nodded.

"Okay. How much money do you think Elia left?"

"Money?" I stared at her. "How would I know? I couldn't even take a wild guess."

"Over three hundred thousand dollars."

I gaped then. "Elia? How, for heaven's sake?"

Jenny sat back in her chair, content with my reaction.

"He lived in a one-room furnished apartment," she said. "One set of winter clothing, one set of summer clothes, none of it new. Other than books, he didn't seem to want to own anything. Over the years he banked and invested the greater portion of his salary. All of it earning interest."

"Plus interest on the interest," I said enviously. I've never had money long enough to earn interest on interest. "Okay. I'm convinced. Now, what's the scholarship thing?"

Jenny hunched forward, her eyes glowing.

"We're going to use the interest as a scholarship fund."

"We?"

"Elianna, David, and I. We're trustees. Or executors. Whatever." She waved the details away with an airy hand.

"We'll put one person at a time through college, all expenses paid. I'm to be the first. When I graduate, we find some other sterling character and *they* use the money. And so on and so on. Forever. Elia will live forever through the Elia Strohan Scholarship Fund!"

I nodded, caught up in her enthusiasm. "He would have liked the idea, I think."

"We've made a couple of stipulations. One, every beneficiary must know Elia and Anna's story. That's where you come in. Will you write it?"

"Of course."

"We'll pay your regular fee."

"Don't be silly," I protested. "I don't want . . ."

"We're doing it right," Jenny interrupted firmly. "We'll keep books, records, like any business. We're hiring you."

"All right, all right. What's the second stipulation?"

Jenny shifted in her chair.

"Maybe it sounds silly," she said self-consciously. "Or maybe we're being idealistic. But the people we pick have to be planning to work in a field where they'll be influencing children. Teaching. Pediatrics. Child psychology. We don't think we're going to change the world. But it has to start somewhere, doesn't it?"

Her eyes searched mine for any trace of the cynic.

"Tolerance. Respect. For *everybody*," she said. "For life itself. It has to start somewhere."

"And you're going to light one small candle." It was a quotation I knew would mean nothing to Jenny.

It didn't. She glanced at her watch.

"Look, Mum. Do you mind if I take off?" she asked. "I promised Elianna and David I'd help catalog Elia's books. They're donating them to various ethnic librairies."

"I don't mind. Go ahead."

She bent across the table and pecked at my cheek.

"I should be home by midnight," she said.

She was at the door when I stopped her.

"Jenny?"

I was about to ask if Rick was history when a new and startling idea crossed my mind.

If she were Cia, or any other woman, would I be prying into her private thoughts and emotions?

"Yes, Mum?"

"I love you" was all I said.

Epilogue

*F*ifteen years have passed since I wrote Elia's story for the beneficiaries of his educational fund.

Jenny was the first. She was seventeen then, she's thirty-two now, a counselor in the trauma center of the Children's Hospital. Of the five who followed, one is a minor league hockey coach, another a journalist, a third owns and operates a day care center. The other two are junior college teachers.

Anna and I became friends. She was a sharp, earthy woman with a derisive sense of humor, with which she transformed her experiences, even in the slave labor camps, into acidly funny stories. She died last week, two days before what would have been the sixty-second anniversary of her marriage to Elia.

She was eighty years old. I'll miss her.

Elizabeth Cantrell
April 1997